D1583906

IF IT
HADN'T
BEEN FOR
GRACE

Written By

BRENDA HELTON

ISBN 979-8-88751-886-2 (paperback)
ISBN 979-8-88751-887-9 (digital)

Christian Faith Publishing
832 Park Avenue
Meadville, PA 16335
www.christianfaithpublishing.com

All the names and places in this book are either the product of the author's imagination or used in a fictitious manner. Any resemblance to actual persons, living or dead, is purely coincidental.

Printed in the United States of America

This book is dedicated to Grace's six children,
who inspired me to write her story.

Contents

Santangelo Boardinghouse

Briarton, Illinois
1918–1919

GRACE'S LONG DARK HAIR RIPPLED in the warm summer air like a satin ribbon unwinding from its spool. What was the reason again that she was summoned to the front porch to stand like a sentential? Grace tumbled a few small pebbles around with her black midcalf laced shoes as she remembered the reason for her assignment. Today was the day her family's boardinghouse was getting another boarder. Boarder number 3. Although she was only fifteen, she was the oldest in the family, and Mamma said that it was time she started sharing in the responsibilities of their boardinghouse. Her assignment was to wait on the front porch until the new guest arrived. Mamma always said it was important to make a good first impression.

"Greet him on the front porch, Grace," Mamma said. "Smile, shake his hand, and offer him a cool drink. The more he feels welcomed, the longer he may stay."

Grace was thankful that this would be the last new boarder for a while. Once he arrived, the house would be full to capacity. As she stood on the porch, obediently following her mother's orders, she wondered what this boarder would be like. The only information they had received was that he was a twenty-two-year-old immigrant from the region of Bari in Italy. His two older brothers, Nico and Tony, came to America six years ago to find prosperity. Shortly after their arrival in New York, the two older brothers moved to Briarton, Illinois, following a lead to start a construction business. They promised to send for their younger brother once the business showed signs of growth. Keeping their promise, they sent for him, and today he was arriving on the four o'clock train from New York. Since the older brothers were already settled in Briarton with wives and children, they arranged for him to stay at the Santangelo Boardinghouse on Watt Street.

Grace chuckled to herself thinking of old man Mahoney's reaction to hearing that an Italian would be rooming right next to him in room number 3. Good ol' Fin Mahoney, her family's first boarder for over three years now with his thick Irish brogue and smell of Irish oak tobacco. He was a good ol' guy although Grace's mamma thought he played his Irish music too loud at times. And when he drank too much sherry, which made him desperately long for his beloved Ireland, he'd dance with such determination in his upstairs room that the crystal chandelier in the parlor swayed from the vibration on the floor.

Mamma didn't have to worry about the boarder in room number 2 dancing. Pearson Wright was a clean-cut, well-dressed, stiff-as-a-board Englishman. Just thinking of him made Grace square her shoulders and stand a little straighter. Grace imagined that his reaction would be to ignore the third boarder. She couldn't imagine Pearson Wright being warm and welcoming to the new immigrant. After all, he had lived at the Santangelo Boardinghouse for two years now and barely engaged in conversation with them. On days when Mr. Wright was the only boarder at the supper table, everyone ate in silence.

She swatted at some late-summer bees busying themselves around the rosebushes as she wished this last boarder would hurry up and arrive. She had work to do inside the house and was growing impatient. As she leaned over the porch railing watching the bees buzz in and out of the rosebushes, she heard the distant roar of a motorcycle. Excited that this may finally be the arrival of the new boarder and the end to her boring duty, she scurried to the kitchen to grab a glass of ice-cold lemonade. She arrived back at the porch door just as he parked the motorbike at the end of the walkway. He looked up and gave her a smile.

"Hello," called the voice in broken English. "Is this the Santangelo Boardinghouse?"

For an uncomfortable moment, Grace locked eyes with the boarder. Her brain was processing much too quickly as she gave him a quick look-over from head to foot. He looked much younger than she expected, certainly not older than maybe his early twenties. He had wavy dark hair, a smile that immediately engaged her, and eyes full of mystery. He wore a clean white collared shirt that was unbuttoned all the way down, exposing his golden-brown chest.

"Is this the Antonia Santangelo Boardinghouse?" he repeated as he grabbed his duffel bags off the back of his bike. His eyes rested on the sweating glass of lemonade she was holding in her hand.

Grace, realizing that she was staring impolitely at this gentleman, snapped to reality and said, "Oh, yes, I'm so sorry. I have been standing on the porch for so long the July heat must have gotten to me. And oh, please forgive me. This cold lemonade is for you."

Grace skipped down the front porch steps to where the boarder was standing and handed him the lemonade. She watched as he drained the glass in one gulp; the sweat from the glass dripping droplets of water like a soft rain on his tan chest, eventually joining together into one fast running stream all the way down to his waistband.

"Thank you, and hello again," he said, extending his hand to her with a jolly chuckle in his throat. "My name is Gio, Gio Rivia. Your family should be expecting me. I believe my brothers, Nico and Tony, called ahead."

Grace looked deep into Gio's eyes. She saw something there that was different—something exciting and scary and adventurous and dark all at the same time. Realizing that she was staring impolitely again, she remembered her mother's words.

Instinctively she reached out to give him a welcoming handshake and said, "Welcome, Mr. Rivia. Yes, we have been expecting you. We hope you will enjoy your stay at the Santangelo Boardinghouse." With that, she gestured the way back up the front steps to the house.

Grace could smell her mamma's cooking wafting out from the front screen door before she was close enough to open it.

"I hope you like chicken," Grace asked shyly, "because that's what Mamma is making for supper this evening."

"Yes, I do, and it smells wonderful. What time is supper? I hope I'll have time to wash up first."

"Mamma serves supper in the dining room promptly at six," Grace offered. "Come on in." Grace gestured inside with a nudge of her head as she held the screen door open for her guest. "Mamma will explain all of the details of the boardinghouse to you before supper. Please follow me, and I'll introduce you to her."

Grace led Gio down the hallway to a wide-open kitchen. After introductions, Antonia Santangelo led her third boarder up the wide central staircase to room 3. Grace stood at the bottom of the stairs watching him carry his bags with ease as if they were filled with pillows. Halfway up the stairs, Gio turned around and gave Grace a broad smile and a wink. Grace stood there, feet weighted to the floor for what seemed like an eternity. Finally she lifted her right foot and commanded her feet to walk to the kitchen. Could it be? Did she see correctly? Did Mr. Rivia just wink at her?

She poured herself a full glass of lemonade and sat down on a kitchen chair. Maybe if she sat real still and sipped the lemonade real slow, her heart would return to its normal rhythm. She did a quick self-evaluation: her feet were tingling, her ears were ringing, and she felt light-headed. What was wrong with her? Grace knew the answer before the sentence was formulated in her mind. She also knew that she better regain her composure before Mamma returned to the kitchen.

Supper was served promptly at six. The aroma of perfectly baked lemon-garlic chicken, roasted potatoes, fried peppers and eggs, and hot homemade bread crept up the staircase, summoning the boarders down to supper like mesmerized zombies. Once all were in place, Grace and her mother moved quickly around the formal dining room, replenishing serving bowls and water glasses.

Table conversation was labored. The two established boarders didn't feel comfortable opening up and sharing as they typically did in the presence of the new boarder, and the new boarder was too hungry to stop eating to join the scant conversation. Shortly after dessert was served, Mr. Mahoney got up and left the table. Grace heard him mumble something about retreating to his room for an aftersupper sherry. It wasn't long after that Mr. Wright stood, offered his thanks for supper, and strolled off toward the parlor to read. Grace and her mother sat in silence as Mr. Rivia finished his second helping of rice pudding and drank the rest of his coffee.

He politely folded his napkin, placed it on the table, looked in Grace's direction, and said with a broad smile, "Thank you. The supper was wonderful, and the company was even better."

Again Grace felt that weighted feeling enter her body. It was as if she didn't have the strength to respond thank you or stand and say good night.

Grace could hear her mother saying, "You're welcome, Mr. Rivia. We hope you enjoy your stay here at our boardinghouse."

Grace and her mother cleared the supper table in silence as Mr. Rivia stood and excused himself to his room to unpack and organize his belongings. It wasn't until they were standing side by side at the kitchen sink washing the dishes that her mother finally spoke.

"So what do you think of the new boarder?" Mamma let out a muted laugh. "He sure was hungry."

Grace kept her head down for fear that Mamma would be able to see straight through to her heart. She pretended she was more interested in having her arms elbow deep in suds, washing silverware, than discuss Mr. Rivia.

"He seemed nice enough" was all she could force herself to reply.

Mamma knew better than to be fooled by the nonchalant response. "Grace, I think Mr. Rivia may be taken with you."

"Mamma, don't say such a thing," Grace said as she continued scrubbing the silverware with fury.

"Grace, stop scrubbing the silverware before you permanently remove its shine, and look at me," Mamma said with a chuckle in her throat. "I saw the way he looked at you during supper. He has a fancy for you."

Only fifteen years old, Grace was not sure if Mamma was right or not. She was too young and inexperienced with men to confirm if Gio had a fancy for her. But as the humid dog days of summer slowly faded into colorful fall afternoons, Grace realized that Mamma's intuition was correct. Gio's quick winks were replaced by long, soft stares from across the parlor; friendly teasing was replaced with subtle compliments. Occasionally Gio would pat Grace on the arm to emphasize a point while talking or put his arm around Grace's shoulder for a brief moment before going up to his room after dinner.

When the colorful trees of the fall rendered their leaves and the air turned brisk, Gio suggested that Grace greet him at the front door each day when he returned to the boardinghouse from work. Grace was only too delighted to oblige. She would busy herself in the morning hours with helping Mamma prepare meals, clean the boarders' rooms and common bath, and do laundry; but as the afternoon hours approached, she chose to do chores close to the front room, where she could occasionally glance out the big picture window to watch and listen for Gio's arrival. He would come to the door and hand her his lunch pail, hat, and wrap in exchange for a steaming cup of coffee and one of Mamma's freshly baked cookies. They would sit in the parlor and talk—reminiscing about the past, reflecting on the now, and sharing dreams of the future—until it was time for Gio to wash up for supper and time for Grace to help Mamma in the kitchen.

As this daily routine continued, Grace learned many things about Gio. She learned that he came to America for prosperity. He was so happy to be in the USA that he kissed the ground at Ellis Island when he got off the ship. He came to be a bricklayer for his brothers' construction business but wanted to start his own construction company someday. Their talks showed her that he was a visionary and a dreamer. When he talked about his future, he spoke with such detail and determination that it was as though he was speaking of the present. No matter how big or small the job, he took pride in what he set out to accomplish. He always finished what he started, often amazing the construction company with his ability to produce a better finished product than what was originally drafted. He was organized and logical, a workaholic, and a perfectionist, often demanding these traits from others he worked with, and was intolerant of those who did not comply. Grace was certain that Gio would accomplish all of his life's dreams, knowing that, with his pointed personality, he would never let his dreams rest as unachieved.

One day in mid-November, Grace noticed that Gio was exceptionally quiet as they sat in the parlor. His mind seemed to be on things far away from the present.

"You're so quiet this afternoon," Grace spoke her observation aloud.

"Yes" was Gio's terse reply.

"Why so melancholy? Did you have a difficult day at work today, Gio?" Grace asked in a tender voice.

"No," he replied in a staccato-like manner.

"What's on your mind then?" Grace asked curiously.

Gio slowly turned, looked Grace directly in her dark eyes, and took her hands in his. "Dance with me, Grace?"

Grace stood obediently as she watched Gio slowly walk over to the music player and turn it on. He turned and stared at her with such intensity that Grace felt he could look straight through to her soul. Grace, never experiencing a man look at her in such a way, stood completely still. Gio half danced, half walked back across the room to where she was standing and gently took her hands. He wrapped one of her hands around his back and tenderly held the other in his own hand. He stroked her long, straight hair.

Finally he smiled and whispered, "I love your freckles, Grace."

Grace could feel her face turning red. She hated that she was so shy. Gio's dance moves paralleled his personality. He held her firmly against his body and moved her around the front room with confidence as if his every step was well thought out and the unseen dance path was organized and logical. Grace relaxed in his arms and let him lead her wherever he wanted to lead. Gio spoke softly but confidently in her ear. He confessed what was burning in his heart for weeks now.

"Grace, I have been boarding here for four months now. I realize that is not a very long time, but from the first day I saw you on the porch holding that glass of lemonade, I knew you were the one for me. I felt something for you that day. I have been watching you closely over the past few months to try to determine if you feel the same way for me. My reason for asking you to meet me in the front room after work each afternoon was for that intent.

"I realize you are only fifteen, and I am twenty-two. I hope that does not present a concern with your parents, but I am confident that, if I speak to them, they will oblige. I am not convinced that they would approve of you dating an immigrant. Again I am confident that they would give their blessing if I told them that I am in love with you. I trust I am not making a fool of myself by being so bold in confessing this to you, but I know what I want, and I know who I want to share my future with. And I am certain that person is you."

Grace's heart was beating so fast and loud she could hear it pounding in her ears. Although she was not experienced with courting men, she was aware of Gio's growing feelings for her. Their friendship and comfort with one another had developed over the past months to the point where she felt she could talk to him about anything. Love? Did he say that he loved her? Did she hear correctly? She took a second to replay his confession over in her mind. She could feel her eyes and mouth open wide in surprise. She wanted to speak but felt frozen in time. Gio stopped dancing, oblivious to the music that continued to play in the background, and held her hands tenderly, eyes steadfast on hers as he waited patiently for her reply.

"I do not know how Papa would react to your confession, but Mamma would not be surprised," Grace finally said with a throaty giggle. "Mamma guessed this for us all along."

"But what do you think, Grace? How do you feel about me? If you don't tell me soon, I don't know what I'll do. I might go crazy!"

Grace pulled herself together and confessed from her heart, "I love you too, Gio. I think I liked you from that first day too but was not confident enough to admit it. I have not been around many men and felt too inexperienced with love to identify my emotions. It was Mamma who first put my feelings into words for me. When you asked me to meet you at the front door each afternoon after work, I was very excited. I was excited because I was hoping that would lead to a stronger relationship. I have enjoyed spending time with you alone. It has confirmed my feelings for you."

Gio's face brightened with a smile. Before Grace had a change to continue, Gio tenderly smoothed Grace's straight dark hair back from her cheeks. He cupped her face in his hands and gently kissed her on the mouth.

"Grace, will you marry me?" Gio asked in a whisper.

"Gio, you want me to be your wife?"

Grace could hardly get the words out and could feel her face getting red again. She wanted to jump. She wanted to run and tell Mamma she was right all along about this new boarder. She wanted to shout at the top of her lungs, "Of course I will be your wife!" But her thoughts wouldn't turn into words. They silently stuck in her throat.

After a long silence, Grace turned her eyes toward Gio's waiting face and whispered, "Yes."

Gio drew close and softly kissed Grace on the forehead, but before he could kiss her with any more passion, Mamma called from the hallway, interrupting the intimate moment.

"Grace Elizabeth, where are you? I need you in the kitchen immediately." Mamma came around the corner and entered the room. "Mr. Rivia, it is time to wash up for supper now. The pasta is almost done, and it is almost six. Mr. Mahoney and Mr. Wright will be down for supper soon."

Gio let go of Grace's face. "Later," he mouthed.

Grace hurried to the kitchen to help Mamma.

Winter was mild that year for northern Illinois. Gio and Grace took advantage of the unusual weather by taking every opportunity to sneak away from the boardinghouse for long walks in beautiful neighboring parks and along the lakes. Gio loved to sing and dance. Grace's favorite moments alone with Gio were when he would start singing in Italian and pull her close to him and they would dance along the walking trails or at the edge of the lake.

During the day, Mamma kept Grace busy caring for the boardinghouse, fitting and sewing her wedding dress, and cooking and baking for the upcoming late-July wedding. In the evenings, Gio kept Grace busy planning their future. Gio's vision was to start their marriage in a brand-new home. He was able to purchase a piece of land for a fair price not far from her parents' boarding-house. He had a business friend that owed him a favor, and he cashed in on the deal by exchanging the favor for land to build a house.

Gio worked diligently through the mild winter and spring months at the new property in anticipation of its completion for late July. By midsummer, the house was completed to Gio's speci-fications. It felt like years had passed since Gio's proposal and the formal meeting with Mario Santangelo to ask for Grace's hand in marriage. They were each a year older now. Grace felt like she had grown years in just a few short months, and Gio assured her that she was ready for a lifelong commitment with him by her side.

Late July was hot but not humid. Gio and Grace stood in the neatly groomed backyard of the boardinghouse under an over-burdened arbor weighted down with pink clematises. Antonia sat quietly next to Mario as she solemnly watched her oldest daughter join her life with Mr. Rivia. She watched and listened as the couple stood hand in hand before the minister and the audience of family and close friends, vowing their love for each other in good times and bad and in sickness and in health.

The reception was a grand celebration. Antonia and her younger daughter, Elena, spent the morning decorating the parlor with lights and flowers from the garden. It was the perfect setting for the lively celebration. Everyone ate, drank, and danced. Grace danced first with her father. Next she danced with Elena, thanking her for the fine job she did decorating the parlor. She was so enamored with the grand celebration that she moved on to dancing with her cousins and then some friends.

Gio was watching from across the room, letting Grace have her fun. He knew he should be out on the dance floor enjoying this special moment with his new wife and her family, but he was tired. The past few weeks of wedding planning had exhausted him to the point that he just wanted the day to be over so he could start his life with Grace alone. Standing on the sideline, patience wearing thin, he made his way over to her and grabbed her arm.

"Hey, remember me?" he said in a feel-sorry-for-me type of voice.

Grace chuckled under her breath. "How could I forget you? You are Gio Rivia, my husband. That word feels so strange to say aloud. I hope I get used to saying it soon. I wanted to tell you how handsome you look in your suit. You look perfect—your hair, suit and tie, and your shoes—just like you came off a newspaper page. I promise the rest of the night will be spent with you, husband." Grace let out a short giggle at the new word added to her verbal vocabulary just a few hours ago. "Will that make you happy?"

"Nothing would make me happier. But do you think we could leave soon? I am anxious to get my wife home. If all goes as I planned, we will have many happy days in our new home starting tonight."

"Gio, I feel like we need to stay a little while longer since these relatives and friends came to celebrate with us. Let's dance. I don't have to dance with another relative or friend. I will only save the rest of the dances for you. Then I promise, as soon as the party begins to slow down, we will leave." Grace knew that this was not what Gio wanted to hear but said it anyway.

"You go right ahead and dance with every person in the room. I will be over there waiting for you," Gio said in a harsh voice. "Just make it fast so we can head home."

Grace was uncomfortable with his response but made the best of the time she had left of the celebration. Not long afterward, Gio and Grace bid their family and friends goodbye, promising that they would come to visit often. As Grace stood on the very same porch where, just a year ago, she first met Gio, she was both excited and nervous. What would the days ahead hold for her as Mrs. Gio Rivia? She knew that, as soon as she walked off the porch of her parents' boardinghouse, she would be leaving her childhood behind, only to begin her new life in her new home as a married woman.

Kristine Avenue House

Briarton, Illinois
1919–1926

"LOOK AT HOW SMALL HE is, Gio," Grace whispered in a breathy, tired voice. "Just seven pounds, seven ounces. So tiny," Grace observed. She was surprised at how well the baby had latched on and was nursing like a champ. "What name are we going to give this little one?"

"You are well aware of the answer to that, Grace. You know, as Italians, we will follow the customs of naming our children using the traditions set before us for generations," Gio answered in a stern voice.

Grace shifted uncomfortably in the bed. She had only given birth a few hours ago. She was very tired, weak, and sore. The midwife Marino was still in the room. She was just finishing up cleaning the birthing area and gathering the last of her belongings. Grace was embarrassed for her to hear Gio's voice.

"He has to be named Vincenzo, after my father," Gio continued. "It is the Italian tradition that the firstborn son be named after the father's father. If the baby was a girl, she is to be named after the father's mother. Vincenzo. No middle name. That will be his name," Gio replied without taking a breath or a second to think.

Midwife Marino finished her duties and walked over to Grace's bed. "Congratulations again, Grace! You delivered this baby like a wonder!" Midwife Marino released a quiet giggle. "You certainly did better than most woman delivering their first child. Now please get some rest." She signed and handed Grace baby Vincenzo's birth certificate and said, "I will return tomorrow to check up on you." She bent down and gently kissed Grace on the forehead before she exited the bedroom.

Gio waited until she was out of earshot and walked slowly to the bed, where Grace was nursing the baby. "He really is small, isn't he?" Gio looked apologetically into Grace's eyes. "Sorry for being so short with you a while ago. I am tired and cranky from being up all night with you while you were in labor. I thought you would have remembered what we discussed months ago about the importance of following traditions of naming a baby in an Italian family."

Grace remained still and quiet. She knew better than to speak. She knew, if she gave her opinion, he would raise his voice and startle the baby. She remained still and stared into Gio's eyes. Gio gently kissed her, told her how sweet the baby looked nursing on her breast, and left the room. Once baby Vincenzo was done feeding, Grace swaddled him in the blanket that her mother knitted for him and sat, watching him sleep.

"Oh, sweet Vincenzo, I have so many dreams for you," Grace whispered tenderly. "Vincenzo, that is not the name I would have chosen for you, but I guess it is important to follow tradition. I wanted you to have a middle name too. Someday I will share with you the names I had picked out for you and will tell you the story of how you became a Vincenzo with no middle name." Grace quietly giggled under her breath. "My wish for you, my son, is that you grow up to be strong and confident like your father. I pray to God that you do not grow up to have my personality, shy and timid, afraid of everything, and nervous to speak your mind. Looks, they come and go with age, my sweet boy, and they do not matter to me. I will love you no matter what you grow to look like, but as a man someday, my prayer for you is that you grow up to have that strong, confident personality of your daddy."

Grace held Vincenzo close as he peacefully slept and gently traced his face with her finger. When she stopped, Vincenzo opened his eyes for a brief moment and locked eyes with his mommy. Grace looked down at him and smiled. The baby was staring at her so intently. It was as if he wanted to say something.

"I left something out of my wish, didn't I, Vincenzo? I can tell you want me to add something very important. You are right, sweet baby. I want you to be educated. Good in arithmetic and reading and writing. I want you to have a smart, quick mind…like me."

Grace cherished every moment she spent with Vincenzo. She enjoyed doting on him through the day, reading him books, playing him music, and getting down on the floor to play with toys. Gio was gone long hours in the day working as a bricklayer at his construction job and often came home to a sleeping baby. Grace did not mind getting up to tend to the baby's needs in the evening as Gio slept soundly through the night. She surprised herself at how fast she recovered from giving birth and how easily she fell into her new mommy role. She never considered herself the motherly type but seemed to fall solidly into the role from the very beginning.

To Gio's dismay, Grace started talking about having another baby before Vincenzo was even two.

"I don't know, Gio. I have surprised myself with this whole mothering thing. I think I am ready to try again. Vincenzo is almost two, and I want him to have a little sister or brother to play with," Grace poured from her heart. "I want the kids to grow up close in age so they can relate to one another and be playmates. Please say you are ready too, Gio," Grace pleaded.

It was not long afterward that Grace announced that she was expecting their second child.

"It's a girl," the midwife Marino announced. "She's seven pounds and five ounces. I will go clean her up and be right back to hand you your new baby. Any names in mind for this one?" the midwife questioned with a smile, remembering the curt conversation regarding Italian traditions on baby naming that Gio had with Grace after the birth of Vincenzo.

Midwife Marino knew that Grace lost the battle at the last baby naming two years ago and was eager to see who would win the naming of this baby girl. She quickly and professionally whisked the wailing baby girl out of the birthing room and rolled her eyes back at Gio and Grace. The midwife knew Gio would win the naming of this baby too.

"I have been thinking of naming her Bella," she said sheepishly. "I thought that would be close enough to your mother's name to satisfy the strong tradition you feel obliged to follow, and we could give her the middle name of Anne. Bella Anne, doesn't that sound like a precious name for our daughter, Gio?"

"Grace, you know the answer to this ridiculous question. We followed tradition when Vincenzo was born, and we will follow tradition again. The first female child is to be named after the father's mother. Mother's name is Isabella Carla!" he said with a shout.

Gio stood up from where he was sitting on the bed next to Grace and started pacing the floor. His face grew redder with every step. Finally he stopped and turned back to look at her.

"We will call her Carla. That's as far as I will budge with breaking tradition, and that's all there is to this conversation," Gio sputtered and rushed out of the room.

Grace wanted to continue the conversation, but she could hear midwife Marino coming back down the hallway carrying baby Carla. The baby never stopped wailing from the minute she was born. Grace hated to admit it, but the loud crying gave her a tremendous headache.

"Would you like to try calming your new daughter, Grace?" the midwife asked in a sweet voice. "It seems I am having no luck soothing her. Perhaps she desires the closeness of her mother."

She placed the new baby girl in Grace's arms with a smile. She was glad the labor and delivery were over for Grace and that it turned out positive. Being Grace's midwife two years ago when she delivered Vincenzo, she recognized that this delivery was a bit more difficult.

Midwife Marino smiled tenderly at Grace and told her again as she did two years ago at the birth of Vincenzo, "You did a wonderful job birthing this sweet baby, Grace. I will return tomorrow to check up on you." She bent down and kissed Grace on the forehead, handed her Carla's birth certificate, and exited the bedroom.

Grace was excited to be a mother again and that the baby was a girl. It was obvious that Carla had a lot to say. She cried and whimpered for an hour after she was born. It took some effort for Grace to get her new baby to settle down and finally rest peacefully. As she looked down at the new baby, cleaned and swaddled in a new blanket, she realized that she had just as many dreams for Carla as she had for Vincenzo. Grace tenderly stroked Carla's dark hair and round face.

"Oh, Carla, I have so many dreams for you," Grace whispered, feeling a moment of déjà vu. "When I held your brother for the very first time, I looked into his eyes and wished for him to be just like his daddy, strong and confident."

Grace continued to stroke Carla's face as Carla started to whimper again. With some adjustments to the blanket and some gentle rocking, Carla finally stopped wailing and fell asleep in her mother's arms.

"My dream for you is that you will grow to be a strong, confident woman with a good education and show the men of this world that women are needed for other things beside cleaning, cooking, and having babies. I don't want you to be a scared, quiet, or a timid girl inside," Grace closed her eyes and whispered, "like your mother."

She sat, rocking Carla, dreaming of this little one's future, until she grew too tired to hold her any longer. Placing her gently in her crib, Grace smiled. One thing was certain—she could not deny that Carla had her same dark complexion, nose, and round face.

Shortly afterward, Gio brought Vincenzo in to meet his new baby sister. Gio and Grace sat back and watched the interaction.

They took turns holding the baby, kissing her and combing her thick dark hair.

"I think she looks like you, Grace," Gio commented. "She definitely has your coloring and hair," Gio said with a giggle in his throat. "I hope she turns out to be a good housewife and cook like you too," Gio said.

Grace averted her eyes.

Although Grace loved being a mother, she did not fall into motherhood as easily this time as she did after the birth of Vincenzo. The addition of Carla to the family brought many demands with it. Carla was a different personality than Vincenzo. Vincenzo was content playing with his toys or looking at a book on the floor, but Carla was more demanding. She was more sensitive, crying often, and required more one-on-one attention from Grace. With a two-year-old and a newborn in the house, Grace found it more difficult to keep up with the demands of the house and spend as much time with the children as she wanted. Many days, she felt overwhelmed with the daunting new role of mother of two and hated to admit that she often had a raging headache by the end of the day. Her biggest fear was that Gio would want another baby soon. She was content with the two she had.

However, two years later, on a sunny summer afternoon in late June, midwife Marino confirmed to Grace that she was pregnant with her third child and due in the spring. This confirmation took Grace by surprise. She was trying to be so careful to put a few more years between pregnancies. When she finally told Gio the news, he was excited and was hoping for another boy. It felt as though Grace no sooner found out she was pregnant than she was beginning to show. She soon could not fit into her regular clothes; and before long, it was more difficult to get down on the floor to play with Vincenzo and carry Carla, who needed her mother's nonstop attention.

Early one January morning, Gio came running into the house shouting and waving a piece of paper in his hand.

"Grace, Grace, where are you?" he called to her, out of breath. "I got a letter from New York today. My mother and baby sister, Sofia, are coming for a visit!"

Gio could hardly contain himself. It had been six years since he had seen his mother and youngest sister. When he left Italy, his mother hugged his neck, not knowing when she would see her son next. Years later, Gio got word that she arrived in America and settled in Brooklyn, New York. This was convenient for his mother but hundreds of miles away from Illinois. With meeting Grace, getting married, building a house, starting a family, and working night and day, Gio never had a chance to travel there to visit. He barely knew his sister, Sofia. She was only a skinny young girl of twelve when he left Italy.

"Grace, you will finally have the chance to meet my mother and sister." Gio closed his eyes and hugged the letter tightly to his chest. He mumbled something in Italian that Grace could not understand.

"Gio, I am seven months pregnant and big as a house with this one. I don't feel well most days. I look terrible. Vincenzo and Carla are underfoot, and I have no idea where we will squeeze two more adults in this two-bedroom house. I would never say no, but..." Grace looked deep into Gio's eyes and spoke in a tender voice, "I would be honored to have your mother and sister come stay here for a visit. I am excited to meet them and to get to know them. Please explain the situation before they come so they know what they will be walking into."

Grace giggled as she hiked Carla up higher on her hip, wiped her tears, and gave Vincenzo's trucks a shove with her foot at an attempt to make a path back to the kitchen.

"How long are they staying? Did they give any indication?" Grace shouted back at Gio, who remained in the front room hugging the piece of paper to his chest.

"The letter says one month!" Gio shouted back.

Grace was glad Gio remained in the front room. She didn't want him to see the look of shock and horror on her face or hear her response.

19

Instead she replied, "Oh, that will be a nice long visit for you and your family."

Grace sat at the kitchen table, face in hands, dreading the visit before they even arrived. How was she going to prepare for their visit? She hardly slept. Most days, she had a tremendous headache and was bigger with this baby than she ever was with either Vincenzo or Carla.

In the week that followed, Grace made accommodations for her mother-in-law and sister-in-law to sleep in the children's room. For the next month, Vincenzo and Carla would have to sleep in the same room with her and Gio. Grace was too big to be moving beds and carrying baskets of toys from one room to another, but she did it anyway. Gio seemed to always be at work and never around to help. Vincenzo, age four, and Carla, almost two years old now, were either into everything, crying, or arguing with one another.

It was challenging for Grace to prepare the house, grocery shop, cook, and stock the freezer, as Gio ordered, and keep an eye on the children too. She felt overwhelmed and tired and always had a headache. Sometimes she couldn't take it anymore and would stop and weep. It was a good thing during that week of preparation that Gio was not home because, besides the small children who were too engaged in playing or arguing, Grace was able to vent her frustrations audibly to an empty house.

The day finally arrived. Grace's stomach was in knots as she watched the car carrying her mother-in-law and sister-in-law pull up into their driveway. She stood at the front door with one hand gently rubbing her swollen pregnant belly and one hand rubbing her head. Vincenzo and Carla circled at her feet. Gio ran out the front door before the car came to a stop. She watched as her mother-in-law slowly emerged from the car. She had a wide smile on her face and leaped into Gio's arms as they kissed and exchanged greetings in Italian. Grace noticed that her mother-in-law was toting a white box tied with twine. Cookies from a New York bakery was Grace's guess. She looked warm and had an engaging smile. She was laughing and holding her son that she had not seen in years. It was a tender moment for Gio and his mother and for Grace as well as she watched from the door.

However, there was nothing that could have prepared her for seeing her sister-in-law for the first time. From the front door, Grace could see a small-framed girl struggling with her skirt to scoot across the back seat of the car. Grace watched as an elegant leg wearing a butter-soft gray leather midcalf shoe emerged from the back seat. A stunningly beautiful young lady with light-brown hair was standing in her driveway. Her sister-in-law's hair was curled to perfection and pulled to one side with a wide navy satin ribbon that matched her dress. The neatly tied bundle of curls hung down almost to her waist. Every twist and turn of her long curls enhanced their natural highlights. She had big blue eyes and fair skin.

Grace had never seen clothes like the ones Sofia was wearing. They looked handmade by an accomplished New York seamstress. The fabrics were like nothing Grace had ever seen in Illinois. Navy and gray swirls with accents of silver metal threads that caught the sunlight ran through the design. The neckline and hem were both trimmed in navy lace. Sofia's stockings were lace and matched the pattern of lace on her dress. Grace could feel her mouth drop open. Gio did not prepare her for this. He described his youngest sister as a skinny girl with poor skin and spaced teeth. Grace was not mentally prepared to see this lovely young lady.

Grace corralled Vincenzo and Carla and headed outside for them to greet their grandmother and aunt.

"Welcome to our home," Grace heard herself say as she hugged her mother-in-law. "I trust you had a good trip."

"Yes, it was long but worth every minute to come and see my Gio and his family," Isabella said in a broken English accent. "This is Sofia, Gio's sister." Isabella turned and grabbed Sofia by the arm to pull her closer to meet her new sister-in-law.

"Hello" was all Sofia said in a soft voice.

"Hello," Grace answered as she leaned toward Sofia to give her a hug. "Welcome to our home. I hope you will find it comfortable here in spite of sharing our small home with two young children." Grace gently pulled Vincenzo and Carla from behind her skirt to introduce them to their grandmother and aunt. "This is Vincenzo, and this is our daughter, Carla," Grace announced proudly.

Isabella scooped both up in her arms at the same time and started speaking to them in Italian. She slathered them with kisses and hugs and even pinched their cheeks a time or two.

"And soon I will be greeting this new baby with kisses and hugs," Isabella said with an excited shine in her eye.

Grace looked down at her swollen pregnant belly, gave it a pat, and just smiled.

"Oh, don't you worry, Grace. Momma and Sofia will be fine here." Gio put one arm around his mother and the other around his sister and led them to the front door of the house.

Gio carried their luggage to their room and gave them a quick tour of the house. Grace watched and listened from the kitchen as Gio took his mother and sister around the house, Vincenzo and Carla following close behind. She chuckled to herself as she stood in the kitchen doorway watching. She had a flashback of how big she once thought this house was—how big it seemed to her and Gio when they first moved in. Now, with two more adults crammed into the space, it's going to feel like the walls are caving in. Just thinking about it made it hard for Grace to breathe.

"Breathe, Grace. Just relax and breathe," she mumbled under her breath.

The visit with Gio's mother and sister went by faster than Grace expected. Vincenzo and Carla found it delightful to be able to sleep in their parents' bedroom; and Isabella helped Grace each day with the cooking, household chores, and watching the children. It was interesting to hear Isabella's stories of Gio as a baby and young boy, their life in Italy, and coming to America. Grace, in return, filled her mother-in-law in on how she met Gio at the boardinghouse and their courtship days.

Grace was interested in getting to know Sofia too, but she never seemed to be around. When Grace would ask where Sofia was, Isabella would answer that she was either in the bathtub soaking, brushing out her hair, or was outside talking to one of the neighbors. Grace felt badly that she was missing out on spending time with Sofia, but she was too busy with all the other demands of the house to try to hunt her down. It would have been nice if Sofia would have helped too, but at least Grace had Isabella helping. For that, she was very thankful. Grace was getting bigger each day. Even Isabella noticed the increase of Grace's girth since she arrived.

"This baby is going to be ten pounds, Grace," Isabella said one day in her broken English accent as she watched Grace going around the house picking up toys.

The baby was active with strong, aggressive movements. It often kept her up at night, preventing her from a good night's sleep. Her headaches were more frequent and lasting longer now too. Grace mentioned her weight gain and headaches to the midwife; but any concern was quickly passed off as lack of sleep, the demands of Vincenzo and Carla, and the extra weight she was carrying from this bigger baby. Grace tried to relax, but it was getting more and more difficult to do so. She was looking forward to the delivery of this baby and the end of this particular pregnancy.

One night, close to the end of Isabella and Sofia's visit, Gio and Grace were woken up by Isabella shuffling around and whispering loudly to Sofia in Italian in their living room. Grace could not understand what she was saying, but she knew it had something to do with Sofia coming home late.

"Gio, why don't you go out there and see what's going on?" Grace asked with concern.

"No, I think my momma and Sofia are arguing about Sofia going to our neighbor's house again." Gio put his finger to his lips to quiet Grace and took a few minutes to listen more carefully. "It sounds like Momma is upset because Sofia was out drinking with him this time and came home drunk. She's upset because she doesn't feel Sofia has spent quality time with us during this visit. Momma is telling her that she's either primping to go out on the town with our neighbor or she's at his house. I do not want to intrude on their conversation. Momma sounds very upset," Gio whispered back to Grace.

Before long, the loud whispering escalated into loud speaking.

"Gio, your mother sounds really upset. She's getting louder. If she gets any louder, she's going to wake Vincenzo and Carla," Grace whispered.

"All right, I'll go out there and see what's going on."

Gio got out of bed, threw on some clothes that were folded on a chair, and went out into the living room. Grace could hear Gio trying his best to calm Sofia and his mother down. Gio had to raise his voice louder in order to be heard over their voices. Grace was nervous because she did not want Vincenzo and Carla to wake up. Her head had been raging with pain all day, and the last thing she wanted was the children to wake up. The baby inside her was definitely awake and demonstrating his disagreement of the situation by rolling and kicking her. She sat up in bed, trying to balance her round body, waiting for the commotion to stop and for everyone to go back to bed. But the yelling and scuffling about in the living room continued.

As Grace sat there in her bedroom, she could hear Isabella shouting at Sofia, calling her a disgrace to the family. She was shouting that they were here to visit Gio and his family; but all she wanted to do was leave the house, get drunk, and flirt with the neighbor. Grace knew she was going to have to go out to the living room and join forces with Gio in trying to calm things down before the children woke up. She decided to give it a few more minutes. She really did not want to confront Gio's family, but she didn't want this commotion in her house at this late hour either.

Grace was puzzled when she heard the arguing move from the living room to her kitchen.

"What on earth is going on out there?" Grace mumbled to herself as she rolled her body out of bed to a standing position.

She tried to pull her robe close over her large frame and tie it in place with the belt. She discovered the robe no longer fit her correctly; but she figured, with all the commotion, the last thing anyone would notice was a gap in the front of her robe. She felt around on the floor near her bed with one foot to try to find her slippers. Having no luck feeling for them, she slowly bent over with a moan to take a look for them. It was official—she now could no longer see over her growing belly.

She waddled out of her bedroom in slow motion and narrowly missed being knocked over by Sofia, who ran past her in a flash on her way to the bedroom she was sharing with her momma. From the panicked look on Sofia's face, Grace knew that Sofia realized she was in serious trouble this time. Grace could not see Isabella or Gio but knew that they were in the kitchen. She could hear Isabella yanking open drawers and rummaging through them, looking for something. Whatever was going on, Gio was shouting at his mother to stop and calm down. From Isabella's half-English, half-Italian response, Grace could sense that she was not going to give up this time until Sofia learned her lesson.

Grace stood in the living room, not knowing what to do. She decided to stand there and wait for either Gio and his mom to come out of the kitchen or Sofia to come out of the bedroom. When neither happened, she decided to step back a few steps and lean her heavy body against the living room wall for support. Just as she settled there, Isabella came flying out of the kitchen like a bull out of its corral, swinging a butcher's knife high above her head. Her face was as red as the apples Grace had sitting in a bowl on her kitchen table. She was out of breath from angrily rummaging through the kitchen, and she was yelling something in Italian at Sofia that Grace was sure was full of threats and promises.

Even though Grace knew Isabella was running after Sofia, she seemed to be running straight for Grace. Grace froze in place. Her feet felt nailed to the floor. Her whole body turned cold from a fear that she had never experienced before. Grace felt like she was watching this scene from outside of her body. She heard herself let out a bloodcurdling scream. Isabella ignored Grace's scream and ran right past her, nonreactive and emotionless, and ran straight toward the bedroom where Sofia was hiding. With a mixed look of disgust, determination, and anger pasted on her face, sweat dripping profusely down her once-peaceful, loving face, Isabella chased Sofia out of the bedroom and back into the living room.

Grace felt her shaking knees buckle beneath her as her pregnant body collapsed to the floor with a thud. She lay there curled in a fetal position up against the wall where she once stood. She continued screaming until her throat could no longer render a sound. Her eyes and mouth remained wide open in shock. Her head was pounding like the drumline of a band during a major competition. Grace did not move or speak but was very aware of Isabella's yelling and actions. Grace could see her mother-in-law chasing her sister-in-law with the knife raised high in the air, taking swipes at Sofia, and Sofia crying hysterically, disheveled and drunk, and clumsily circling the living room a few more times before Gio finally caught his mother by the arm and stopped the disastrous scene. Vincenzo and Carla woke up confused and crying.

"Mommy, Mommy, what is going on?" cried Vincenzo.

Grace could hear Carla crying. She wanted to unfold her body and get up to comfort her children, but she had no voice and was frozen in the fetal position she collapsed in on the floor. Fear like she had never felt before washed over her body. Hot, burning pain stabbed though her chest as her heart raced to an unfamiliar beat, and her head felt like it exploded and was in pieces on the floor. Her dry mouth was open. She could not scream, call for Gio, or move. She lay there, seemingly watching herself from outside of her body.

"I am no longer a baby, Momma. I am eighteen years old. If I want to be with a man, I can. You no longer have to watch out for me or stay up waiting for me!" Sofia screamed in a drunken, slurred voice to her mother.

Realizing everyone was awake now, including the children, Isabella no longer felt an obligation to be quiet. "You are nothing but a drunk and a whore, Sofia. You promised me that you would not do this when we came to visit your brother. You have men in New York, men everywhere you go. Now even in Illinois, you do this to me?" Isabella yelled in a hateful voice. "You are an embarrassment to this family. We will leave in the morning for New

York. Get in the bedroom and start packing so we can leave first thing in the morning."

Adrenaline finally evened out with exhaustion to follow, and Isabella and Sofia retired to the bedroom to start gathering their belongings. Gio returned the knife to the kitchen and then joined his mother and sister in their bedroom. He remained with them until he felt it was safe that they would not start up again and walked back into the living room.

With all the commotion, Gio did not realize that Grace had left the bedroom and that the children had woken up. As he reclined on the couch, holding his head, trying to erase what he had just seen and heard, he caught a glimpse of Grace's slipper out of the corner of his eye. Startled to see her out of the bedroom and horrified that she may have witnessed the whole ugly event, he jumped off the couch and ran to her. Gio was not prepared for what he saw. Grace was collapsed on the floor, and Vincenzo and Carla were huddled around her, resting their tired heads on her swollen pregnant belly. Gio gathered up the sleepy children and put them back in bed, giving each one a tender kiss on the forehead. He quickly ran back to attend to his wife.

"Grace, are you okay? Grace, look at me," Gio pleaded.

Grace remained frozen on the floor, eyes and mouth wide open as if in shock.

Gio tried again, "Grace, are you okay? Will you please look at me. Say something!"

When Gio was not able to get Grace to respond to him, he gently unfolded Grace's body without moving her from that spot, trying to make her as comfortable as possible on the floor. He ran in the bedroom and grabbed a quilt to throw over her shivering body. Gio left Grace on the floor and rushed to the kitchen to call midwife Marino. Once he knew that she was on her way, Gio returned to his wife. Grace continued to be unresponsive to Gio's voice and touch, staring into space, frozen. All he could do was hold her and stroke her hair and talk calmly to her as he waited for the midwife. He knew she was breathing, but the best Gio could guess was that she was in some kind of shock. It felt like an eternity. The midwife finally arrived thirty minutes later.

Gio sat on the floor next to Grace as he explained the situation to the midwife. He explained that he was too distracted with getting his mother and sister to calm down that he actually did not see Grace come out of the bedroom. With the help of the midwife, Gio was able to half carry, half walk Grace back into bed. She stayed until Grace semi came out of her frozen state and was able to nod her head and point in response to questions asked. The midwife tightly wrapped Grace's head with a dish towel to relieve some of her headache. At five in the morning, she left the Rivia home, stating that Grace needed some time to calm down and get a good night's sleep and that she was optimistic that she would find Grace recovered by midmorning the next day.

As promised, midwife Marino returned at noon the next day. She was happy to find that Gio's mother and sister left earlier that morning. She knew the stress of having them out of the house would be good for Grace. However, after a quick assessment of Grace, the midwife did not find much improvement. Grace was able to whisper, but her speech was slow and staggered. Her eyes were full of anxiety and darted back and forth in a worried pattern around the bedroom. She sat in bed, wringing her hands, and she had frequent bursts of weeping. Midwife Marino asked Grace if she would like to walk to the living room, where it would be more comfortable to sit and talk. It was apparent to her and Gio that Grace was having difficulty lifting her left leg when walking.

"How did you sleep last night, Grace?" the midwife asked in a calm, sweet voice.

"My head pounded like a drum. It has felt like this almost this whole pregnancy, but for the last week or so, it has pounded nonstop," Grace answered in a slow, barely audible, slurred voice.

"I will rewrap your head in a tight towel before I leave. I will add some ice chips to the back of the towel. That often helps relieve pounding. How about if we try that, Grace?" she offered.

"Anything you can think of to give me some relief," Grace agreed in a slow, soft voice.

"You rest here on the couch, Grace, while I go to the kitchen and prepare the ice wrap for your head. Gio, may I speak to you in the kitchen, please?" the midwife said as she motioned for Gio to follow her out of the room.

Grace was so exhausted she did not even respond. She reached for a pillow at the other end of the couch, placed it under her head, and was asleep before midwife Marino and Gio left the room.

Once in the kitchen, she did not waste any time or words. "Gio, it is my recommendation that you call their family doctor as soon as I leave and get Grace in for an evaluation as soon as possible. She has suffered some sort of emotional trauma, shock, or possibly a mild stroke from the scene here last night. I am not a medical doctor, but something is not right. Her speech is not normal. Her eyes are full of fear. She is weeping on and off, and she is dragging her left leg. It will not be long before her body will be giving birth. She needs all the strength she can muster for that, especially since this is going to be her biggest baby yet. Please do not delay, Gio. I am very concerned."

Midwife Marino gave Gio a promise-me nod, prepared the ice wrap, and returned to the living room. By the time Gio put a call into the family doctor and returned to the living room, she was gone.

Dr. Denero was able to see Grace the next afternoon. He listened to Gio's seemingly endless story of the additional stress in the home due to his mother and sister's visit. Gio explained in detail the events of the previous night. He told the doctor that, long before last night, Grace had severe headaches. In fact, she had headaches throughout this entire pregnancy. Dr. Denero listened as Gio explained how he would give her pain medication, would wrap Grace's head with a tight towel, and make her rest in a darkened room. Nothing seemed to help.

He went on to tell the doctor that he had witnessed Grace being tired and showing stress over caring for their two children. However, he made it abundantly clear that Grace's reaction to the previous night's event was the first time he had ever seen her react in that manner.

Dr. Denero listened and waited patiently for Gio to complete his account of the story. The minute he could get a word in the conversation, he turned away from Gio and addressed Grace. As the doctor turned his chair toward his patient, he saw a withdrawn, scared woman—head down, eyes closed, and arms wrapped around her swollen body. She sat so quietly that, if the doctor had not been looking straight at her, he would have never known another person was in the examining room.

"Grace, can you tell me, in your own words, how you are feeling?" Dr. Denero asked in a soft, kind voice.

He listened carefully to Grace as she explained the differences with this pregnancy versus the others. She explained the overwhelming demand of two small children running around and the unbearable headaches that were coming more frequently, were more powerful, and were lasting longer. She gave an account of the previous evening. She explained in detail the scare she felt of what she thought she was going to see but didn't. She explained how she dropped down to the ground and the weakness in her left leg. The doctor was very still and silent during Grace's time to talk, but his mind was speaking volumes. When she finished telling Dr. Denero everything that she thought was important for him to hear, she dropped her head on her chest, closed her eyes, and waited for the doctor to speak.

"Grace, I'm going to start by giving you a physical exam. That will determine our next step. Mr. Rivia, would you please wait out in the waiting room until I call for you?" Dr. Denero said with concern.

Thirty minutes later, Dr. Denero called for Gio to meet him in his private office. Gio walked into the doctor's private office but did not see Grace.

"Where's Grace, Dr. Denero?" Gio asked as he gave the lavishly furnished office a questioning glance.

"She's still in the exam room getting dressed. I wanted to speak with you privately first," Dr. Denero replied as he sat down with a thud in his big leather office chair. Dr. Denero sighed. "I completed a thorough physical exam on Grace. All seems to be well with the baby. Movement, heartbeat, all fine. One thing I can tell you with surety is that this baby is going to be very big. My guess would be that this one is going to be a minimum of ten pounds.

"This is your wife's third child, so I am not as concerned with her having a ten-pound baby as her third baby as I would be if it was her first. Also, I know that she has had midwife Marino with her for the other births. That will be comforting for Grace this time around since delivering a ten-pound baby is not going to be easy. Grace can rely on the midwife for reassurance since she has had birth history with her," Dr. Denero recited as if all in one breath.

"However, Mr. Rivia, I am very concerned about Grace's health. The severity and frequency of her headaches and the physical reaction to the events of last evening are concerning to me. She still has not regained full strength in her left leg, which was first noticed after last night's scare, and her blood pressure is way too high. Therefore, I am going to write an order for you and your wife to go see a specialist for evaluation immediately.

"I am going to mark the order urgent. I do not want you to wait until the baby is born to see this specialist. Since I am marking this order as urgent, you and Grace should be able to confirm an appointment this week. The sooner the better. You can set up this appointment at our front desk before you leave my office today." Dr. Denero stood up slowly and waited until Gio was looking him straight in the eye before speaking, "Here is the order. Please show it to the ladies at the front desk, and they will help you get scheduled with a specialist."

Gio could see and hear the urgency in the doctor's demeanor. "Thank you, Dr. Denero. I will get this appointment set up immediately."

Gio met Grace in the hallway and explained to her all that the doctor told him. As suggested, Gio stopped by the front desk of Dr. Denero's office and scheduled the appointment with the specialist. The appointment was in two days.

Grace's baby did not cooperate. At 2:30 a.m. the very next day, Grace woke up in severe pain. She woke up dreaming that she was being repeatedly hit by a truck. Her water broke sometime in the middle of the night, but her exhausted body and mind did not wake her up. She was lying in the middle of a soaked bed. By 3:30 a.m., Gio was on the phone with midwife Marino, instructing her to come quickly. Even though this was Grace's third baby, Gio did not know what to do to comfort her while they waited for the midwife to arrive. Finally Grace demanded that he go to the children's bedroom and stay there until the baby was born. He didn't know how to comfort her, and frankly she was tired of all of his excuses in trying to diplomatically get out of being with her while she was in labor. She was never so happy to see midwife Marino.

"Grace, you and I already know this is going to be your biggest baby. You do exactly what I say, and we will work together delivering this one," midwife Marino said in a reassuring voice and questionable smile.

"Okay, okay, thank you," Grace squeaked out in a raspy, breathless voice.

She had been a midwife for fifteen years. She was trained well, and she loved her job. She had helped many women deliver their special bundles of joy over the years, but helping Grace deliver her third baby, she felt inadequate. Between 3:30 a.m. and 3:30 p.m., Grace and midwife Marino sweat, cried, walked, rocked, and moaned; but finally after twelve hours, Grace's ten-pound, one-ounce baby boy was born.

The bedroom was a mess when Gio was finally called in to see his big baby boy. The midwife did not bother cleaning up the room before his entrance. She did not think Gio would mind seeing the soiled towels, sheets, pillows, and the birthing instruments strewn all over the floor and dresser. She thought he'd be excited to finally see his newborn baby after the long night and half of the next day. Midwife Marino was sure Gio would oversee the mess and would run to his wife with tenderness, hugs, kisses, and congratulations.

Instead Gio entered the room and shouted, "What a mess! It looks like a war went on in here!"

Midwife Marino was in shock. She knew how hard Grace had worked to birth this baby. Her experience as a midwife told her that delivering a baby of this size was not easy for any woman, let alone a woman in Grace's unhealthy state. The midwife was tired and hungry. It had been a long night and half the next day with several touch-and-go moments where Grace lost a lot of blood. She could not believe Gio's reaction to walking into the room. She could not hold her tongue. This was the third birth she had supervised in this home for this family. She had kept her mouth shut in regard to Mr. Rivia's actions for all the others, but today was not the day to test her. She was tired and covered in blood, and she had not eaten or had anything to drink for over twelve hours. She stood up, feeling confident that it would be okay to leave Grace while she nursed her newborn baby independently, and asked Mr. Rivia to step out in the hallway.

"I am sorry you feel like your bedroom looks like a war zone, Mr. Rivia, but frankly, it was. Your wife had a very difficult time delivering this big baby. She lost a lot of blood. She tore and has many stiches. As you know, she is not in good health. Her blood pressure was high every time I checked her vitals. She had an extreme headache the entire delivery but continued to push with such force that blood spots formed in the whites of her eyes, not to mention that her left leg is not strong and could not hold the birthing formation needed to push the baby out. I will quickly gather my instruments, and I will clean up the room as much as possible. I will be on my way before you come in to introduce the new baby to his brother and sister."

Midwife Marino gave Mr. Rivia a stern look, turned on her heels, and stormed back in to check on Grace. She gathered her items and soiled laundry and left Grace's house. True to her word, she left the house before Gio was back in the bedroom with Vincenzo and Carla.

"Gio, what do you think of this big boy?" Grace asked in a tired voice.

She was sore and weak, but she did not want to show that to Gio. She was just so happy that the delivery was over. She was excited to see Gio's reaction to his big new son. His reaction was not what she expected. Gio was quiet and looked upset. Grace decided to keep talking to try to get him to react.

"What will we name our son?" Grace asked. "Italian tradition says this one should be named after my father, right? He'll be named Mario." She giggled. "It fits. Such a strong name for this big, strong guy!"

"Yes, that's correct, Grace. His name will be Mario," Gio replied, still thinking of midwife Marino's stern comments. "He's sure a big boy. I will go get Vincenzo and Carla to come in to meet their brother!" Gio shouted over his shoulder as he left to retrieve the two little ones.

Mario's brother and sister were intrigued with the new addition to the family. They both took turns brushing his baby-fine hair and holding him on their laps with Gio's guidance. Vincenzo helped Grace put a blue cap on baby Mario's head while Carla gave him soft kisses on his arms.

Later that night, when Grace was alone in her room with her new baby, she held him tenderly; and as she had done with her other two children at birth, she gently spoke over Mario.

"Mario, you are a big, strong baby with a big, strong name. Holding you at birth is like holding a three-month-old baby." Grace giggled at her observation. "I know already just by hearing your loud, strong cry and your determined look that you are going to be a boisterous, confident leader someday." Grace continued to giggle as she gently stroked the soft hair of her biggest baby. "Just look at the size of your chest. You will probably not even fit in the newborn clothes I have for you. No problem, they are just hand-me-downs from Vincenzo anyway."

Just then, Mario let out a loud cry. Grace rocked him tenderly.

"What's the matter, Mario? Did I offend you? Are you trying to let me know that you didn't want to wear Vincenzo's hand-me-down clothes anyway? I can see that you are going to be my child that will only want to wear nice brand-new clothes. I watched you earlier as Vincenzo was brushing your hair. You liked that, didn't you?" Grace giggled at her projected image of her newborn son as a grown adult.

Just then, Mario opened up his little eyes, looked straight into Grace's soul, and let out a loud, long cry.

"Oh my, you sure have a set of good lungs on you, young man. Are you trying to let me know that you are going to be a singer too?"

Mario abruptly stopped crying.

"Message received!"

The next few weeks after Mario's birth were difficult for Grace. Her left leg was uncooperative. It felt numb now more than it ever had, and her headaches sent her to bed with a tightly wrapped head and the lights off. It was difficult to care for a newborn and two active younger children. The demands of the children, the house, and Gio caused Grace to be overwhelmed and spend a lot of her day in tears. Midwife Marino came to do her follow-up visit. Grace unloaded all her cares on her now-good friend. After examining Grace, the midwife expressed her concerns.

"Grace, did Gio ever take you to the specialist that Dr. Denero referred you to?" she asked, trying to not sound alarming.

"We had a scheduled appointment, but I ended up going into labor before we could have our visit. I will tell Gio to reschedule the appointment," Grace said with confidence.

That evening, Grace reminded Gio that they needed to reschedule the appointment with the specialist. She told Gio that, since Mario's birth, she noticed that her left leg was getting more and more difficult to lift. She told Gio that it was difficult to get in and out of the tub, she had difficulty getting up off the floor after playing with Vincenzo and Carla, and sometimes she even tripped from not being able to lift her left foot when walking. She confessed to Gio that, even though she thought it impossible for her headaches to get worse, they had. She told Gio that many days were spent in tears trying to deal with the children while he was at work. Gio listened and made an appointment with the specialist for that same week.

Grace felt nervous as she walked into the specialist's office. She did not want to hear bad news or end up admitted to the hospital. Who would watch Vincenzo, Carla, and baby Mario? Gio tried to calm her down by reminding her how bad her headaches were and how she recently started dragging her left leg.

Dr. Springer was a middle-aged brain specialist that came highly recommended by Dr. Denero. He was light haired, tall, and thin and spoke with a steady, calm voice. His demeanor instantly put Grace at ease. He asked her questions about her health, and she answered in honest, detailed answers. Gio was surprised at her answers. He learned more about Grace's health issues by listening to her talk to the doctor than he knew himself. Her answers painted a clear picture for the doctor. At the end of the question and answers and a physical exam, Dr. Springer announced that he was going to set up a battery of tests for Grace at the local hospital. He explained that the battery of tests would be outpatient and would take approximately four hours. Dr. Springer wanted Grace to complete the battery of tests and scans as soon as possible, so he scheduled the appointment for the next day.

The battery of tests and scans were not as bad as Grace anticipated. Dr. Springer met her at the hospital, and again Grace's anticipation of the tests went right out of her mind as soon as he started instructing her as to what would be forthcoming.

A few days later, Grace and Gio were back in Dr. Springer's office for the results of the tests and scans. In his usual calm voice and noncommittal expressions, Dr. Springer revealed to them that Grace had a blood clot in her brain. This was the main cause of her headaches. At the moment, the blood clot was not completely shutting off oxygen but had already caused some damage, resulting in the numbness and movement in her left leg. No operation was suggested, only medication to treat the blood clot. If the medication did its job, no further damage would be done; and therefore, no further ramifications would result.

The damage that had already taken place was not reversible. Dr. Springer suggested that Grace not have any more children due to the stress and strain on her body from carrying it as well as the delivery. The doctor also gave Grace a second medication for her headaches. Dr. Springer wanted to see Grace back in his office for regular checkups, tests, and scans to make sure the medication was working and that it was agreeing with Grace.

Grace left the office in a happy mood. Hearing that she had a blood clot in her brain was not the best news, but at least, it did not require surgery. She got medication for it and for her headaches. Gio was quiet on the walk back to the car. He looked upset. Grace broke the silence.

"What are you thinking, Gio?" Grace asked in the sweetest voice she could muster.

"I don't like any doctor telling me when my family is complete. What if I wanted more children? What if I wanted a sister for Carla? Family is important. Family is all we have, Grace." Gio angrily unlocked the door to the car and swung it open.

"Dr. Springer was only looking out for my well-being. It is a lot to carry a baby for nine months, not to mention labor and delivery too, Gio. It takes a toll on a woman's body. After three children, I thought we were done anyway. Mario was over ten pounds. What if I have another baby that big?" Grace said tenderly to Gio. "Don't you care enough about me to want me to be well?" she continued.

Now seated in the car, Gio turned and looked at Grace. "I will tell you when we are finished having children. As the leader of our household, I will be the one deciding when that will be. The completion of our family will not come from a doctor," Gio said sternly. "Remember what I said, Grace. The final decision about having other children rests with me!"

Grace rested her head on the back of the car seat for the rest of the ride home. She knew that, when Gio got in these power moods, he was impossible to reason with.

Over time, Grace had fewer and fewer headaches. She noticed that it had been months since she had to tightly wrap her head and dismiss herself from the family to go sit in a darkened room. The medication that Dr. Springer gave her for her headaches was clearly working. Now that she was feeling better, she'd get Vincenzo off to kindergarten and spend the rest of the morning hours reading and playing with Carla and Mario. Sometimes they'd play outside, or sometimes they'd just take a drive. Each day, Grace would plan some activity with the children. It felt so good to be free of her headaches and be able to spend quality time with the children again.

One night, while she and Gio were in bed, Grace brought up something that had been weighing heavy on her heart—Mario's baptism. Since she was feeling better now, maybe it was time to have Mario baptized in the church. It was typical to baptize children within a few weeks of their birth. Vincenzo and Carla were baptized in the church at one week old. However, with Grace being sick, plus taking longer to recover from delivering such a large baby, they decided to wait. With Grace's tests and scans, the time just got away from them. Gio honestly forgot all about having Mario baptized. His birth seemed so long ago. It felt like years since midwife Marino scolded him for stating that their bedroom looked like a war zone after his birth.

Gio thought it was a great idea to go ahead with the baptism. He thought the church would be understanding of the circumstances behind their waiting. Grace contacted the church in the morning and had the arrangements made. Grace and Gio planned a celebratory get-together after the church ceremony at their home with family and close friends. Grace bought Mario a new outfit and hat for the celebration. She combed his thick, curly hair to one side. He looked as darling as any picture of any baby in any magazine. Mario giggled and waved at all the guests. He strutted around as if he understood the party was just for him.

After seeing how crowded they were in the house at Mario's baptism party, Grace came to the conclusion that she and Gio had outgrown their home on Kristine Avenue. What once was a cozy home for them as newlyweds was now busting at the seams. Mario was one and sleeping in a crib in their bedroom. There was barely any room to walk around in there without bumping your toe on something.

Vincenzo was five now, and Carla was three. They shared the second bedroom, but that was also the room that had their toys. It was not unusual for Vincenzo and Carla to wake up in the middle of the night and start playing with the toys in their room. Before long, the whole household was awake due to their laughing and carrying on. Gio would get upset because his sleep was disturbed and he had to work in the morning. Grace was upset because oftentimes their noise would wake up the baby and it took her a while to get him back to sleep. Mulling all this over in her mind, she decided to speak to Gio about moving to a bigger home tonight after supper.

"Gio," Grace called sweetly after she finished cleaning up the kitchen from supper, "I was playing with the children today, and I could not help but notice how crowded we are in this tiny home. Their toys alone consume their room. Remember how big it felt when we first moved in? We hardly had enough furniture to fill up the space," she casually mentioned.

"We're not moving, Grace!" Gio rudely yelled back at her.

"The toys are in their room, and Vincenzo and Carla get up in the middle of the night to play. They wake you up. They wake up Mario. Don't you think it would be better to have a bigger home where they could have a separate area for their toys?"

Without warning, Gio vaulted out of his chair, bounded over to where Grace was standing, and slapped her in the face. "Now you listen to me. We are not moving. I do not have enough money saved to buy us a new house. I had to pay your doctor bills, remember? When the time comes for us to move, I will tell you. Meantime, you watch these kids, clean this house, get dinner on the table, and let me figure out when the time is right for us to move."

Gio walked back to his chair with no regard to what he had just done. Grace quietly retreated to the bedroom. She came out to get Vincenzo and Carla for bed but went right back in the bedroom and closed the door. She had a pounding headache.

When Gio came in the bedroom later that evening, he woke Grace up from her sleep. "Grace, I am so sorry for what I did earlier. I had a terrible day at work. Every time I turned around, someone else had a problem. I took it out on you." Gio tenderly kissed Grace's head. "I hope you forgive me. I have never put my hands on you before, and I'm not starting now," he confessed.

"Gio," Grace whispered. "I love you so much. I have never seen that look in your eyes. I was scared," she muttered.

"I know, Grace," Gio whispered back. The last thing he needed now was for Mario to wake up. "Listen, I have a friend that owes me a financial favor. I will speak to him tomorrow and see if he will repay me the favor in some land and housing materials," he replied. "We can talk about this some more tomorrow. I need to get some sleep. It has been an awful day!"

With that, he kissed Grace good night and fell fast asleep. Grace quietly opened her nightstand drawer and pulled out one of her headache scarves. She made sure it was extra tight before she lay her head back down on the pillow.

Gio came home from work the next evening in a happy mood. With a big smile on his face, he announced to the family that they would be moving to a brand-new home on Imlay Avenue. The construction would take a few months, but then they would be able to move to a home that would give them more space. Grace just stared emotionless at her husband. What a powerful, determined man.

Imlay Avenue Duplex

Briarton, Illinois
1926–1932

GRACE LOVED THE NEW HOME Gio built for them. It was two bedrooms, like the house on Kristine Avenue, but the children's bedroom was much more spacious. Mario was old enough to sleep in a regular bed now, so he shared a bed with Vincenzo. Carla had her own bed across the room. The house had a basement. It was great for storage, and it had a walk-out basement too.

Gio and Grace had a nice-sized room. Grace was thankful to finally have the crib out of her bedroom. She felt more comfortable sleeping with her husband without children in the same room.

The outside of the house had a lot of curb appeal. The front of the house was all brick and had a large front porch. In the back, Gio built a four-car garage. The second floor had a balcony. Gio planned on renting out the upstairs, and his family would live on the main floor. He had a professional Italian artist come in and hand paint murals of Venice on the walls in the living room.

The first piece of mail that Gio and Grace received at their new home was a wedding invitation from New York inviting Gio and Grace to the wedding of Gio's sister, Sofia. There was a letter included in the invitation personally written by Sofia explaining that she met a wonderful man named Thomas and she would love for them to attend the wedding so she could introduce them to her new husband.

"I would love to go to New York, Gio," Grace said with a big smile on her face. She was light-headed from the anticipation of going on a vacation there.

"There is no way we can attend this wedding. We just moved into this house. There is so much to do here and at work too. We just can't attend, Grace," Gio answered with a sigh. "We will send a gift this week with a decline to the wedding. That way, they will get the decline and gift before their special day. Maybe we can travel there and meet Thomas once things settle down here," Gio said as he placed the invitation on the table and left the room.

Grace hung her head in disappointment. She had never been on a vacation anywhere, and the opportunity to go to New York seemed so exciting. But she understood what Gio was saying. She picked up the letter from the table and filed it away with their bills so she would remember to send a gift as Gio instructed.

"Well"—Grace signed heavily to the now-empty room— "that sure was a short-lived vacation in my mind."

However, that was not the only thing that was short lived. Exactly one year after Thomas and Sofia married, Thomas had a heart attack and died. He died at home. Sofia found him dead in his chair. Isabella called Gio and Grace to tell them the news. Sofia was too heartbroken to talk to anyone. She had just finished setting up their home, and now he was gone. That night, Gio and Grace sat quietly on the couch into the late evening hours. They sat holding hands. Gio was in deep thought and sorrow for his sister. Grace sat praying that nothing like that ever happened to her.

It was not long after Thomas's death that Gio heard the news that Sofia met a new man named Theo and that a wedding was coming in the near future. Again Gio and Grace decided to decline the wedding invitation. They sent their well wishes with the decline. A few weeks later, they had a chance to see pictures of the simple small wedding.

Shortly after the wedding, Gio received news that Sofia was pregnant. Gio and Grace were excited for Sofia. She had so much heartache over Thomas's sudden death. They were thrilled to hear this happy news, and Gio was excited to become an uncle.

During the fall, Grace got very ill. She caught a cold from Vincenzo and Carla, who must have brought it to their house from school. She spent every chance she could in bed. Her body was achy. She was coughing and had a runny nose. As soon as she got the children to sleep, she went to sleep herself. The weather was cold and dreary. It seems as though Grace would no sooner get over one cold than another would come upon her. On the cold, dreary nights of fall and winter, Gio would join her early in bed too. They'd snuggle under the warm blankets and share events from their day. When Grace was not feeling better after a month of flulike symptoms, she went to see Dr. Denero for some relief.

"Grace, you have the common cold," Dr. Denero said after examining her. He continued to speak to her in a flat voice with his head lowered. "Your immune system is suppressed, weakened, right now due to your pregnancy," he reported.

"Pregnancy? I'm pregnant?" Grace shouted in a squeaky voice. "I made this appointment because I have had one cold after the other recently. I'm pregnant? Are you sure, Doctor?" she replied in a shocked, tear-filled, sheepish voice.

"I'm absolutely certain, Grace," he replied with a stern face.

He knew what this meant for her. She was not having headaches like before. However, her tests and scans showed that the blood clot was still there. The medication had not treated it like he and Dr. Springer had hoped. The extra stress of having a baby was not recommended by either doctor.

Grace went home and shared the news with Gio. He was extremely excited. He wanted to celebrate. He wanted another child and was happy to later report to Dr. Springer that no one tells him when his family is finished. Grace was sick most of the pregnancy. It was a cold, miserable fall and winter in Illinois; and she caught every bug that Vincenzo, now seven and in second grade, and Carla, now five and in kindergarten, brought home from school. Mario, who was now three, was the only child home during the day. Grace did not gain a lot of weight with this pregnancy. This was the smallest her belly had been with any pregnancy. Even though her left leg was weak and she walked with a limp, on most days, she was able to keep up with Mario.

School was out for the summer for Vincenzo and Carla in June. By that time, Grace was eight months pregnant. She did not have a big belly with this pregnancy, so it was easier to get around. But she was worn-out from being sick all the time. It continued all pregnancy to be one head and chest cold or the flu back to back. Having the two older children home for the summer was overwhelming for Grace. She had a nice routine going with Vincenzo and Carla off to school in the morning and having only Mario home during the morning hours. Grace was not ready for the change that came with the summer months.

One afternoon, when Grace had enough of Vincenzo and Carla arguing over who got the bigger apple for breakfast, who was better at catching the red ball, and who was smarter, Grace sternly sent them both outside to play. The yard was not fenced in, so she warned them both to stay in the backyard until she had a chance to change Mario's diaper. Then she would be right out there with them.

Vincenzo and Carla were very happy to go outside to play. They were used to having recess at school. They thanked their mother, and before she could add a second warning to remind them to stay in the backyard, they were gone. Grace was confident that Vincenzo and Carla would listen to her warning. After all, Vincenzo was seven now, and Carla was five. They were old enough to play outside by themselves for a few minutes.

Grace took her time changing Mario's diaper and decided to change his clothes too since he had some food on them from breakfast. She was walking through the house with Mario in her arms on her way out to Vincenzo and Carla when she heard their truck engine roar. Grace quickened her steps. She looked out the back window of the house but did not see the children. She ran to look out the front window just in time to see the neighbor from across the street jump his fence like an Olympic hurdle jumper and run to their truck that was reversing down the driveway with Vincenzo at the wheel.

Grace froze in place. She watched the neighbor jump on the running board of the truck, stick his arm through the open window, and cut the wheel just in time before the truck rolled out into the city street. Their mailbox was demolished to toothpick-sized boards, but the truck was stopped. Grace flew through the front door of the house and down the porch steps screaming all the way. Mario, being jostled in her arms, giggled at the "ride" he thought his mother was giving him.

"Are you all right? Please tell me that you are all right," Grace heard her neighbor shouting at Vincenzo and Carla still seated in the truck. He opened the door of the truck and scooped both Vincenzo and Carla effortlessly from the front seat with one arm.

"We're okay," Vincenzo and Carla replied in unison.

"It was all Vincenzo's fault," Carla said in a tattletale tone.

Grace made her way to the truck. She was still screaming. She handed Mario to the neighbor and screamed and pulled her hair as she scolded her two older children, "What did you two do? Get out of the truck right now and march yourselves back into the house. I will deal with you in a minute."

After hearing his mommy's screams and stern voice, Mario realized the "ride" was over. He started crying in his usual loud cry and turned his head so that he was crying right into Grace's ear. Her head started pounding. Her throat hurt from screaming. She felt flushed, and she was shaking. She wasn't sure if she was shaking because of the danger Vincenzo and Carla could have been in with reversing the truck out of their driveway or the trouble she'd be in with Gio if something happened to the children. Gio must have left the keys in the truck's ignition. Vincenzo knew how to start the truck. Gio had shown him many times, but Vincenzo had never put the truck in gear.

The neighbor saw how shaken up Grace was from the incident. He saw that her face was red and her voice and hands were shaking. He tried calming her down by telling her that he and Gio would take care of the mailbox when Gio came home from work that evening.

Grace walked into the house, put the children to bed without lunch, told them Daddy would deal with them when he got home from work, and collapsed on the couch. She did not clean up after the children. She did not make dinner. The Rivias ate leftovers for dinner that night.

In late July, midwife Marino reported to the Rivia home to help Grace deliver her fourth baby. This baby came so quickly both Grace and midwife Marino barely did any work. Gio was called back into the room shortly after she went into labor.

"It's a girl, Gio!" Grace announced with pride. "A sister for Carla!" she beamed.

Gio held his daughter for the first time. "She's so small! How much did she weigh? I guess any baby after delivering Mario would seem small in comparison." Gio laughed out loud.

"She was only five pounds and six ounces," reported midwife Marino. "What name should I print on her birth certificate?"

"Antonia, after my mother," Grace whispered. "That is such a big name for such a tiny baby. How about if we call her Toni for short?" Grace questioned.

"Toni, I like that," responded Gio. "That's exactly what we will call her. She sure does not have much hair, does she?" Gio laughed. "With a little bald head of just peach fuzz, you watch, Grace, this one will grow up and be a beautician," Gio said with a chuckle in his belly and a broad smile.

Midwife Marino was encouraged to see Gio so lighthearted, talkative, and almost happy at this birth. She tended to Grace, and Gio went and gathered the other three children to meet their new sister. They each took a turn sitting on the bed with their mommy and holding baby Antonia in their arms. One by one, they each gave their observation of her. Vincenzo thought she was cute because she was so small but looked like a turtle. Carla, who refused to call her Antonia or Toni, insisted that she would call her "sister." She demanded Gio to put her down on the floor so she could play with her right then. When he didn't, she stormed off pouting. Mario was concerned that she was red, wrinkled, and cried too much.

The midwife laughed under her breath as she listened to the children's first reactions to meeting their sister. This made her so much more relaxed since the last time she was with the Rivias to supervise a birth. She certainly did not want a repeat of what happened at Mario's birth here at Antonia's. As soon as she thought that thought, she knew that the situation and delivery of this baby was extremely different than the day baby Mario was born. Mario was a very difficult delivery for both Grace and the midwife. She closed her eyes and shook her head, remembering that nerve-racking night. Since Mario's birth, midwife Marino made a point to apologize to Mr. Rivia regarding her short, snappy attitude. Her demeanor reflected her exhaustion. Mr. Rivia said he understood and accepted her apology.

Newborn Antonia was half Mario's birth weight. Of all four children midwife Marino had supported Grace through, this baby was the fastest and easiest delivery. However, upon examining Antonia immediately after birth, she noticed that the baby had a rattle in her chest and her eyes would not stop exuding pus. In addition, she took note that Grace was much quieter after this birth. She was still, with a frozen, fakelike smile on her face, eyes staring off in the distance. She looked worried. She did not readily join in conversation or initiate conversation with Gio or the other children as she noted with Grace's other deliveries. Wanting to remember all her observations, she pulled out her birthing log and made a note to watch for these concerns when she made postpartum visits over the next six weeks. For the fourth time, midwife Marino prayed that this would be Grace's last child.

Gio agreed to put the three older children to bed that night so Grace could rest with the new baby. Once Antonia was settled and Grace was alone with her, she gently unwrapped the baby's blanket and examined the baby's little fingers and toes. She gently kissed them. She stroked her soft, bald peach-fuzz head and examined all the curves of her little ears. The baby was so small the blanket swallowed her up.

"Antonia," she whispered, "I don't care that you are considered small today as long as you grow into a strong, confident woman."

Grace tenderly rocked the baby in her arms until they both fell asleep.

Grace expected to recover quickly after having Antonia. After all, this was her smallest baby. She was sick most of the pregnancy with colds and the flu, but the delivery was fast and easy. However, Grace soon realized the toll another pregnancy took on her body. She noticed that her left arm was not as strong as it used to be. When she would pick up or bathe Antonia, Grace noticed the weakness. She noticed the difference while doing daily chores around the house too. It was difficult to reach up to hang the clothes out to dry, mop the floor, and make the beds. When getting dressed, it was difficult to pull up her stockings or raise her arms to comb her hair. She did not remember her left arm being weak before having Antonia, only her left leg.

Grace wanted to look at the calendar to see when her next appointment was with the specialist. She knew it had been a long time since she had followed up with tests and scans. Getting pregnant with Antonia and then being sick most of the pregnancy interrupted her routine of seeing him. She made a note to check her calendar to see just how long it had been since she visited with Dr. Springer and then made a mental note to talk to Gio about this when he got home for dinner.

Grace was on her way to glance at her calendar in the kitchen when she heard Antonia coughing in her crib. This was not unusual. Antonia seemed to always have a rattling sound in her chest and a slight cough. Most of the time, even her cry sounded raspy. This had been noted since birth. Grace could not help but think that Antonia was born sickly because of how sick with colds she was while pregnant with her. The baby was now a few months over a year old and was still wrestling with respiratory issues and seeping eyes. However, this deep, barklike cough that Grace was hearing right now sounded different.

She waited outside the bedroom to listen and see if it would subside. When the coughing did not stop after a reasonable amount of time, she entered the room. She looked down at Antonia in the crib and noticed that she was red and sweat drops were rolling off her almost-bald head. Grace picked up the baby to find that her sleeper was damp from sweat. She knew without even taking her temperature that she had another fever. She called the doctor for a house visit. Within a few hours, Dr. Denero showed up at the house to check her out. The diagnosis was croup. Medications were administered, and a follow-up visit was scheduled.

Once the medication started to work, Antonia fell peacefully back to sleep in her crib. Grace was thankful that Mario was quiet while she dealt with Antonia and the doctor. She was even more thankful that Vincenzo and Carla were still in school. She decided to go check on Mario. She knew he was napping, but that was before the doctor arrived. Grace walked to the children's bedroom and quietly opened the door. She could hear music playing. She opened the door to find Mario standing on the bed with a pencil in each hand. He had drawn pictures all over the wall all around the room. Grace was so overwhelmed with this day that she sat on the floor, put her head in her hands, and cried.

No sooner did she have all the walls washed clean than it was time for Vincenzo and Carla to come home from school. They both wanted to tell her about their day at the same time, and they were both hungry. Grace made them a quick snack. While they were eating, she could hear Antonia waking up. She sounded cranky and was coughing again. Grace went to check on the baby. Antonia had coughed so hard that her little face was puffy and she had red blotches all over her cheeks. Grace struggled to pick her up with her weak left arm but managed to get her close to her body and soothed her until the baby was quiet. Meanwhile, Mario found another pencil and was off in the corner of the kitchen singing to himself and scribbling in Vincenzo's spelling book.

This was not the end to Mario's shenanigans. Grace understood the "terrible twos," but now Mario was three. She had heard about the "thunderous threes." Maybe that was what was wrong with him. Maybe he was going to be even more active and mischievous in his threes than he was in his twos. Grace could not even imagine. She often asked herself if Mario was so rambunctious because of his age or if he was more rambunctious because of her. She was tired most of the day. Recently she began noticing that she could not walk, get up and down stairs, or up off the floor as fast as she used to. Her left leg seemed weaker.

Whatever the reason, Grace was running out of patience with him. Just this week, she had to give Antonia a second bath because Mario got into Gio's hair gel and rubbed it all over Antonia's head. He told Grace he did that to help Antonia grow some hair. That same week, he dropped three balls down the toilet and not only plugged it up but flooded the bathroom floor. Grace could not unclog the toilet. She decided to go ahead and mop up the water and sanitize the floor again, but they'd all have to wait until Gio came home before the family had a functioning toilet.

"Frustrating and inconvenient" was all she kept muttering to herself as she mopped.

It seemed that, no matter what she said or did and no matter the amount of scolding, nothing affected Mario. He was a strong-willed child, and Grace was overwhelmed.

The next morning, Grace got Vincenzo and Carla off to school with ease. Mario and Antonia ate their breakfast without incident. Grace was amazed at how well the morning was moving along. It was almost as if she was waiting with anticipation for things to come crashing down in front of her. But as the morning turned into afternoon and it was nap time for the children, she started to think maybe this was going to be a smooth day after all.

She put Mario and Antonia down for their naps and decided to do some straightening up around the house. She started in the living room and moved to the children's room. Once that was all straightened up, she moved on to her bedroom. She had her room all organized in a short amount of time. Since Mario and Antonia were still napping, she decided to go through some of the drawers that she noticed were getting rather full of papers. She sat on the bed and started digging through some old property contracts and papers, school papers and awards of Vincenzo and Carla that she wanted to save for them, when she came across the children's birth certificates.

"Here's Vincenzo's birth certificate," Grace said in a low whisper. She did not want to wake Antonia, who was napping in her crib right next to where she was sitting. "Here's Carla's birth certificate," she said as she continued rummaging through the stack of documents. "Here's Antonia's," she said. Then she stopped and made a questioning face, drawing her eyebrows together. "Where's Mario's?" she almost said in full voice.

Antonia turned over and stretched a big stretch in her crib. Grace decided to bundle and carry all the documents found in the drawer out to the kitchen table. His birth certificate had to be in this stack somewhere. Once in the kitchen, she went through the whole stack again one document at a time. No birth certificate for Mario.

When Gio came home from work that evening, Grace told him about her day. Gio was excited to hear that it was so productive. Most days, when he got home, all he heard over and over was how overwhelmed she was with Mario. She shared with him that she was not able to find Mario's birth certificate. She handed the stack of important papers to Gio and asked him to take a look. Perhaps she just missed it somehow. Gio took his time looking through all the papers but did not find it either.

"I found his baptism certificate but not his birth certificate," Gio reported as he held up the church document with its shiny gold seal.

"You found the baptism certificate?" Grace questioned. "Let me see it," she asked.

Grace gently held the church document, remembering that special day when Mario strutted around his party making all the guests laugh. "Oh, my goodness, Gio!" she shouted as she stood up from her chair. "Look, they recorded his birth year wrong. They recorded that he was born in 1924. Mario was born in 1925."

"Let me see that," Gio demanded.

Silence filled the kitchen. The wheels were rolling in Gio's head. Gio sat quiet looking into space as if he was reliving that day in March when his son was born.

Finally he spoke, "We do not have a birth certificate for him, and I have a good idea why. First he was such a big baby that his birth was much different than the others. The labor and delivery was long and difficult. Second midwife Marino was tired and on edge after the birth. Remember she left the house in a rage? She was upset because I told her our bedroom looked like a war zone after the birth," Gio said as she looked questioningly at Grace.

"Yes," Grace replied. "I was so sore and tired, but I remember her gathering her items and leaving quickly. I do not remember signing his birth certificate now that I am thinking of it," Grace said. "Do you remember signing anything that day?"

"No, I don't. If we do not have a birth certificate for him, we will have to use the baptism certificate as proof of birth, and since the church document has the birth year recorded incorrectly, that means we could start him in school one year early. Grace, we could start Mario in kindergarten at four years old. He can start in the fall. That will help you with having Vincenzo, Carla, and Mario in school all day. You could spend some quality time with Antonia," Gio said in an excited voice.

She is such an easy baby. She is quiet and peaceful. Maybe if it worked and the school would take the baptism certificate as proof of age, Gio just might see a happy wife when he got home from work.

Grace listened in silence. She sat at the kitchen table, document in hand, eyes and mouth wide open as she processed what this could mean for her. Finally she smiled a slow, soft smile. She let out a breathy sigh.

"Yes" was her only reply.

Gio and Grace went to the school together to plead their case regarding Mario's missing birth certificate. The school was very understanding of home births and accepted the baptism certificate as proof of age. They knew that children in the Catholic church were baptized within a week or two of their birth. They did not question the incorrect year on the document.

Mario began kindergarten that next fall. The imposter five-year-old was not developmentally ready to compete with his peers.

Four-year-old Mario was not completely potty trained and exhibited immature characteristics for a kindergartener. These actions created concerns for the teacher. Disregarding any notes that trailed home from school, Gio and Grace stood by the deception that Mario was, in fact, five. They knew that their boy was a proud, strong-willed child and would eventually be able to compete with his peers. By the end of the school year, Mario had proven Gio and Grace correct. He no longer had separation anxiety from home. His speech and language greatly improved, and he was completely potty trained.

When the phone rang during dinner that night, Gio got up from the couch to answer it. After a brief conversation, he returned to the living room to report that Sofia had her baby, a baby girl. She and Theo named her Vera. Gio was excited that she was not much younger than Antonia. Maybe they would grow up to be close cousins—close friends. Gio was hopeful. Grace did not think that would happen. Knowing Antonia's personality and having that short experience with Sofia back when she was pregnant with Mario, she could not see Sofia's daughter and her daughter being close. Grace knew to keep her mouth shut and not give her opinion.

One night, several weeks later, when the children were in bed and the house was quiet, Grace realized that she never checked her calendar to see when her last appointment was with the specialist. Between Antonia being sick, leading to doctor's house visits, and all the disruptions with Mario, she completely forgot to check the calendar. Grace decided to wait until morning to look at it. She promised herself that she would check first thing in the morning. She decided not to say anything to Gio about seeing the specialist until she checked her calendar first. Then she would be able to give him an accurate date as to the last appointment and show him that a follow-up appointment was needed. She also decided not to bring to Gio's attention that she recently noticed that her left leg was feeling weaker and was now feeling a difference in the strength in her left arm.

Grace got up early and, as she promised herself the night before, checked her calendar. She quickly realized that her last visit with Dr. Springer was long overdue. She was expecting to see that. However, what she was not expecting to see was that her period was late, very late. Grace froze with fear. She did a quick calculation replay in her mind and realized that it was definitely possible that she could be pregnant.

Vincenzo and Carla sauntered into the kitchen looking for their breakfast.

"What's for breakfast?" Vincenzo casually asked.

There was no response from Grace.

"I'm hungry," reported Carla.

Grace did not respond. She stood at the counter, looking out the kitchen window, tears rolling down her face. Later that day, she called Dr. Denero's office.

"I would like to make an appointment with Dr. Denero," Grace barely choked out.

"Is Antonia under the weather again, Mrs. Rivia?" asked the receptionist sweetly.

"No." Grace cleared her throat. "She's doing much better. Thank you. This appointment is for me."

"And the reason for the appointment?" asked the overly cheerful receptionist.

"Pregnancy test," replied Grace.

Silence filled the phone line.

"I see," responded the less cheerful receptionist.

Once again, Grace's appointment to the specialist was put on hold.

Time went fast for Grace with this pregnancy. She kept busy with Antonia, and before long, the children were out of school for summer. Since only Gio had to be up early, Grace encouraged the children to sleep in. She slept in too. It felt so good to stretch out in the bed with the fan blowing down on her. It was a warm summer, and it wouldn't be too long before she delivered this baby.

One morning, when Grace was enjoying the extra morning sleep time, the phone rang. She pulled herself out of bed and made

it to the phone before it stopped ringing. She could barely understand the woman on the other end of the phone. The lady was
hysterical. She was not sure, but she thought it was her sister-in-
law, Sofia.

"Grace, Grace, there has been an accident," the lady reported.
"Theo is dead. There was a fire at his work last night. He was in
the room where the fire started. The fire was so hot and intense
that the firemen were not able to get inside until this morning.
When they opened the door, there was Theo on the landing." She
stopped and cried harder. She said a few phrases in Italian that
Grace did not understand.

Grace realized now that this was Sofia and understood what
she was saying. Grace's heart sank. Sofia was speaking so fast and
hysterical Grace did not have a chance to respond. She listened
quietly.

"Oh, Grace, Theo was right there at the door. He was right
inside the door on the landing. He was almost out of the building.
The firemen think that the smoke overcame him and that, by the
time he got to the door, he was too weak to reach up and turn the
knob to get out," she cried into the phone. "How am I going to tell
Vera?" She sobbed. "She is only a little girl. She will never know
her daddy." Sofia cried harder at this thought.

Grace stood in her kitchen at that early morning hour and
cried silent tears of sorrow for her sister-in-law. How could all of
these terrible things happen to one person?

Grace tried consoling Sofia, but as she talked, she could hear
how ridiculous she must have sounded to Sofia. She never experienced anything remotely similar to this in her life, and she was
telling Sofia that she understood? She had a husband and was
pregnant with her fifth child. Grace stopped talking, took a deep
breath, and reassured Sofia that she would tell Gio the news as
soon as he got home. She told Sofia that he would give her a call
later in the evening. Grace stumbled back to bed, but there was no
more sleeping with Sofia and Vera heavy on her mind.

It was a hot summer morning in early July when midwife
Marino was called back to the Rivia home on Imlay Avenue to

support Grace in delivering her fifth child. Grace was already in active labor when the midwife arrived. She hurriedly gathered what she needed for the birth. If this baby came as fast as Antonia, she would have to work fast. With it being summer, all the children were home. Vincenzo was now nine years old. He was quiet, studious, and a deep thinker. Both Gio and Grace recognized that he had a sharp mind. Carla was seven. She loved to talk, chew gum, and play outside. She loved school from the very first day she set foot in the door. Her favorite subject was math. Mario was five and just finished kindergarten. He calmed down quite a bit as a result of being in school. He learned how to share, wait his turn, and understood having limits. Antonia was two. She still had bouts with bronchitis and the croup, but her eyes finally stopped weeping.

It was not long, and Grace delivered her fifth baby. It was a girl. Gio and Grace named her Virginia after a sweet elderly neighbor that lived a few doors down. Virginia the neighbor was small in stature but was mighty with a heart filled with kindness and generosity. Her smile and laugh lit up a room. She had a positive spirit and an uplifting mannerism—a true gift of encouragement. They could only hope that their brand-new daughter would take on the personality of their neighbor for whom she was the namesake.

"Grace, this baby has so much black hair," midwife Marino commented as she suds up Virginia's little head. "Wow, so different than Antonia's nearly bald head, right?" She gave a little giggle and continued speaking to Grace.

After a while, the midwife realized she was not getting a response. She glanced back over her shoulder at Grace lying in the bed behind her and realized that she had fallen back to sleep. Even though this labor and delivery was not unusually difficult, it was horrific for Grace. Having helped Grace through labor and delivery five times now, she recognized the difference in Grace's health. Grace was only twenty-seven years old but looked much older to the midwife.

Virginia was washed, dried, and comfortably sleeping in her bassinet next to Grace's bed. The midwife quietly gathered all the soiled sheets and towels and placed them in the hamper. She took a quick glance around the room to make sure she retrieved all her birthing instruments and placed them in her bag. She did not want to wake Grace, but she knew she needed to get her signature on the birth certificate. Gio had been in and out of the room several times during the delivery, but when it was time for Virginia's bath, he stepped out of the room to be with the other children. He told the midwife he would be back to show them their new sister once Grace woke up.

The room was all cleaned, sanitized, and back in order. Grace continued to sleep. The midwife grabbed her bag and walked out to her car. She was trying to give Grace as long a time as possible to sleep, but it was getting late. Her job here was finished. She returned to the bedroom and gently nudged Grace.

"Grace, Grace, it's time for me to leave," the midwife spoke as she continued to gently nudge Grace.

"Oh, I am so sorry," Grace apologized in slurred speech. "I fell asleep, didn't I?"

Midwife Marino noticed Grace's slurred speech immediately. She also noticed that the left side of her mouth was drooping.

"I'm going to step out and come back with Mr. Rivia. You both will need to sign the birth certificate, and then I will be on my way," she said in a calm voice.

The midwife had a semblance of calmness, but her insides were churning. It was apparent that Grace did not realize her speech was slurred and her mouth was drooping.

The midwife spoke to Mr. Rivia about Grace's condition.

"What do you mean her speech is slurred and her mouth is drooping?" Gio asked in a concerned voice. "I never noticed that. She wasn't like that this morning when she went into labor. I thought those pills she was taking for the blood clot in her brain were working. She hasn't had a headache for a long time," Gio continued.

"The medication for the blood clot in her brain is different than the medication for her headaches," the midwife explained. "It has been a very long time since she had a follow-up visit, including new tests and scans, with the specialist. Look, Gio, I'm not a specialist or anything, but even I can tell that, since her last visit, her left leg has gotten considerably weaker. Grace told me that recently she has noticed a weakness in her left arm too. Now today we are seeing the left side of her mouth dipping down and hearing slurred speech. She needs a follow-up visit with Dr. Springer as soon as possible, Gio. Once she is examined and the tests and scans are updated, the specialist will be able to determine where to go from there," she advised.

Midwife Marino returned to Gio and Grace's bedroom to clean and pack up her bag to leave. Gio signed the birth certificate. He thanked the midwife for her help and promised her that he would call and make an appointment for Grace to see the specialist within the next few weeks. After she left, Gio went and got the children to come and see their new sister.

Vincenzo was the first one to enter the bedroom. He was nine years old and the most curious of all of the children. He was intrigued by Virginia's full head of black hair. He kept repeating to Gio that poor Antonia was two years old and still did not have any length to her hair. Carla entered next. She was seven now and very excited to have another sister. She held Virginia close and told her all her stories of Vincenzo and Mario bossing her around. She whispered to her new sister to hurry and grow up so she could have some backup against her brothers. Gio and Grace just listened and smiled as they heard her confession. However, they both knew that Carla was speaking the truth from her heart and hoped that the three girls did grow up close, watching each other's backs.

Wiggly Mario bounced into the room next. He was five and very eager to tell Virginia all about school. He held her on his lap, telling her that she did not have to be afraid to go to school. He and Vincenzo would protect her. Antonia walked sheepishly into the room. She was two now and not so sure that she wanted to give up her crib to this baby. She was not sure she would like leaving

Mommy and Daddy's room to go share a bed with Carla. She was quiet as she held her baby sister. She stroked Virginia's silky dark hair. This action made Grace tear up.

"You'll have hair before long, Antonia. You just watch and see," Grace mumbled slowly.

Gio decided to take a few days off of work to help Grace after the birth. He wanted to use these days off to speak to her about the recent changes in her health and to see if he could get her in to see the specialist before he had to return to work. That afternoon, he found the chance.

"Grace, why didn't you tell me you have noticed a worsening in your left leg and new weakness in your left arm?" questioned Gio.

"Oh, Gio, we have been so busy. You work so hard during the day I didn't want to bother you. I started to say something several times but got interrupted. I wanted to remind you months ago that I was overdue in seeing the specialist for updated tests, scans, and a medication check. We have both been too busy with life to stay on track," she responded.

"Have you looked in the mirror since you gave birth to Virginia? Have you noticed that the left side of your mouth is drooping? Do you hear your slurred speech?" Gio fired off the questions with more aggression.

"Yes, I know my speech is not clear. I think it will go away in a few days. I'm sure it's just a reaction to childbirth. I did not notice that my lip is drooping," she answered in a quiet voice. "Do I look repulsive to you, Gio? Is that what this is about?" Grace nervously asked.

"I'm calling the specialist today. I am going to demand that we get an appointment with him before I go back to work," Gio said as he hurriedly got up from the bed without making eye contact with Grace.

Grace did not know what Gio said to the specialist. She never left the bedroom to listen to his conversation. All she knew was that it was not very long afterward that Gio returned to the bedroom and informed her that an appointment with the specialist was scheduled for early tomorrow morning.

Dr. Springer's heart dropped with he saw Grace. Without looking at her chart, he remembered her and noticed the difference in her appearance. He had not evaluated her since right after Mario was born. That was five years ago. They made small talk at first about Mario and his shenanigans and the fact that she had two additional pregnancies since his birth. Dr. Springer's eyes opened wide with surprise as he stared at Grace in disbelief.

Gio looked at him and mumbled under his belly chuckle, "No one tells me when my family is complete."

The specialist set Grace up for outpatient services to have new tests and scans run to evaluate the blood clot in her brain. The doctor scheduled a follow-up visit at his office for the next week. Gio announced that he would not be able to attend that visit since he took a few days off for the birth of Virginia. There was no way he could take off any more days from work. Grace was not upset about that, and the doctor did not see it as a requirement that Gio return with Grace. With that, everything was squared away, and they left for home.

Grace was not ready to hear the doctor's report the next week.

"In the five years since I have seen you, Grace, there has been some decline in your condition," Dr. Springer said in a serious voice. "The blood clot is still in the same spot. Instead of it beginning to dissolve and reduce in size, which was the purpose of the medication, the blood clot has increased in size and is now occluding more blood flow to the brain. The decrease in blood flow is what is causing the new symptoms you are noticing, weakness in your face muscles causing the left side of your mouth to droop, the new weakness in your left arm, and, of course, the increased weakness in your left leg. I am going to change your medication. Also, I am going to give you a higher dose than before. I would like to see you back in one month for a new set of tests and scans. That will give enough time for us to evaluate the new medication," Dr. Springer said with a calm smile as he extended his hand to Grace.

She reached out and shook his hand. They both stood up at the same time and momentarily caught each other's eye. Grace could not dismiss what she saw there. His eyes spoke volumes. She did not like what she saw deep in his eyes.

That evening after dinner, Grace shared Dr. Springer's findings with Gio.

"I don't know, Gio," Grace began. "I didn't like the look in Dr. Springer's eyes when he gave me my test and scan results. His eyes were sad, even worried looking," she confessed to her husband. "His eyes were telling me something that his mouth was not. I think he was trying to tell me that I am not going to recover from this," she said in a choked-up voice.

"Now don't you start worrying about something that he didn't even say, Grace," Gio said, trying to calm her down before she went into full crying mode. "I am sure there are many things we can do to help this weakness of yours. Maybe we need to change doctors, or maybe we need to demand to be seen sooner than one month. In fact, now that I am thinking about this, just the other day, I was talking to Robert, a buddy of mine from the bricklaying mill, about you. He was telling me that he had an aunt with similar weakness issues like yours. He told me that his uncle finally decided, as a last effort for his wife's health, to move out of the city and into the country. He told me that his uncle and aunt have been out there a year now, and they both see a big difference in her health. All the clean air, farming their own vegetables, and quiet changed their lives," Gio reported with confidence.

Out of nowhere, a thought came to Gio. He was thinking of his conversation with Robert that day at work. He remembered that his buddy Tony was there too. It was lunch break, and the three of them were talking about land in the country. He remembered Tony saying that he had some corner acreage on a farm in New Hamfield, Illinois. He was looking to get it off his hands. Tony owed Gio several favors. A year ago, during some downtime at the mill, Gio did some special brickwork as a side job on three different homes for Tony's family. Maybe he could take this time to collect on his favors.

Gio closed his eyes and tried replaying the lunch conversation in his head. He tilted his head back and fell quiet for a few seconds. Gio's head was whirling. He processed the deal in his head without saying anything out loud where Grace could hear. If this deal worked, it could change everything for them.

"Maybe we could find a place in the country that would do you good, Grace," Gio said, knowing that his words were falling on deaf ears.

"I am not moving again, Gio," Grace said with emphases on the word *not*. "We have five children. That means we would have to switch Vincenzo, Carla, and Mario's schools. We would have to register them again. It is just too much to pack everything up for seven people and set up in a new place all over again. Anyway, we have only been in this house four years," Grace argued her case.

By the look on Gio's face, she knew she went too far in speaking her opinion before she could stop things. His neck was bright red, and the unnatural flush of color was slowly creeping up into his face like a white dish towel absorbing red food coloring. He clenched his teeth and, without warning, stood up from his chair with such force that it tipped over behind him. He stood there for a second and then lunged at Grace across the table and caught her by her dress collar.

"You listen to me. You think you know everything. If I say the country air will do you good, it will do you good. If I say we will move, then we will move. You drag your left leg. It is weak. Now you are saying that your left arm is weak. After Virginia, your face became weak, and your mouth is drooping. Do you hear your speech? It's slurred. If I say the country air worked for my buddy's aunt, it will work for you," Gio said all in one breath. He abruptly let go of her dress collar, causing Grace to teeter backward. He picked up the chair and sat back down. "I have a buddy that owes me favors. I will start working a deal with him about his land in the country," Gio said without looking Grace in the face.

"Okay" was all Grace could squeak out.

After Gio walked out of the kitchen, she walked to the bedroom, shut the door behind her, and buried her head in a pillow and sobbed.

Grace was interrupted by Mario's knock on the door.

"Mommy, the iceman is coming down the street. I can see him just a few houses away. How many pounds do you want me to set the diamond card in the window to? Twenty-five, fifty, seventy-five, or one hundred pounds?" he shouted.

"Set the card to seventy-five pounds, Mario!" she shouted back in a slurred, shaky voice. "It's been so hot this summer we are going to need more ice than usual. I'll be right out to pay the man," Grace called out as she got herself off the bed, wiped her face, and straighten her dress and hair.

No sooner had Grace paid the ice man than Vincenzo, Carla, and Mario took off at full speed hooting and hollering as they chased the ice truck all the way down the street. This was the three oldest children's routine every two days when the iceman came to deliver the much-needed cold ice to the homes on Imlay Avenue.

The hot summer months passed, and before long, it was time to think about school again. Vincenzo and Mario were all excited to return to school to see all their friends. Carla was excited to return to school to learn. She loved school more and more each year. She often sat and talked to Grace about her dream of becoming a math teacher.

One afternoon, shortly after the school year began, Grace received a phone call from Carla's third-grade teacher, Mrs. Fredricks. Grace was in the kitchen feeding Antonia and Virginia their lunch when the phone rang.

"Hello, Mrs. Rivia," said the kind voice on the other end. "This is Mrs. Fredricks, Carla's teacher," she continued.

"Hello, Mrs. Fredricks," Grace answered in a wondering voice. "I hope you are not calling to report a behavior problem with Carla," Grace spoke into the phone as she quieted Virginia.

"Well, Carla can be mischievous at times, but I think I understand why," Mrs. Fredricks continued in a calm voice. "Carla has been caught several times since the beginning of school sneaking penny candy and gum into the classroom. She comes to school each day with a pocket full of goodies. She often sneaks and hands them out to other children in the classroom, and before long, the whole class is chomping down on Carla's penny candy and gum. I am not sure if she has reported this to you at home yet, but she has been put in time-out three times this week alone for carrying on this way," Mrs. Fredricks reported. "Also, Carla loves to talk. She has been sent to the corner several times already this school year because she will not heed my warning to stop talking during class instruction," the teacher continued.

"I am so sorry," Grace said in a voice full of embarrassment. "I will certainly speak to her about this when she arrives home," Grace fumed.

"I appreciate that, Mrs. Rivia," the teacher said, returning to her original kind voice. "However, I think I have discovered an answer to all of this mischief," she reported, clearing her voice so she could be heard clearly. "Carla has a bright mind. I feel she is acting out this way because she is bored with school. One of the reasons I am calling, Mrs. Rivia, is to get your permission to have Carla act as a classroom tutor in math. Several of the other students are struggling, and I feel Carla might be able to help them since she understands all of the math concepts. Do I have your permission to move forward with this request?" Mrs. Fredricks asked as she waited for Grace's response.

"Well, absolutely, Mrs. Fredricks," Grace said with pride. "I am sure Carla would love that. She often has shared with me that she wants to be a math teacher someday," Grace gloated.

"Wonderful," Mrs. Fredricks responded. "I will set Carla up as a classroom math tutor to her peers. She will tutor in the cloakroom in our classroom," the teacher informed. "Also, Carla shared with me that you see the importance in education. She tells me that you are good in math as well. She said that you give her hints on how to remember her math facts. I wanted to thank you for your support at home, Mrs. Rivia. Please continue this routine. Carla is reaping the reward," Mrs. Fredricks said as she smiled and nodded her head.

"Thank you for calling and offering this tutor position to Carla. I know this will make her feel good about herself," Grace said in a quiet voice and smiled.

She hung up the phone and took a moment to gather herself. She was so happy for Carla. Maybe she really would grow up to be a math teacher. Grace couldn't wait to see her this afternoon to let her know proud she was of her.

Grace could watch the children get off the bus at the bus stop down the street from her kitchen window. She wished Carla would run home instead of walk today because she was very excited to tell her the news from her conversation with Mrs. Fredricks earlier in the day. However, from the way Mario and Carla got off the bus, she could tell something was wrong. Their body language told Grace that something happened on the bus or in school that set them off. From the way they were walking down the sidewalk, she could tell they were upset with one another. Vincenzo trailed behind the two hotheads.

By the time they reached the housedoor, they were shouting angry words at one another, and Carla was swinging her schoolbook at Mario's head. Mario kept dodging, and the book never made contact. Vincenzo looked at Grace, shrugged his shoulders, and retreated to his room to do some reading. Grace asked Mario and Carla what was wrong, but they both were talking at the same time defending their case against the other. She received no clear answer. All she could gather was that it had something to do with a boy named Dominic and the game they played at recess.

Their loud arguing filled the house. Before Grace could get them to calm down and tell her the whole story, their noise woke Virginia up. Grace shuffled to the bedroom to tend to the baby. While she was in there, she decided to change Virginia's diaper and clean her up a bit from her afternoon nap.

As Grace took care of Virginia in the next room, she kept an ear out for Carla and Mario. They continued to fuss with one another. Grace could hear them in the kitchen now. What apparently started with a situation from school continued with a situation in her kitchen. She could hear cabinet doors opening and slamming shut. Grace fumbled as she tried to work faster getting Virginia dressed. She could hear the commotion escalating.

"Mario, I am hungry too!" Carla shouted at her older brother.

"If you're hungry, you go get the olives yourself!" Mario shouted back.

"That is so stupid, Mario. You are right there getting the olives from the big jar under the sink for yourself. You know I want some too, so why are you putting the jar away?" Carla half asked, half shouted as she pushed Mario aside and reopened the cabinet door to get the olive jar out again.

Mario slammed the cabinet door and shouted back at Carla, "I am the only one who is allowed to get the olives out of the big jar under the sink! You are not allowed."

"Mario, move away. You are not the boss of me!" Carla shouted as she pushed Mario aside.

She opened the cabinet door under the sink and carefully lifted the big jar of olives out again. She placed the jar on the kitchen table. That was when Grace heard Carla scream.

"*Cosmo!*" Carla cried out. "Why did you do that?" Carla screamed and cried.

Grace put Virginia back in her crib half-dressed and rushed out to the living room. Carla was standing by the kitchen table with blood streaking down the back of her head. She reached back to touch her wound. She looked in shock as she looked at her hand full of red blood. Her face was wet with tears. Carla's sad big eyes met Grace's.

"Mommy, Mario stabbed me in the head with his pencil," Carla sobbed.

Grace took Carla to the bathroom and cleaned her head with soap and water, applied medicine, and a bandage. She sent Carla to her bedroom to rest.

Grace looked everywhere for Mario. She looked under beds, behind furniture, in the backyard, and down the street. He was nowhere to be found. Finally she gave up. Grace decided to have Gio take care of him when he got home.

Gio had just finished taking care of Mario when Mr. Leonard came to the door to drop off the rent to Gio. He had rented the upstairs part of the duplex for almost five years now. He was single, and the space provided upstairs was just what he needed. Mr. Leonard was an easy tenant. He was quiet and always paid his rent on time. Gio was pleased to have such a great person living above him and the family.

"Mr. Rivia, I wanted to come down to give you my rent and to ask you if it would be okay to have my younger brother come live with me in the apartment upstairs for a short time. He has fallen on hard times, lost his job at the steel mill. He needs a place to stay until he gets back up on his feet," Mr. Leonard spelled out for Gio.

"Sure, sure, no problem at all," responded Gio. "Thank you for letting me know. I look forward to meeting him," Gio said with a kind voice.

Mr. Leonard brought his younger brother, Tom, down to meet Gio the next evening. Tom looked much different than Mr. Leonard. He was very thin with a sunken in face. He was unkept: dirty hair, nails, and clothes. When he was being introduced, he would not look Gio in the eye. If Tom had come looking for a place to rent by himself, Gio would have never rented to him. But since this was Mr. Leonard's younger brother, Gio was okay with him living in his upstairs duplex. After all, it was only temporary anyway. Gio remembered that Mr. Leonard said that his brother had fallen on hard times. Perhaps he just needed the care of his older brother to get back on track.

However, Tom moving in with his older brother was the end of the quiet rented apartment in the Rivia duplex. It was not long after Tom moved in that Grace's quiet days with only Antonia and Virginia at home came to an end. Grace would try to put the girls down for a nap in the afternoon, but Tom's loud music would keep them awake. It was difficult for Grace to climb the stairs up to Mr. Leonard's apartment to see what was going on because of her weak leg, so she would get a broom and hit the ceiling to get his attention. It rarely quieted things down.

Grace noticed girls entering the apartment during the day. There would be loud music and pounding on the floor. Grace was not sure what they were doing, but she knew that it needed to stop. She had no peace in the lower apartment during the day anymore. The noise would keep the girls from napping, and the stress was causing Grace to have headaches.

"Gio, please do something about Mr. Leonard's brother living upstairs," Grace pleaded to Gio one evening. "The noise is crazy. It used to be so quiet here during the day when it was only Mr. Leonard living up there. He would be at work, and I never heard anything. Since his brother moved in, it has been crazy," Grace explained.

"Let's give it a little longer, Grace," Gio said. "He has only been here one month. Mr. Leonard said his brother lost his job. Maybe he needs a little more time to find one, and then he will be out of the apartment working in the day like his brother," Gio rationalized.

One month turned into two, and two months turned into six. There was no change. Grace was still complaining to Gio each evening about all the noise coming from upstairs and the women that were going in and out all day long. Gio finally went to speak with Mr. Leonard.

"I am sorry to tell you this, Mr. Leonard, but while you are out working during the day, your brother plays loud music and brings women into your apartment," Gio explained. "Grace is upset about the noise. It's difficult for her to get the girls to nap with all the noise," he went on to report.

"I am sorry for that, Mr. Rivia," Mr. Leonard said with regret. "My brother is having a difficult time finding another job. He claims he is searching each day but has not found one yet," Mr. Leonard said in defense of his brother.

Mr. Leonard promised to speak with his brother about the situation and said he would make sure things changed.

However, a few days later, Gio came home from work not feeling well. He experienced firsthand what Grace had been experiencing for months now regarding the noise and commotion coming from the upstairs apartment.

Gio stomped up to the apartment and banged on the door. No answer. He called out Tom's name. No answer. Gio balled up his hands and banged on the door with both fists. When there was no response again, Gio went back down to his apartment and brought up the spare key. He opened the door and gasped in horror. The music was so loud the windows were vibrating. He could feel the bass vibrating the hardwood floor under his feet. Gio looked around the apartment and saw filth. Dishes were piled in the sink, clothes were tossed over all the furniture and on the floor, and empty liquor bottles and trash covered the floor. He saw no one in the apartment. He kept calling out for Tom. Gio walked over to the closed bedroom door. He knocked and called out for Tom. No answer. Gio slowly opened it. There inside draped across the bed like knotted pretzels were Tom and two women passed out drunk.

Later that evening, Gio evicted Mr. Leonard and his brother from the upstairs apartment.

"Grace, start packing," Gio announced with authority at breakfast the next morning. "We are moving to the country."

This time, Grace answered, "Okay!"

Gio went to work at the bricklayer mill that morning with nothing else on his mind but sealing a deal with Tony for land in the country for Grace and his five children. Before 10:00 a.m., the deal was in motion. Gio collected on his favors: fourteen acres of land in New Hamfield, Illinois, that included a farmhouse, a barn, chicken coop, some chickens, a vineyard, and two fruit orchards. Gio also bartered with his buddies for them to help him build a gas station, oil pit, car wash area, and a bar with eat-in capacity to be built on the corner of the front lawn of the farmhouse acreage once the family settled in. But for now, he'd settle for enough quiet and country fresh air to heal Grace.

The Farmhouse

New Hamfield, Illinois
1932–1936

IT WAS EARLY DECEMBER WHEN Gio, Grace, and the five children finally moved into the farmhouse. The truck holding the first load of their belongings slowly made its way down the long driveway to the two-story white farmhouse with wraparound porch and big front door. Grace stared out the window in disbelief.

"How many favors did Gio cash in on to pay for this farm?" Grace whispered to herself. She knew better than to ask.

The truck barely came to a stop before Gio jumped out of the truck. He immediately started directing the men that had come to help them move place the furniture and boxes in the house.

While Gio directed the men, Grace decided to take a look around. She grabbed a long stick from the yard to help her balance, and she headed on foot around the large farmhouse. The house was on a corner lot, so the front had a lot of lawn. She could see in the distance, closer to the road, where Gio's buddies already started digging to build the gas station, oil pit, car wash, and bar that would serve a light lunch and drinks. As Grace headed toward the backyard, the first thing she saw was the grapevine. The wood trellises were pregnant with concord grapes. Although the grapes were deep purple in color and the seeds a dark brown, they were overdue for good wine making. The grapes should have been harvested in early fall, around September, but with the house being vacant for so long, harvesting never happened. Grace could see that they would be missing out on making wine this year.

The acreage in the backyard was filled with a peach orchard, an apple orchard, an overgrown garden, a chicken coop, and a barn. Grace leaned on the stick she was using to balance herself and drew in a deep breath. The crisp late-fall air felt good being pulled into her lungs. She stood there, closed her eyes, and dreamed of feeling well enough to tend to all the possibilities before her. Her daydreaming was interrupted by the sound of a few clucking chickens that come sauntering out of the chicken coop. By the way they looked, Grace knew they must have been hungry. They probably came out to see if anyone was going to feed them. As she got a better look, it was clear that they were not getting proper nourishment. She made a mental note to correct that right away.

Grace circled around the outside of the house and decided to take a look at the inside next. She climbed up the front porch steps. The wraparound porch was vacant of porch furniture; but in Grace's mind, she could visualize pots filled with colorful flowers, draping fern plants, chairs and tables filled with pitchers of lemonade in the summer and cups of hot chocolate in the cooler months, and friends, family gatherings, and, maybe in the far future, even weddings on this charming porch. Grace was excited to see the inside of the house.

There was no preparing Grace for what she saw inside. She pushed open the big front door to see an open staircase with an intricately carved wooden handrail leading to the upstairs. She had never seen anything like it before. To the right of the stairway was a wide-open living room. Behind that was an elegant dining room. Grace continued walking to the back of the house to find two kitchens. One was the main kitchen, and the other was a summer kitchen. Both kitchens faced the orchards and garden in the backyard.

Once Grace circled around the main floor, she ended up at the front door and the open staircase again. This time, she turned left. Here, she found a large room that was closed off with French doors. It looked like it would be a very private room, maybe a study or library. Grace had no idea what they would use this space for. It did not have a closet. She knew it was not a bedroom. She knew this for sure because the one and only thing Gio shared with her about this farmhouse was that it had five bedrooms, and they were all upstairs. Grace slowly climbed the stairs to take a look.

Just like Gio told her, the house had five bedrooms—plenty of room for them. No more being crowded into a small space. There was one bathroom, and it was the largest bathroom Grace had ever seen. She knew the girls were going to love soaking in the big, spacious tub.

When she thought she had seen every inch of the house, Gio told her the farmhouse also had a full basement. Grace threw her hands up to her face in utter disbelief and closed her eyes.

"How much more perfect could this house be for the seven of us, Gio?" Grace half cried, half spoke out.

"So you like it?" Gio said with a voice full of pride for his accomplishment.

"Yes, Gio, it's perfect. I love it!" she whispered in his ear as she pulled him close. "I can't wait to show the children their new home," Grace said happily.

"And I can't wait to see you get well," Gio said hopefully.

Grace, Gio, and a few friends from the mill worked long hours over the next few days to get all seven of them settled into their new home. The first night the children slept in their new home, they slept like babies. The house was quiet, away from the noise of city sounds. They had plenty of room in their new bedrooms. They played jacks, jump rope, and marbles in the full-size basement; and they ran all over the fourteen acres outside. They loved their new home. Grace told the children they could stay out of school for a few days to get used to the house and yard but, the next week, they would get enrolled in school and start their new school.

True to her word, Grace went to the country school to enroll the children in their second half of the school year. She enrolled Vincenzo in fifth grade, Carla in third grade, and Mario in second grade. From the look of the setup of the school, Grace knew this was going to be an adjustment for the children. First they would have to walk one and a half miles each way to and from school. Second there were only four classrooms in the entire school. The entrance was an open area. The stage was at the end of the building. There were two grades per classroom: first and second, third and fourth, fifth and sixth, and seventh and eighth. Each classroom had four rows of desks. Two of the rows were for one grade, and the other two rows were for the other grade.

Since Grace and Gio did not get the children's records from their pervious school, the children needed to be tested for placement at the new school. Test results showed that academics would be relatively the same for Vincenzo and Mario. They would continue with the last half (semester B) of the grade they attended at the city school. However, test results showed that Carla fell within the average range for spelling and English and therefore would continue where she was in the city school for those subjects but would skip half a year in math. Grace was very pleased to hear this and shared with the teacher that she was used as a classroom peer tutor in math at the city school.

It did not take the children long to adjust to their new school. This pleased Grace. She knew their education was important. They didn't seem to mind the long walk to and from school. In fact, they used it as a cooldown time, transitioning from the active school day to quiet homelife. Each day, they would return home excited to share something new they learned in school.

One day, Vincenzo came home from school all excited about a story he read in school about William Tell. He told Grace all about the famous marksman with his crossbow. Carla was listening around the corner.

"Antonia, would you like to take part in my story about William Tell?" Vincenzo asked in an animated voice to his four-year-old sister.

"Who's that?" Antonia answered.

"He was a famous marksman, and he put an apple on his son's head and shot it off using a crossbow. Doesn't that sound exciting? You like apples, right, Antonia? Would you like to pretend you are William Tell's son and put the apple on your head?" Vincenzo asked excitedly. "I'll even let you pick out the apple in the refriger-ator all by yourself."

"Okay, Vincenzo," said Antonia.

"Hey, Vincenzo, I want to play William Tell too," Carla said as she came out of hiding from around the corner. "Do you want to shoot the apple off my head instead?" asked Carla in a begging voice.

"You're too tall, Carla. I need a shorter person. Antonia is just the right height," explained Vincenzo. "But I do have an idea, Carla. Will you be the referee?" Vincenzo asked in a questioning voice. "I will get the bow ready and take aim, and you can say shoot when it is time," Vincenzo delegated, hoping Carla would buy into the idea.

"That sounds great, Vincenzo," Carla said breathlessly. "I would love to be the referee. When do we do this?" she asked.

"Tonight, after dinner," Vincenzo replied.

Vincenzo, Carla, and Antonia waited until dinner was fin-ished and the kitchen was cleaned. Then they went into the kitchen, and Vincenzo let Antonia pick out the apple. Gio and Grace were drinking coffee and talking in the living room. The other children were playing here and there inside the big house.

Vincenzo walked Antonia out to the front yard. He told her to stand under the big tree. He carefully balanced the apple on her head and told her to stand very still. Quiet and trusting, Antonia listened and followed all directions. Vincenzo took his place sev-eral paces in front of Antonia. He turned around to face her. He picked up his bow and took aim. He looked over at Carla and gave her the signal.

"*Shoot!*" shouted Carla in her newly appointed referee voice.

The arrow left his fingers with sufficient speed. It soared across the open space between him and Antonia in a textbook-per-fect arch. The silver arrow sailed through the air without inter-ruption. Vincenzo and Carla were elated. They jumped up and down in celebration. All was well. The release of the arrow was perfection; and Antonia was standing under the big tree, perfectly still, just as Vincenzo had instructed her. However, as the arrow covered the distance between them and Antonia, Vincenzo and Carla's cheering came to an abrupt end. The arrow began to drop lower than expected before reaching its target. By the time the arrow reached Antonia, it was too low to hit the apple on her head. The arrow made a bull's-eye for her left eye and went straight through. Antonia dropped to the ground. Vincenzo dropped his bow, and Carla covered her eyes.

Antonia lay on the ground and screamed in pain. Grace and Gio came running outside to the front yard. Once Grace saw Antonia, she froze in her tracks, covered her mouth, and started screaming. She reached up with her right hand and pulled at her hair in disbelief as to what she saw. Gio ran to Antonia, picked her up in his arms, and ran back into the house with her climbing two porch steps at a time. He laid her on the kitchen table and, without missing a beat, pulled the arrow out of her eye. Grace took a few minutes to calm herself down outside on the front porch. After she could hear that Antonia had stopped crying, she walked into the house.

"Gio, Gio," Grace stumbled over, saying his name. "We need to get her to the hospital right away. I'll go get out coats!" Grace shouted over her shoulder as she went into the next room to retrieve their coats from the closet.

"Just grab a towel and ice, Grace," Gio directed.

Grace hesitated, but she did as she was told. By the time Grace returned to the kitchen with the requested supplies, Antonia was sitting up.

"Gio, let's get her to the hospital," Grace spoke a little louder and with more conviction.

Gio whirled around and glared at Grace. Keeping his left hand on Antonia's shoulder, he took a swipe at Grace. Due to his limited reach, no contact was made. Grace froze.

"I will take care of Antonia," he said in a low, growling tone. "I am not taking her to the hospital, so stop begging. You just stay here and be my assistant," he said to Grace in a stern, staccato voice.

Once Gio and Grace cleaned and bandaged Antonia's eye, they gave her some medication and sent her to bed with an ice pack. Grace sat by her side until she fell asleep. Meanwhile, Gio grabbed his five-inch-wide, twelve-inch-long razor strap that he used to sharpen his razors and went on a hunt to find Vincenzo. Gio returned with a broken strap.

The next morning, Gio felt foggy. He did not sleep well. He replayed the actions of the previous night over and over in his head. He was overcome and disturbed. Before he went downstairs to get some coffee, he peeked in on Antonia. He walked over to her bed and put his hand lightly on her forehead. He was thankful to see that she was cool, no fever. He quietly tiptoed out of the room.

Next he wanted to talk to Vincenzo. He knew he would be downstairs getting ready to leave for school. He picked up his pace and went downstairs. He walked into the kitchen to find that the three school-age children had already grabbed their lunches and started walking to school. Grace was standing at the counter making coffee.

"How was Vincenzo this morning?" Gio asked Grace in a questioning voice.

"Quiet. Didn't say much," she answered. "I think he was still shaken from last night's actions," she added.

Grace poured Gio some coffee, and they both sat at the kitchen table in silence.

Grace broke the moment. "Aren't you going to be late for work if you don't hurry up and leave?" she asked. "It's not like you to be home this late in the morning."

Gio did not answer. He did not need to be reminded by Grace. He knew he was going to be late for work if he continued dragging his feet like this, but he was worn-out. He finally finished his second cup of coffee and stood to put the cup in the sink when the phone rang. He didn't feel like talking to anyone this morning. He wanted to be left alone. The phone kept ringing.

"Aren't you going to get that, Gio?" Grace asked, not clear on what was wrong with him this morning.

Gio did not answer her. Instead he mumbled something under his breath that Grace could not understand. He shuffled over to the phone and finally picked it up on its seventh ring.

"Hello," Gio growled into the phone.

"Hey, Gio, this is Jimmy. Sorry to bother you so early in the morning, but I thought you would want to hear this news. The construction at the corner of your front lawn is finished. All structures passed final inspections late yesterday afternoon. You're good to go, buddy," he reported.

"Wow, Jimmy, wonderful news!" Gio said, sounding awake for the first time since he woke up. "I needed to hear some good news this morning. I will walk down there later today and take a look," Gio said happily as he hung up the phone. He turned to tell Grace the good news. "Grace, that was Jimmy, the head of the construction crew for the front lawn project. It's completed and passed all inspections late yesterday afternoon. All we have to do now is build the tables, get some chairs, buy supplies, and we're in business," Gio reported with a smile on his face.

"That's great news, Gio," Grace cheered for her husband. "You had a vision and went after it. I am proud of you. I know this project has been one big burden for you, especially since you started it so soon after we moved into the farmhouse. I know you pushed to have this completed so that it could start being a moneymaker for our family. So many families are struggling with the Great Depression upon us. I am happy the project is completed and can be lifted off your mind," she said in a soothing voice.

Jimmy's good news gave Gio the energy he needed to put the event of last night behind him and look forward to what today would bring. He grabbed his lunch off the counter, threw on his hat, and left the house for work.

That evening, Gio walked down to the front lawn corner of his farmhouse lot to check out the new structures. He walked into the bar first. The front eating area was large enough to hold four round wooden tables and sixteen chairs for their customers. They would sell beer for five cents a glass, Gold Tip gum, candy, sandwiches, chips, and soda. In the back of the bar was a private room for families or small parties. It was large enough to hold another four round tables and sixteen chairs.

Gio looked around at the space. He thought to himself, *I think this might be a great place for a cot too. I might have to bring one down from the house to use as a resting area for when I get tired.* He chuckled aloud to himself.

Next Gio checked out the gas pump area, oil pit, and car wash area. He was thrilled to see that all structures met his specifications. It was exciting to see his vision in tangible form. He knew financial hard times were coming to America, and he knew this corner was going to make all the difference for his family and for the community too. This was going to be the corner in New Hamfield, Illinois, where any family could drive and receive full service for their car, eat homemade food, and drink as well. Gio smiled and was pleased at the end result. He would order all the supplies they needed by the end of the day with the hope of having these structures up and running by a few weeks' time. He couldn't wait to tell the boys when they got home from school.

When the supplies finally arrived, Gio, Vincenzo, and Mario got busy building tables for the bar. They built a total of eight tables and put porcelain on the tops of each of them. They set up four tables with four chairs around each of them in the front bar area and another four tables with four chairs around each for the back party-room area. Next they stocked the bar. With prohibition still around, they were only permitted to stock the bar with 3.2 beer. Gio was adamant about abiding by the law and not serve any wine or whiskey. The boys helped Gio stock the food area of the bar. They unpacked boxes of Gold Tip chewing gum, penny candy, candy bars, and soda. The sandwiches they would sell would be made in the kitchen of the farmhouse. They would carry them down a dozen at a time for sale.

Gio taught Vincenzo how to tap the kegs of beer. Vincenzo was the main person behind the bar. Mario would work in front of the bar selling food. Gio would pump and sell the gas. It did not take long for everyone to understand their jobs and to organize the bar and eating areas. They were all very excited to open the corner business. They decided that the bar would be open Monday through Friday, five o'clock in the evening until dark. This would give Gio enough time to get home from work before going down to the bar to pump gas. It would also give the children enough time to get home from school, do their schoolwork, and go down to the bar to help him out. On Saturday and Sunday, the bar would be open from early morning until dark.

On the targeted day of the opening, Gio announced that, before they turned on the "Open" sign in the front window, there was one more thing that needed to be done. He told Vincenzo and Mario to wait at the bar and not to turn on the "Open" sign yet. Gio walked up to the farmhouse and carried down a cot. He placed it in the back room of the bar.

"Mario, you see this cot?" Gio asked.

"Yes," answered Mario.

"This cot is going to stay here in this back room. When I get hot from standing outside pumping gas, I am going to come back here and rest on this cot. It will be your job to fan me until I cool down," Gio instructed. "Do you think you understand what I am asking you to do?" Gio questioned.

"Yes," Mario obediently answered. "It would be my honor."

On opening day for the business, Grace got up early to make a dozen sandwiches for them to sell at the bar. Gio, Vincenzo, Mario, and even Carla spent the morning running back and forth between the bar and the farmhouse bringing down last-minute items. Finally all the running in and out of her kitchen stopped. The "Open" sign had been turned on, and the bar was actively receiving customers.

Grace took a break from all the morning activity and sat at the kitchen table. Antonia and Virginia were quietly playing in the basement. She sat at the kitchen table drinking some lemonade and happened to look down at her kitchen floor. There was dirt, mud, and even some grass that was tracked in from Gio and the older children running in and out this morning carrying things down to the bar. As tired as she was, she decided to wash the floor. After she swept it, she felt a little bit more energetic and decided to wash the floor by hand on her hands and knees instead of using the mop. Using a scrub brush and bar of Murphy's Oil Soap always made the floor shiny and smell good too.

She eased herself down on the floor using one of the kitchen chairs for balance, getting down on her knees. She used a scrub brush and long bar of Murphy's Oil Soap to suds up an area, then went back over it with a wet rag, removing all the suds and dirt. She rinsed her rag in a bucket of clean, warm water and repeated the process. It was jobs like this that reminded Grace just how weak her left leg and left arm really were. However, all the hard work was paying off because she was loving the results. She looked back over the part of the floor that had been washed and noticed the sheen. She smiled. She was almost finished with the floor when her rag hit something sharp. She let out a little yelp and dropped the rag. She looked at her hand and saw blood. She wiped it away and took a closer look. She saw the eye of a sewing needle sticking out of the meaty part of her hand.

"My sewing needle!" she exclaimed. "I must have dropped it on the floor in here when I was sewing that button on Mario's school coat the other day," she said out loud to herself.

At that point, Grace finished the job quickly. She carefully pulled herself up off the floor, drained the bucket of dirty water, and put all the cleaning supplies away. Then she sat down at the kitchen table to better evaluate her hand. By that time, Grace saw that the eye of the needle was no longer visible. It had worked its way completely through her hand. She knew it had to come out, but it did not look too bad right now. It was uncomfortable. She could feel it in there, but it did not hurt that badly that she needed to call Gio back to the house from the bar. She convinced herself that she would be okay. She decided to just wait until Gio came home from pumping gas to see if he could help her remove the needle.

By the time it turned dark and Gio and the older children came home from working their first day at the bar, Grace could barely move her fingers. Her hand swelled up to twice its original size. It was tender to the touch, and it felt warm. Her sore, swollen hand made it difficult to tend to Antonia and Virginia. Grace was in severe pain. There was no way to see or feel the eye of the needle in her hand anymore. There was a deep red line forming from the wound site, continuing up past her wrist. When she pressed on it, puss seeped out.

"What happened?" Gio asked in a concerned voice when he saw her later that evening.

Grace told him the story from earlier that day. They decided to take a ride to the hospital. Grace was reluctant to go, but Gio insisted. He realized that this was infection and needed to be treated right away. Vincenzo was put in charge of the children.

Several hours later, they returned home. The doctors were able to remove the sewing needle and treat Grace with antibiotics and a bandage. The ride home was very quiet. Grace assumed that Gio was tired from the long day at work and then pumping gas at the bar after work. She was the first one to break the silence.

"Why are you so quiet, Gio?" Grace asked in a soft voice.

They continued traveling several more miles in silence.

Finally Grace repeated, "Gio, why so quiet?"

Gio took a deep breath, and then took a few seconds to sigh a deep sigh.

"This incident has made me start thinking, Grace," he said in a slow, deliberate voice. "You need help around the house. You are not able to do all that you were able to do just a few years ago. Your leg is not getting better, and your left arm is almost frozen in a bend position. That makes it difficult for you to do everyday household chores that are needed for a family of seven. I know it is difficult for you to get up and down from the floor, lift and push things, hang the clothes on the line outside, and even dress yourself some days.

"I also know that you have not been ironing. Mario came complaining to me the other day about not having a starched white shirt to wear to school. I took a look in his closet, and he was correct. So I went to the laundry area and saw the basket of clothes that needed ironed," he said in a careful voice. "I think I am going to start looking for someone to come in to help with at least the ironing. What do you think about that?" Gio questioned.

"It is difficult for me to iron," Grace confessed. "It takes me a long time since I do not have the full use of my left arm," she continued. "I guess, if you really want to pay someone to come in and help, that would be fine. The sooner the better, I guess. I am really not going to be able to do much now with my right hand bandaged," she said in a sad voice. "I feel so helpless," she cried. "Almost like I am not a good mother or wife anymore. I can't keep up with the needs of the children anymore," she confessed. "I barely feel like a wife," she half whispered to herself.

Gio heard her but did not respond.

The next day, Gio hired on a young lady named Litch to come and help with cleaning and ironing for the Rivia family.

It did not take long for Grace to realize how much stress had been lifted off her shoulders by having Litch at the farmhouse to help out. She was wonderful. She anticipated things that needed to be done around the house without Grace having to follow her and direct her. She instinctually knew what needed to be done and how to do it. With Litch at the house, Grace had more time to spend with Antonia and Virginia and to rest.

One day, not long after Litch was hired, Elena, Grace's youngest sister, called on the phone.

"I'm calling to see how you are healing from your hand wound," Elena asked. "I've been thinking about you and wondering how you were getting along," she said.

"Oh, I'm doing fine, Elena. Thanks for calling and checking up on me," Grace answered. "Gio hired a young lady named Litch to help me out during the day. She's wonderful, really helpful. She spends the day doing some cleaning and ironing. I am so thankful Gio hired her," Grace said in a happy voice.

"That's wonderful, Grace. I am so happy you are doing well. I was concerned with you moving to that big farmhouse. I thought that might be overwhelming," Elena said in a concerned voice for her older sister. "Anyway, Grace, I am calling for another reason too. I was thinking that I would like to come and pick up the children for Mass on Sunday," Elena said in a questionable voice. "Virginia is two years old now, and I think it would be a good idea to start getting the children involved in the Catholic church," Elena proclaimed.

"I don't know, Elena. I don't think Gio will like the idea," Grace answered in a timid voice. "Plus, now with the bar being open, Gio needs Vincenzo and Mario down there to help him."

"I know he doesn't see the importance of church. He doesn't attend himself, but what would he have against his children attending the Catholic church?" asked Elena. "He has the boys helping him at the bar all the other days of the week. He can let them have two hours on Sundays off. That's not that much time away from helping him," Elena continued.

"I'm not exactly sure what he will say about all of this, Elena, but I will ask," Grace said to her sister. "For that matter, I would be willing to help Gio at the bar until the children return from Mass," she said willingly. "Elena, you need to be clear on something. I don't think Gio hates church. I just think he's had some bad experiences with it. He told me a story one time about when he was nine and living in Italy. One time a year, during festival season, his family would attend the festivals that the Catholic church would organize. He remembers seeing a mule pulling a cart with statues on it. As the cart made its way thought the crowded streets of the festival, people would toss money or attach money to the statues as it came near them.

"He was curious to know what happened to all that money. So he decided to follow the mule-drawn cart. The mule pulled the cart to the iron gate of the Catholic church. Then the cart went behind the gate, and the iron gate was shut and locked. The cart never came back out. Gio did not like that he was not able to see what happened to the money. No one told the crowd how their donation was going to be used. This made him not trust the church," Grace explained.

"And that's why he doesn't like the Catholic church or will let his children attend?" Elena asked in a squeaky, high-pitched voice.

"I guess, Elena," Grace answered. "He also told me that, when he was a teenager, he found out that his mother, Isabella, was the result of an affair that her mother had with a priest," Grace answered in a quiet voice. "I think, between these two things, Gio has been turned off by the church. He always says that he will not go to a church that puts money first or puts on a show, whether it is the preacher or the music director. He wants to go to a church that preaches about God and then shows God through the actions of the church," Grace further explained.

"I am sorry that Gio had those negative experiences with the Catholic church," Elena sympathized. "However, I am still asking if you would allow me to start picking up the children for Mass every Sunday," she asked kindly. "It would only be for a few hours. I will return them as soon as it is over so they can go help Gio at the bar," she said, pleading her case with her sister.

"I will ask Gio," Grace promised.

To Grace's surprise, Gio agreed for Elena to pick the children up for Mass on Sundays. It was arranged that all five of the children would attend under one condition. Grace had to walk down to the front corner of their lot and help him tend to the bar during the hours that the boys were at Mass. Grace agreed. She thought it might be fun to actually do something together with him. Grace called Elena to let her know that Gio agreed.

Elena arrived early at the farmhouse on Sunday. All of the children were dressed and ready to go to Mass with their aunt Elena. The older children were excited to get out of a few hours of working at the bar. They were even more excited to experience this new thing called Mass.

When Elena drove the children home, she asked them to sit on the front porch with her for a while and handed each of them a small box. She told the children to open the boxes before going into the house. Vincenzo and Mario received Saint Christopher medals to wear around their necks; and Carla, Antonia, and Virginia received gold crucifix necklaces in their boxes. Elena eagerly helped the children put their necklaces on. She told them that, as long as they wore them, they would be protected from harm. They each thanked her and gave her a hug goodbye. Elena was fulfilled.

Time moved quickly on the farm. They were all so busy between caring for the farm animals, family garden, and orchard and tending the bar and car services at the corner of their lot. Before Grace realized it, six weeks had passed. The children continued to attend Mass. Litch continued to work for them, and it was time for Grace's sixth-week follow-up visit for her hand wound. Grace made an appointment.

Dr. Denero unbandaged Grace's hand and confirmed that the wound had healed nicely. He reminded her to continue taking all of the antibiotic until the bottle was empty, gave her a big smile, and patted her on the back in a friendly gesture.

"While you are in the office today, would you like to schedule an appointment at the front desk for current tests and scans of the blood clot in your brain?" Dr. Denero asked Grace. "It has been quite a while since your last set of scans with the specialist. I know you have been busy with moving out to the country and all, and I saw that you built a business at the corner of your farmhouse lot too. I just thought, since you were in the office today, it would be a good time to get those on the schedule," the doctor suggested.

Grace opened her mouth to answer, but Gio's response superseded hers.

"That's exactly correct, Dr. Denero. You heard correctly. We moved out to the country in December. With spring in the air, we would like to watch and see what affect the country air has on Grace. There will be no scheduling of tests and scans with the specialist. The country air will take care of Grace's health." Gio smiled as he answered the doctor with confidence.

"But, Mr. Rivia, even though the country air may give Grace a quieter, more peaceful environment and perhaps rosy cheeks, it will not help dissolve the blood clot in her brain and prevent further damage. Her regularly scheduled tests and scans are the only way we can monitor the blood clot, as well as manage her severe headaches," the doctor tried to explain. However, Dr. Denero quickly realized by the look on Gio's face that his medical opinion was falling on deaf ears.

"Grace and I appreciate all that you have tried to do to help her along, but we will handle this situation the way we see fit. We moved to the country on the recommendation that country air is best for these type of health situations," Gio quickly answered, hoping this explanation would be the end of this discussion. "So with that, we will be on our way," Gio politely said as he motioned to Grace that they were finished here and stood up.

"Mr. Rivia, you do realize that, without these regularly scheduled appointments as well as tests and scans, Grace's medication will not be permitted to be refilled," Dr. Denero announced with the most professional voice he could muster in this most aggravating confrontation.

"Yes, Doctor, we are aware. The country air will do Grace good," Gio said in a voice that told the doctor that this was the last thing he wanted to say on this topic.

The doctor, realizing that he was wasting his breath, hung his head and quietly exited the exam room. Grace hung her head and felt invisible.

It was a quiet ride back to the farmhouse for Grace and Gio. In her mind, Grace's voice was screaming to be heard. Gio embarrassed her in front of the doctor. She wanted to shout at Gio that, even though her left leg and arm were weak, she still had good, functioning ears and a mouth that could hear and speak for herself. It was not his tests and scans on his brain; it was all hers! She did not need him to make decisions for her health. What was she going to do without her medications that were specifically prescribed as a result of the tests and scans? Grace trembled at the thought. It was so irritating when Gio made her feel invisible, microscopic, and unseeable. Recently this was a constant feeling.

In his mind, Gio was celebrating. Grace cowered in front of the doctor. He put the doctor in his place. He set him straight. No more tests and scans. The country air would take care of every health issue Grace had. Grace needed him to make decisions for her. She was quiet and trusting. She was not a risk-taker. He did not need her voice or opinion. He would take care of everything. What would she do without him? He trembled at the thought. It was rewarding when Grace made him feel dominant, masterful, and imperious. Recently this was a constant feeling.

Grace was happy to finally reach home. When she got to the kitchen door, she heard Vincenzo talking to someone on the phone.

"Oh, wait, Aunt Sofia. They're just arriving home from the doctor now. I'll give the phone to my dad," Vincenzo said as he obediently handed the house phone to his dad. "It's Aunt Sofia, Dad. She's calling from New York."

"Sofia, hello," Gio called out in a happy voice. "How are you and Vera doing?" he asked with a big smile on his face.

Grace shook her head as she walked past Gio, through the kitchen, and into the living room. She desperately needed to rest. She strategically positioned herself on the couch propped up on a fluffy pillow. She could hear their conversation from where she was sitting. She tried not to listen or even care, but Gio's happy, carefree voice kept her engaged. She couldn't help but feel hurt as she listened.

"He sure doesn't sound like this when he's talking to me." She couldn't help but compare. "All I hear is the demanding, overbearing Gio, the Gio that won't let me voice my opinion," she whispered to herself.

Gio and Sofia talked on the phone for another five minutes. Grace waited patiently on the couch for Gio to be finished. After he hung up, he joined Grace in the living room.

"You should have heard Sofia on the phone, Grace," Gio said excitedly. "She sounds great, really upbeat. You know, full of hope and love for life again. I think she has peace in her heart and mind. She must have found a way to cope with the loss of her two husbands and has moved on with her life. She said Vera is doing well too. I am so happy for her," Gio announced with glee.

"That's great, Gio," Grace said with happiness for her sister-in-law.

"With us being so busy moving and starting the business these past few months, I have stopped calling and checking up on her. I want to get back into the routine of calling," Gio said with promise in his heart.

"That would be nice, Gio," Grace said with sincerity. "I'm sure she would appreciate you calling regularly to check up on her. She sure has been through a lot these past few years. I couldn't even imagine raising a child all by myself," Grace shuddered at the thought.

True to his word, Gio continued calling his sister in New York on a regular basis. Grace would overhear them from the living room sharing stories about family, work, and life in general. However, there was never a conversation with Sofia that Gio did not share his dreams for the farmhouse and the bar. Grace would perk up and listen more attentively to that part of their conversation so that she could hear his dreams too. He never spoke to her about his dreams for anything. This was the only time that she was privy to this subject.

"Yes, Sofia," Gio began a conversation about the farm with his sister one Friday night, "I just traded a bricklaying favor with a buddy of mine for a horse, cow, and two goats. He's going to deliver them in his truck tomorrow."

"Who's going to take care of the animals?" asked Sofia.

"The boys," Gio replied with a little giggle in his belly. "I've already spoken to them about tending to the animals. The chickens will stay in the chicken coop, and the barn is big enough to house the additional animals. All I have to do now is teach Vincenzo and Mario to muck out the stalls and feed the animals. They're excited, Sofia," Gio said with confidence.

"Well, what about the garden, grapevine, and peach and apple orchards?" Sofia continued to ask her brother.

"Carla will help me tend to that. Antonia is coming up in age to help too, and the older girls will be a good example for Virginia to follow in their steps someday when she is a little older," Gio answered.

"What about Grace?" Sofia asked in a half-whispered voice. "What will she do to help?"

The phone line went quiet for a while as Gio thought.

"She'll fill in as she can," Gio answered in a quiet voice.

"How is her health anyway?" Sofia asked in a sheepish voice.

She didn't know if it was right to ask. She knew this was a tender subject with Gio, but she wanted to know.

Gio sighed a long, breathy sigh. "I was hoping that the country air would take care of her health issues right away, but so far, I have not seen a change. My plan is to give it one year, sort of take a look at the situation at that time and then decide if living in the country is doing its trick," Gio said as he stopped to take another breathy sigh. "Her left leg is weak. Almost drags it now. Her left arm is frozen in a bent position. Her face has some weakness too," Gio reluctantly answered. After a few seconds of silence, he confessed, "Let's just say that I am mother and father to the children."

"Oh, Gio, I am so sorry to hear that," Sofia said with sorrow in her voice. "If there is anything I can do to help, please let me know. I will be praying for her. I know how difficult this must be for you and for the children too," Sofia said.

Gio paused and replayed what Sofia said in his head.

Pray for her? Did I hear correctly? Gio quickly replayed the conversation in his head. *Yes, I am sure that she said she would be praying for Grace,* Gio thought to himself.

A little confused to hear Sofia say those words, Gio sprung back to life and dropped the conversation.

"Thank you, Sofia," Gio replied in a kind voice.

"Yes, definitely, Gio. Just let me know if there is anything I can do to help. You know, it is only Vera and me. It wouldn't take much for me to travel to Illinois to help you out," Sofia offered sweetly.

Shortly afterward, they said their goodbyes, and his conversation with Sofia came to a close. Gio hung up the phone and sat there. He couldn't move. Typically, when he was finished talking to his sister, he would jump right up and get on with his evening. Sometimes he would go find Grace and tell her parts of their conversation. Not this time. Gio sat there replaying the conversation. *Content*, that was the word. That was the word he would use to describe Sofia.

The next day, the farm animals arrived. Not only did Gio's buddy trade him the animals for his bricklaying favor, but his buddy threw in bags of vegetable seeds to help Gio get started with planting the family garden. Gio was elated and appreciative for this unexpected gesture. While Gio, Vincenzo, and Mario spent the afternoon getting the animals placed in their stalls and fed, Grace sat around the kitchen table with the girls, sorting vegetable seeds.

"We are going to grow our own vegetables," Grace explained to Carla, Antonia, and Virginia. We will sort these seeds today, and tomorrow we will plant them. We will water them and watch them grow. In a few months, we will have a full family garden of potatoes, lettuce, beans, peppers, cucumber, tomatoes, garlic, and onions. Then we can take baskets out back and harvest all the vegetables for our dinner table," Grace continued to explain to the girls.

All the children were on board to begin the new farm projects that were ahead of them. The animals were nestled in the barn for the night, and all the vegetable seeds were sorted for tomorrow's planting. Gio and Grace listened in amazement as the conversation at the dinner table that evening bounced between why cows have so many stomachs, why tomato seeds were so small, why baby goats were called kids, why onions grow underground, and why you measure the height of a horse with your hand.

Gio and Grace openly laughed as they sat and tried to follow the conversation that was created by the arrival of the animals and seeds at the farm earlier in the day. Gio and Grace ate up the innocence of the conversation. They were thankful that the children were willing to help with the new jobs and were taking interest in the farm. The conversation was light and fun, and Gio could not remember the last time they enjoyed a family dinner this way.

The children were still giggling about this and that when dinner was finished. Gio loved the light feeling in the air. He wished the kitchen had this feeling more often. He sat sipping on his coffee as the children, one by one, asked to be excused from the dinner table. Grace had just finished her coffee, and he knew it wouldn't be long before she would want to get up and start cleaning the kitchen. Gio tipped back his cup to gulp down the last of his coffee when Grace pushed herself away from the table to stand up, but before she was completely standing, she fainted and dropped to the floor.

"Grace!" was all Gio could shout. "Vincenzo, Mario, come and help me pick up your mother!" Gio shouted to the boys.

Gio ran over to where Grace lay on the floor and cupped her head in his hands. Vincenzo and Mario came running back to the kitchen to help their dad.

"What happened?" called Vincenzo.

"I don't know," answered Gio. "She fainted as soon as she stood up from the dinner table. Help me move her away from the table," Gio requested. "Mario, run and get a wet, cool rag," Gio ordered.

By the time Mario returned with a wet washcloth, Grace was conscious.

"What happened? Why am I on the floor?" Grace asked.

"You fainted," Gio answered the question before the boys could speak. "Let us help you up so you can sit on the chair," Gio said.

Gio, Vincenzo, and Mario worked together to help Grace up off the floor. Before long, she was sitting at the kitchen table sipping some water. They let her sit there for a few minutes to gather herself, then they helped her walk to the living room, where she rested on the couch. Gio called Carla and Antonia to clean the table from dinner and wash the dishes. They knew better than to question what just happened or the job they were called to complete. Instead the sisters worked together getting the job finished. Young Virginia hung out in the kitchen with her older sisters and helped them by drying off the kitchen table and hanging the dishcloths to dry before all three left the kitchen.

Grace retired to the bedroom early that evening. She was exhausted. Gio stayed up late sitting in the living room contemplating his next move. He had a lot to think over. Grace had never fainted before. What if this became a regular occurrence? What if she fainted while he was at work? Finally he decided that he would make a trip to the pharmacy before work on Monday and buy some smelling salts. He would show Carla how to use them and would put her in charge of them should this happen while he was not at home.

On Sunday, before Elena came to pick up the children for Mass, Grace fainted again. This time, Vincenzo and Mario helped their father walk Grace right back to bed. Gio told Vincenzo and Mario that they could not attend Mass that morning. He needed their help at the bar.

That night, Gio barely got any sleep. He was up most of the night strategizing a plan. He had no idea why Grace was fainting. He also had no idea if this was going to stop as quickly as it started or if it would continue happening. All he was clear about was that he had to accomplish two things today.

First he called for Carla to meet him in the living room.

"Yes, Dad? You wanted to see me?" Carla asked nervously. She was worried that she did something wrong and was in trouble.

"Please, Carla, come and sit down with me a minute," Gio spoke kindly.

He told Carla about Grace fainting twice. He told her that he did not know if this was something that would never happen again or would happen frequently from this day forward. Gio explained what smelling salts were and told her that he was going to buy them first thing tomorrow when the pharmacy opened. Together they decided upon a secret place to keep them in the house. He told Carla that she was in charge of them and made her promise that she would be the only one to touch them. Once Gio felt that Carla was clear on the directions, he told her to go back to what she was doing.

Second he called his sister, Sofia.

"Sofia," Gio started out slowly, "I need your help. If you and Vera come and help me with Grace and the children, I will help you by giving you free room and board."

"I'll pack up and come this week, Gio," Sofia answered with a sweet voice.

Later that evening, Gio called the family to the living room for an impromptu meeting. He had Grace and the children sit while he stood over them to explain that his sister, Sofia, and her young daughter, Vera, were coming to help them at the farm. They would be traveling by car from New York and would arrive next Monday. Gio said all this without making eye contact with Grace. However, out of the corner of his eye, he watched her turn pale. He knew this was the first she was hearing this news and was not happy. He did not stop to address her concerns. He continued to announce that their aunt Sofia and cousin Vera would be sleeping in the guest bedroom. Their stay would be indefinite. With this announcement, Grace's mouth flew open, and she glared up at Gio in disbelief.

Slowly Grace stood up to be on the same eye level as Gio. "What are you talking about?" she began. "When was this decided?" she half asked, half scolded. "Who decided that I need help with the children or this farm for that matter?" she asked as she carefully walked across the room to where Gio was standing.

The children did not move or say anything.

"Grace," Gio slowly called out her name in a whiny voice. "You know what is going on. Surely you realize that you cannot take care of the house and the children too. I hired Litch to help out, but that is not enough. With Sofia coming to help, we can let Litch go. Sofia and Vera can stay here to help us, and in return, we would be helping her too," Gio tried his best to explain.

"I don't need anyone coming in to help," Grace protested. "You don't need to point out that I cannot do things like I have before, but my strength will come back, Gio. Isn't that what you proclaimed? Isn't that the reason you wanted us to move to this farmhouse, for the fresh air, quiet, and my healing?" Grace argued.

"You are fainting, Grace!" Gio shouted at a level she had never heard him shout at before.

Grace covered her ears and instinctually jerked back.

"This discussion is closed. I have the say-so here. Sofia and Vera are coming in a week. End of conversation. No opinions are accepted beyond this point," Gio declared.

Grace knew when to shut up. She knew not to argue her point. She sat down on the couch and closed her eyes. She held her throbbing head. She didn't say anything to Gio the rest of the night. When it was time to go to bed, she went alone. She sat in the bedroom and tightly wrapped her head to try to ease her headache. Gio never came to bed that night. He slept on the couch in the living room.

During the week waiting for Sofia to arrive, Gio and the children planted the seeds that never got planted in the family garden due to Grace starting to faint. Gio was excited to finally have this job completed and was looking forward to all the produce that the garden would render. Carla and Antonia helped Gio set up the spare bedroom in anticipation of Sofia's arrival. Gio chose this specific bedroom for Sofia and Vera because it was the most private of all five bedrooms upstairs. Not only was it at the opposite end of the hallway from Gio and Grace's bedroom, but it was around a short corner. It would be perfect.

Sofia arrived at the farmhouse on a Monday afternoon. Vincenzo, Carla, and Mario were in school when she arrived. Antonia and Virginia were napping, so the house was relatively quiet. Grace met Sofia and Vera at the front door since Gio was at work. Grace felt awkward greeting them. Not only did Grace barely knew them, but Sofia was called upon by Gio to come help. She felt so defeated. This was not Grace's idea. She did not agree to this. She felt betrayed and blindsided by her husband. She was resentful. She took a deep breath, as if that would help blow the negative thoughts out of her head, and gave them a gentle hug. She walked then upstairs and showed them their room. Sofia and Vera stayed busy in their room until the rest of the family came home.

By the time the school-age children returned home from school, Antonia and Virginia were up from their naps and eating a snack in the kitchen.

"Where's Aunt Sofia and cousin Vera?" asked Vincenzo as soon as he walked through the door.

"They're upstairs getting settled in," answered Grace. "I'm sure they will be down soon. They have been up there since they arrived earlier this afternoon. Maybe they decided to take a nap or clean up from their long drive from New York," Grace reasoned.

The children were hungry from school and the long walk home. Grace was passing out cheese and crackers when Sofia and Vera entered the kitchen.

"Where are my nieces and nephews?" Sofia shouted, extending her arms as if to hug all of them at once. "How was school?" she asked with a big smile.

Three-year-old Vera peeked out from behind her mother's full skirt.

"Vera, don't be shy. Come out and say hello to your cousins," Sofia said as she reached behind her and pulled Vera out where she could be seen.

Vera reluctantly came out from behind her mother's full skirt. "Hello," Vera said in a quiet voice.

All but Carla gave a giggle at her tiny little hello. They all returned their greetings to their newly met cousin.

Carla stood staring. She could not believe how beautifully dressed this little girl was. Vera was wearing a ruffled skirt that matched her mother's. Her hair was neatly combed and tied back with a satin ribbon that matched her dress. The toe of a pair of tiny black leather shoes played peekaboo from under her fully ruffled skirt and net slips. Carla looked down at her own clothes. She felt embarrassed as she saw her old sneakers that were dirty from walking the long distance to school each day. She had on brownish-green leggings. They needed washing. Her dress was plain cotton and had no ruffles. She inconspicuously reached up to touch her hair and realized that her hair was a ball of knots.

Carla thought to herself, *Maybe Mommy is wrong. Maybe it will be a good thing having Aunt Sofia live with us. Maybe she can help me get rid of these ugly brownish-green leggings.*

As time passed, Carla's wish came true. Not only did Aunt Sofia agree that the ugly stockings needed to go; but she sewed Carla pretty dresses, taught her how to comb and style her hair, and introduced her to wonderful-smelling perfumes from New York. Carla ended the school year looking like a young girl of ten years old instead of an old-fashioned frump.

As the hot summer months flew by, the Rivia family, along with Sofia and Vera, celebrated Gio and Grace's nineteenth wedding anniversary, Antonia's fifth birthday, and Virginia's third birthday. All the celebrations were held at the house. Fresh eggs, vegetables, and fruit were enjoyed from the farm's chicken coop and bountiful family garden and orchard. Sofia did most of the cooking. She always made her handmade noodles for each of the special celebrations. They all agreed that they had never eaten any food so delicious.

"I'd be happy to teach you how to make the handmade noodles, girls. It's easy. It just takes practice," Sofia offered.

All the girls smiled and laughed with glee as they shook their heads, affirming that they wanted to learn.

"Actually, Gio, I was thinking," Sofia said as she turned and directed her request to her brother. "How about if we add spaghetti and meatballs to the menu at the bar? It would be easy to make a big batch of sauce with some small meatballs. If the girls want to learn how to make homemade noodles, they could help me. We can make homemade noodles and sell the meal as homemade spaghetti and meatballs with a slice of bread and butter. What do you think?" Sofia asked, holding her breath that her brother would say yes.

"Hmm" was all Gio uttered. "I love that idea, Sofia," he finally responded. *That would be great to sell at the bar since we are only selling cold sandwiches. If we add the spaghetti and meatballs, the customers would have a choice between a cold or hot meal*, Gio rationalized in his head. "When do you think we could start selling that?" Gio asked.

"I'll start teaching the girls how to make homemade noodles this week," Sofia replied. "How about if you give us two weeks to practice and stock up the freezer with enough sauce, meatballs, and noodles to get started?" she said.

Gio threw back his head and laughed. "This is tremendous!" he shouted and came around the table to give Sofia a big hug.

In two weeks, hot meals were introduced to the community at the bar. In addition to a served-up hot meal of spaghetti and meatballs on a plate, Sofia sold bottled spaghetti sauce as well. Gio thought adding the hot meal to the menu was a genius idea. The community people came at lunch for a cold sandwich and returned for a hot meal or a jar of spaghetti sauce to go at dinner-time. Everything was running smoothly. The gas station had lines of waiting customers. The oil pit and car wash were used daily, and the ice machine was a hit, bringing in its own profit.

During dinner hours, the bar and back party room were crowded with hungry families. Mothers and fathers were sitting together around tables feeding the whole family delicious home-made food and a soda at a cheap price. Babies cried and ran around the room. Fathers scolded, and young ones teased and laughed. It was a community family affair that Gio loved standing back and watching each night.

Then, after dinner hours, Gio would turn up the music, turn down the lights, and bring out the cigars. This was the time of night that Sofia would leave and walk back up to the house. She made it very clear to Gio early on that she wanted no part of this part of the bar. Gio understood and never questioned her. Once Sofia would leave, older crowds of adults would gather for a five-cent glass of 3.2 beer, dancing, woman watching, and a good smoke. Sometimes the bar would be active until the early morning hours. One night, some gentleman drinkers called out to Gio.

"Hey, Mr. Barman," the first gentleman called to Gio, "why don't you get us some white moonshine to drink in here?"

"White moonshine? I can't do that. You know Prohibition rules," Gio answered back. "I am not permitted to sell anything stronger than 3.2 beer."

"Who's going to tell?" called out the second gentleman, laughing.

"As a bartender, I have no intention of breaking Prohibition rules," he said.

That was the end of that conversation for that evening. However, the next night, the same two gentlemen returned and continued their conversation with Gio about sneaking in some moonshine so that they could have something stronger than 3.2 beer to drink at his bar. The two gentlemen made it sound so easy to sneak it in. All Gio had to do was get two barrels of moonshine, keep them up at the house, and bring it down to the bar one jug at a time. He'd keep the jug behind the counter and only serve it if asked for. He would not advertise that he had it in the bar. If Gio got raided, he'd only have a jug of the illegal drink in the bar. The next day, Gio did some asking around and found out where he could pick up a couple barrels of moonshine. Next he called Vincenzo and Mario to meet him in the back party room of the bar.

Once the boys were in the back party room, Gio began his conversation.

"Boys, you understand what Prohibition is, correct?" Gio began.

"Yes, Father." The boys nodded their heads in unison.

"I have a way of bringing in more money to the bar by selling white moonshine for fifty cents a glass. Right now, due to Prohibition rules, that is illegal to sell in any bar," Gio continued.

The boys stood very still and quiet, eyes intent on their father.

"I am having two barrels of white moonshine delivered to the house tomorrow. We will keep it in the basement. I will bring the moonshine down to the bar one jug at time," Gio said quietly as if even saying its name out loud was illegal. "Here is where I need your help, boys," Gio continued. "If the bar gets raided for selling illegal drink, they will only find one jug of it behind the bar. Even with one jug of it on the property, I will get arrested. If that happens, that is your cue to run to the basement, roll the two barrels out to the field, and dump them in the tall grass in the back," Gio instructed. "Do you understand your job?" he asked.

The two boys nodded in agreement with their father.

"One more thing. Mario, would you please stay here with me and fan me as I rest here on the cot?" Gio asked his younger son. "It has been so hot today, and the flies have not stopped landing on me. I would like to just take a few minutes to rest here in this back room," Gio continued.

"Certainly, Father, I would be honored to fan you while you rest," answered Mario.

As the summer continued, Gio sold his white moonshine and 3.2 beer in the bar without event. He was pleased that he took the chance because it was bringing in more money than he ever imagined. The buildings he had built at the empty front corner of the farmhouse lot was making a profit for his family to survive through the Great Depression. His family was thriving when many others were suffering financially. He knew having his sister, Sofia, come to help him on the farm was a big contributing factor to his success. She was bold, energetic, and a true go-getter. She had desire and spunk and did not give up until she got what she wanted. She was driven. Gio realized that the older he got, the more he admired these qualities in a woman. He was so thankful that she said yes to coming to help him on the farm.

Sofia was equally elated that Gio offered her space at the farm. She and Vera had a beautiful room to call their own and all the land she could ever wish for to go on walks or just take a break outdoors. She loved being surrounded by family. She felt fulfilled and needed again after suffering great sadness from burying two husbands unexpectedly. She was once again doing all the things she loved to do: gardening, cooking and baking, and sewing clothes and hair bows for Gio's daughters. Being at the farm, she felt that her life was in sync, running like a well-oiled machine. Sofia was happy.

Grace was sad. Her life could not be running more out of sync. Grace knew that Gio's asking Sofia to come live at their home was to make her life easier—to make her life run like a well-oiled machine. However, since Sofia arrived, Grace's life was more like a train wreck. Grace would watch from the window as Sofia, Carla, Antonia, and Virginia would pick fresh tomatoes and herbs from the family garden in preparation for making hot meals for the bar. She felt so lonely and left out. She did not have a job anymore. She felt useless and invisible, a wallflower that blended into the background of life. Since Sofia's arrival, not only did she lose her job as Gio's sounding board for his latest ideas for success, but she lost her job as mom.

When she asked Sofia if she could help, she was told to go rest. Everything was taken care of. They could do everything faster without her around. She did not have much to do, so she either sat in the living room or stayed in the bedroom with her head tightly wrapped. Her headaches were back in full force. Without any current scans or tests from the specialist, refills of her medication were not available. Grace was timid, a peacemaker, quiet, and private. She had no idea and was slightly afraid to talk to Gio about her feelings. So she internalized everything and became more and more withdrawn.

One afternoon, as Grace sat watching the activity out the window, Mario came to her.

"Mom, what are you doing?" Mario asked.

"Watching everyone work outside on this beautiful summer day. Why, Mario?" Grace inquired.

"I am upset, Mom. I have noticed something that I do not like. Things have changed since Aunt Sofia arrived. She's slowly taking over, Mom. You need to speak up. You are too quiet. Confront her, please," Mario tearfully confessed his feelings to his mother.

Grace sat up straighter in her chair to address her son. "Mario, you give off the impression to others that you are a hardcore boy, but you are really a sensitive eight-year-old who is watching out for his mother," she said, reaching out to give him a hug. "Thank you for sharing your feelings with me, Mario," she whispered in his ear. "It is okay. At first, I was upset that Aunt Sofia was coming here to stay indefinitely, but Daddy feels it will be helpful in the end. She is helping with the farm chores, dinner, and is even helping the girls with clothes for school," Grace answered in a soft voice.

Mario put his arms around his mother, stroking her straight dark hair. He did not say another word; he just held her in his arms. Grace was uncomfortable and did not know how to respond to his tenderness for her. Eventually he let go of his tight hold and just held on firmly to her shoulders. He looked deep into her eyes. Neither of them said a word, but Grace could feel the warning of his nonverbal words loud and clear straight down to her soul. They froze in silence, eyes locked for a few seconds; and then Mario let go, turned, and quietly walked back outside to finish his chores before he got in trouble with his dad.

Before long, the hot summer months vanished, and September turned the community family's attention to the start of the upcoming school year. The nightly bar activities slowed as families began using any extra money on school clothes, shoes, and food to pack lunches. Sofia continued to have the girls make homemade pasta, sauce, and meatballs with her; but the demand slowed to a point where she had more time to spend talking to Gio than serving customers. One evening, when they were alone at the bar, Gio asked Sofia a question that he'd wanted to ask many times before.

"Sofia, why do you hate the late-night crowd so much? As soon as the families leave the bar and I turn up the music and things get a bit looser, you walk back to the house," Gio asked with curiosity. "They're just wanting some carefree adult time in a bar, drinking to relax from their day," he continued.

Sofia drew in a deep breath. "I don't like it because the Bible condemns drunkenness and its effects," Sofia said boldly.

"The Bible?" Gio said softly. "You care about what the Bible says? Do you read the Bible, Sofia?" Gio asked, surprised.

"Yes, Gio, I do," Sofia answered with confidence.

"When did all this happen?" Gio asked.

"When Theo died, I was a wreck. No young girl expects to have her husband die within a year of their marriage, let alone two. Two husbands dead unexpectedly in a very short amount of time. Right after the funeral, Aunt Marinelle pulled me aside. She recognized how lost I was. She told me that I did not have to be scared, overwhelmed, or lonely. She told me about Jesus, His love, and His mercy. She gave me her personal Bible. When I thumbed through it, I saw many scriptures that she had underlined and highlighted. I started reading those places first. I was so interested in what I read that I started reading her Bible regularly, even the unmarked places. With every word, I was filled with peace and hope. His word gave me encouragement. Aunt Marinelle invited me to her church. She started picking me up for church each Sunday. It was at her church where I accepted Christ into my heart," Sofia said, choking up at the marvel of Jesus's love for her.

Gio was silent as he listened in surprise. He never expected to hear this kind of proclamation from Sofia or anyone else in his family. His family claimed that they were Catholic, but that was in name only. Gio remembered the family attending church on a holiday or at festival time, but even that was not consistent. After the holiday, church was never thought of or mentioned again. He'd heard different coworkers talk about God. He always listened but never joined in the conversations. He knew which of his work buddies served God and which ones didn't. He could tell the difference in the way they talked, their actions, and their work ethic.

In the deep, silent parts of his heart, Gio contemplated God. He wondered if God could ever love him knowing all the questionable business dealings he'd been involved in. He often wondered if there really was a heaven and hell. How do you get this personal relationship with God that he'd heard his buddies talk about? He never asked these questions to anyone or sought clarification from anyone. God was a private thing to him, and he was comfortable keeping it that way.

The next morning, Gio got up with the alarm to get ready for work. He realized that the conversation he had with Sofia the night before about God and His mercy never left his head. All night, it played round and round in his head like a record spinning out of control on its turntable. Gio knew what he needed to do to make the spinning come to rest. At the first work break of the day, Gio headed for the break area, where he knew he would find one of his churchgoing buddies. Gio sat down quietly at his table. Several other coworkers were there. It was not long before Gio's buddy started talking about a family issue where God's mercy and faithfulness was so prevalent. Gio listened. He remained silent, but as soon as the group started disbanding to return to work, Gio pulled his buddy aside.

"Hey, I was wondering, Can you explain God's mercy and faithfulness to me?" Gio asked in a simple way.

"Sure, Gio," his buddy answered. "Better yet, I'll put the name and address of my church in your work locker. Come join us sometime. You will learn a lot!" he shouted over his shoulder as he half walked, half ran back to his workstation.

"Okay, thank you!" was all Gio could shout back before his buddy disappeared.

At the end of the day, Gio saw the scribbled note his buddy left him in his locker. It was an Italian church. That immediately intrigued Gio.

Even though the Italian church sounded interesting to him, he decided to attend three churches that were closer to the farm first. He did not share his plan with the family. Over the next few Sundays, Gio attended church for the first time since he was a child. Only this time, he was not attending because it was a holiday or festival or for the fun of chasing and pinning money on a statue being pulled through the streets on a cart. This time, he was attending because he was searching, like a hungry lion, for God's word to feed his soul. After all these years of not going to church or having an adult explain God's simple principles to him, his soul was empty and dry, and he was hungry.

He heard when his buddy accepted Christ. His brick mill was buzzing about it. He watched his buddy at work from afar, and he saw a difference in him. He watched him evolve. He watched him grow in Christ right before his eyes. He saw the bold testimony he developed. Now he recognized the same thing in Sofia. Gio wanted to learn. He wanted to feed on the truth about God—the truth that would answer his questions about God's faithfulness, mercy, and love.

He left the older kids and Sofia to run the gas station and bar while he went off on his secret mission. Elena, Grace's sister, came to the farm to pick up the younger children for Mass.

The first church he attended had a special musical production going on. He did not like this approach to hearing God's word and promptly left. Gio did not give up. The next Sunday, he tried another church.

The second church was very fancy. It had stained-glass windows from floor to ceiling. A big pipe organ filled the front of the church. Gio looked around. Although he recognized the beauty of the room, he was not impressed. He wanted simple. He wanted someone to tell him, in a simple way, the simple truth of God—His mercy, faithfulness, and love. Sitting in this church made him feel uncomfortable. He did not get discouraged. He would try the third church next Sunday.

However, the third church was not what Gio was looking for either. It was formal. The minister wore a robe, and the congregation repeated words after the minister. Gio did not feel a freedom here. He wanted the minister to teach him what was in the Bible. Gio almost felt like giving up, but he remembered there was always the church his buddy told him about.

For the fourth Sunday in a row, Gio attended church. This time, he attended the small Italian church his buddy attended. Since the church was a little farther away than the other three he attended the previous weeks, he was a little late in arriving there. Gio noticed on the church marquee that they were advertising a revival at the church. He did not know what that meant, but he opened the church door anyway and stepped inside. He opened the back door and was greeted by worship music filling the room. The atmosphere in this church was like nothing he felt the previous Sundays. The music in the air was rich. The thick richness of the music hit Gio hard, like he walked into an invisible wall, and it caused him to freeze in place.

He closed his eyes and felt goose bumps form on his arms and back of his neck. He listened more intently. He heard words like "His love is pouring down on us like rain. Jesus is our great friend, protector, and healer." Even though Gio did not know any of the words to sing along, he stood with the congregation and just drank it all in. By the time the minister got up to preach, he was already half fed. The minister spoke on being born again and filled with the Holy Spirit. At the end of his sermon, Gio knew this was what he had been searching for. When the pastor gave the altar call, Gio went to the front to meet the pastor. They prayed; and when they were finished, Gio was a new born-again, spirit-filled Christian, with the evidence of speaking in a heavenly language.

Vincenzo was the first person Gio saw when he returned to the farm. He came clean about what he had been doing for the past four Sundays in a row. Vincenzo was intrigued. Gio invited him to go to church with him the next Sunday. Vincenzo attended with his father and walked out of the little Italian church a new born-again, spirit-filled Christian, with evidence of speaking in a heavenly language at just eleven years old.

Carla got wind of what happened to her father and Vincenzo. She wanted to attend the revival too. The next Sunday, Gio took both Vincenzo and Carla with him to the little Italian church. That Sunday, Carla, at just seven years old, left the church a new born-again, spirit-filled Christian, with evidence of speaking in a heavenly language. The three Rivia family members rejoiced in the altar area thanking God for His mercy and goodness to them. They were excited to return to the farm to tell the rest of the family.

Once everyone sat down at the Sunday dinner table, Gio told the whole family about the revival at the church and how he, Vincenzo, and Carla, became new born-again Christians and filled with the Holy Spirit. Grace and Sofia sat and wept as they listened to the story. They all felt this transformation was needed and would be remembered as a landmark for the family for generations to come. They decided to attend the revival at the church for as long as it was there. This would mean that Elena would have to be told to not come to the farm to pick up the children for Mass and the bar would have to be closed on Sundays for the whole family to attend church together.

They also decided that, from that day forward, they would give thanks to God for their food. They had never done that before. Since the Great Depression began, they had known many families to go hungry when they had never felt denied. They wanted to give back to God by thanking Him for His goodness in supplying all their needs. This prayer before eating their food would be their first prayer together as a family.

Gio delegated a job to each family member to complete by the end of the week. First Grace would call her sister, Elena, and tell her she no longer needed to pick the children up on Sundays for Mass. Grace was to inform her that the whole family would be worshipping together at the small Italian church. Second Sofia would make some signs for the doors of the bar announcing that, starting this week, it would be closed on Sundays. Antonia and Virginia would help her hang the signs. Third Vincenzo and Carla would have the job of praying at the table before each family meal. After giving everyone in the family a job, Gio decided to assign himself a job too.

"The job I will complete by the end of the week will be to buy myself a Bible. Mario will come with me to help pick it out. I realize that, if I want to grow in the Lord and be the Christian leader of this home, I need to read and understand God's Word," he proclaimed to the family.

The week was busy with everyone working on their designated jobs. Sofia, Antonia, and Virginia followed through with their job the very next day. Sofia colored bright, legible signs for the doors of the bar announcing that it would be closed on Sundays, and the two young girls helped her tape them up for all to see. Vincenzo and Carla met in the living room two days after that to make a loose schedule of who would pray for which meal and on what days. Gio and Mario stopped at a Christian bookstore later that week so Gio could buy himself his first Bible.

By Friday of that week, all the jobs were complete, except Grace's job.

"What do you mean you still haven't called Elena to tell her not to pick up the kids for Sunday Mass? It's Friday already. Sunday is two days away," Gio half reminded, half scolded Grace.

"I know, Gio. You don't have to remind me. Elena is going to be so upset. She loved picking up the children each Sunday. I'm nervous to tell her," Grace said in a quiet voice.

"You either call and tell her, or I will," Gio said forcefully. "We are going to start worshipping together as a family. That's the end of this story. Tell Elena today," Gio demanded as he turned and rushed out of the room.

Grace took a deep breath and dialed the phone. Just as she predicted, Elena was upset and even cried when Grace told her the news. She was hurt that, all these years, Gio never expressed or showed a care in the world about God or church for himself, let alone his family. All of a sudden, he changed, and now he not only cared about God and church but wanted the whole family to worship together at a small Italian church. This was very confusing for her to understand. Grace tried her best to explain it but was not getting through to her sister. Elena was livid to think that the children would no longer attend the beautiful big Catholic church with its high ceilings and stained-glass windows but would rather be attending a small church that was not much bigger than her living room.

After fifteen minutes of listening to Grace defend Gio and his choices, Elena hung up on her sister. Grace sat for a few minutes trying to collect herself. She did not like confrontation. Gio was comfortable with confrontation on a daily basis, not Grace. She sat staring at the phone long enough to rationalize that Elena would eventually calm down and forget all about this. When Grace did not hear anything more from her sister for two weeks, she was assured that Elena did, in fact, forget all about the situation.

Gio and the family became regular attenders of the small Italian church. They attended Sunday-morning services, Sunday night, and Wednesday family night. At one of the Wednesday-night family services, Vincenzo won a contest, and the prize was a Bible. He was very excited to win the Bible. Every time he wanted to read or study God's Word, he had to borrow his dad's Bible. This became a problem because Vincenzo studied God's Word for hours each evening. He was fascinated with Bible history; and it seemed that, just when he was in the thick of his studies, his father would need his Bible back. He couldn't wait to find a place for his new Bible in his own bedroom. He was tired of sharing.

The next Wednesday family night, Carla won the contest and received her very own Bible. Nothing could have made her happier. She immediately started studying and memorizing her favorite verses. It was not long before she realized that the scriptures that fascinated her the most were on prayer. As she studied more, she became absorbed with what God taught and instructed regarding Christians and prayer. Carla started spending more and more time in prayer, praying personal prayers, prayers for the sick and needy, and prayers for God to direct her life.

One Sunday after church, when the family just sat down to their midday meal, there came an aggressive knock at the door. Gio was startled and quickly rose from the table to see what was going on.

Gio opened the door. "Elena, my goodness, your knock sounded like pounding. What's going on?" Gio asked his sister-in-law.

"I'll tell you what's going on, Gio. What's going on is you refusing to let me pick up the children for Mass each Sunday. What's this I hear from Grace that you are now a born-again Christian attending church as a family at a little Italian church?" Elena rapidly spit out as her face grew increasingly beet red.

"That's right, Elena," Gio responded in a calm voice. "We attended a revival at that church several Sundays ago, and since then, Vincenzo, Carla, and I accepted Christ in our lives. We each received the Holy Spirit the night we were born again. We are now attending that church as a family," he continued.

Elena stared Gio straight in the face. She froze at the front door for a second and then feigned to the right of Gio, just like a football player seeking a touchdown, and ran to the kitchen, where the rest of the family was sitting around the table like concrete statues, frightened by the commotion at their front door.

Elena entered the Rivia kitchen like a Spanish fighting bull at the festival of San Fermin. Her eyes were wide open and bulging, her face was puffy and red, and her voice was unrecognizable.

"So you're born-again Christians now, are you?" she interrogated Vincenzo and Carla first.

Both children slowly nodded their heads in confirmation. Then Elena took her time examining each niece and nephew around the table, slowly and intentionally, one at a time.

"Your mother tells me that, since you have been attending this new church, you girls have taken off your crucifixes, and you boys are no longer wearing your Saint Christopher medals," she continued.

All the children nodded their heads, too scared to utter a word.

"Well, I have come today to give you all new, shiny crucifixes and medals," she proudly but stubbornly announced as she pulled the new items out of her purse.

"Elena," Gio called out to stop her. "They will not be wearing the new jewelry. We know that Jesus died on the cross like the crucifix shows, but we also know that Jesus rose again. He is no longer on the cross. The boys do not need to wear Saint Christopher medals for protection. Jesus is their protection," Gio said in a nonargumentative voice. "If you do not agree and cannot honor our family belief, then I am asking you to leave," Gio said in an authoritative voice.

"Grace, are you going to let him talk to me in this way?" Elena questioned her sister in front of the whole family. "Grace, I'm talking to you. Are you going to let him talk to me in this way?" Elena asked a second time.

"Elena," Grace called to her sister in a soft voice. "Please understand. We believe in Jesus Christ, who died a cruel death on the cross but rose again. That is how we want to think of Him, in heaven, at the right side of His Father, not still hanging on a rugged cross. Gio and I agree that we do not want the children to wear jewelry where Jesus is still on the cross suffering. And regarding the Saint Christopher medals…" was all Grace got out.

Elena pursed her lips and raised her eyebrows at Grace, and Grace knew not to say another word.

"Grace, you and your family will regret this," Elena said as she threw the replacement jewelry back inside and snapped her purse shut.

She stood for one dramatic moment glaring one by one at each of them sitting around the kitchen table and slowly turned and walked out. No one followed her out. They each remained seated until they heard the front door close.

"I'm not hungry anymore," said Vincenzo.

"Me either," said Carla in a soft voice.

Mario, who was sitting next to Carla, remained frozen in disbelief replaying the scene in his head.

Antonia and Virginia let their emotions rise to the surface, and both started crying. Grace reached over to comfort the younger children. Sofia started clearing the table. It was Gio who smelled it first.

"What's that smell?" Gio said, jumping up from his chair. "I smell burning grass. Do you?" he shouted as he ran to the front window.

They each popped up from their seats to go look outside. Once the front door was opened, Gio could see a fire had been started on their front lawn. He ran out of the house, jumped over the front porch steps, and grabbed the water hose from the side of the house. Vincenzo and Mario ran to help their dad. The women and girls stayed on the porch watching.

"It's our Bibles, Dad!" screamed Vincenzo. "Aunt Elena must have grabbed them from the living room table on the way out of the house. She burned our Bibles!" Vincenzo shouted in anger.

Then he dropped to the ground, hid his head in his hands, and cried in disbelief. Gio and Mario knelt quietly next to Vincenzo. Sofia went back into the house and cleaned up the kitchen. The girls went in the basement to play. Grace grabbed one of her scarfs.

She wrapped it around her head and knotted it extra tight. She went to bed, and no one saw her until morning.

Everyone was moving slowly the next morning. They were all still in shock of what they heard and watched their aunt Elena do the day before. Gio, Grace, and Sofia were just thankful that the children still had a few days left of summer break; so no one had to hurry to get ready for school. Once the children were up and moving around, they announced that they were famished and started demanding breakfast.

"Aunt Sofia, please make us pancakes this morning," asked Carla. "None of us hardly ate anything yesterday. It was a bad day," she continued.

"Yes, I want pancakes too," begged Mario. "I am so hungry. Do we have any bologna to fry with the pancakes?" he asked in a hopeful voice.

Aunt Sofia giggled a belly-shaking laugh. "I will make you pancakes and fry up some bologna too. Remember, your dad only wants you to eat one slice of bread. With us closing the bar on Sundays, it has cut our finances. So one slice only, okay?" she reminded the family.

The children all nodded in agreement.

"Where is Antonia?" Grace asked in her slurred speech.

"I saw her resting on the couch," answered Virginia. "I think she's sick again with a cold or something. I heard her coughing all night in her bed, and she was talking funny," Virginia reported.

"Antonia," called Sofia. "Antonia!" Sofia called a little louder.

Finally weak small Antonia appeared slowly around the corner of the kitchen. She was pale and weak and could barely open her eyes as she stumbled into the kitchen to answer who was calling for her.

Gio was the first one to react. "Antonia, what is the matter?" Gio asked in a sympathetic voice.

"My throat hurts really bad, Daddy," Antonia barely squeaked out as she wrapped her tiny fingers around her throat. "My throat feels like it is on fire," she added.

"Are you hungry?" Gio asked his daughter.

"No, not at all. I just want to go back to sleep," she half whispered, half wheezed out.

"Okay, you can go back to bed, but first I want you to take a few sips of wine. The wine will give you an appetite. You are getting way too thin. Plus, it will make your throat feel better. You have to be well to go to school in a few days. You don't want to miss your first day of school, do you?"

Antonia shook her head no. Then she obediently took three sips of wine from her father's glass. She had no idea how this drink was going to make her feel better. It tasted terrible to her, but she obeyed her father because she wanted to feel better and not miss her first day of school either. She returned the glass to her father, telling him thank you, and slowly left the kitchen to go back to bed.

"I will check on you later to see if you regained your appetite," Gio called after her.

Antonia went back to her bedroom and crawled under the covers of her bed. Gio and Grace checked on her several times throughout the day. However, Antonia did not regain her appetite. By dinnertime, nothing changed. Gio and Grace continued to encourage Antonia to drink and eat. They forced her to sit up in bed and take three more sips of wine. She drank but refused to eat. Gio finally told Grace they would have to call the doctor in the morning.

"You know that is going to be a bad thing, don't you, Gio?" Grace reminded him. "Antonia screams and hollers and carries on so when she sees the doctor. She is so timid and fearful," Grace said.

"You don't have to remind me of that, Grace. I have been with her many times when the doctor has come to visit. If you think about it, I have handled more of these respiratory infections with her than you ever have," Gio responded curtly.

Grace did not say another word. She knew it was true. Due to her poor health, Gio took the role of mother and father to the children.

Gio checked on Antonia first thing in the morning. She was very warm and weak. She barely had the strength to open her eyes. Her throat was almost completely swollen shut. Her cough was harsh. Gio called for the doctor to make a house call. Within a few hours, the doctor knocked on the door of the big farmhouse to check on Antonia. Upstairs in the bedroom, Antonia was so weak and tired she did not even know that the doctor was present.

"She has another respiratory infection. This time, it's worse than any other time I have treated her. Her throat is almost completely closed up," the doctor reported. "I am going to start her on some mediation. Gio, she's probably not going to be better for the first day of school," he continued. "I would say she will need a minimum of two weeks recovery time," the doctor said with a sad voice.

Gio hung his head in disappointment. He knew how much Antonia was looking forward to her first day of kindergarten.

By the fourth morning of Antonia refusing to get out of bed, eat, or drink, Gio announced to the family at breakfast that, regardless of the doctor's medication, Antonia was not doing any better and was going to miss her first day of kindergarten.

"She is very weak and still running a fever. When you call her name, she will not even sit up in bed. Her cough has gotten worse, and her throat is so raw she cannot speak above a whisper. She has been sick with these respiratory problems off and on from the day she was born," Gio recalled.

Everyone got quiet. They all knew that Antonia would be upset to miss her first day of school. That was all they heard her talk about all summer. She was so excited to attend school like her older sister and brothers.

"Daddy," Carla questioned slowly and quietly, not sure how the next thing she was going to say would be received, "why don't we pray for her? Our God is powerful. He is our healer. I think we should gather around her bed, anoint her with oil like we have seen done with the sick and needy in church, and pray for her."

Gio listened to Carla in silence. After a few minutes, he spoke.

"Hmm, that's a great idea. Yes, let's do that, Carla. Would you like to be the one to say the pray over your sister?" Gio asked.

"Yes, I would, Daddy," Carla answered, now sitting straight up in her chair, eyes wide open and bright. "Let's grab the anointing oil and go up to her bedroom and pray for her right now. I know God is going to heal her today!" she shouted with confidence as she scurried out of the room and up the steps to Antonia's room.

The family quietly walked into Antonia's room. She was sound asleep, skin clammy and flushed, and breathing through her mouth. Gio, Grace, Sofia, and all of the children gathered around her bed. They decided not to wake her up. Carla unscrewed the lid of the anointing oil and placed some on her finger. She anointed her little sister's forehead with the oil. Carla could feel the heat from Antonia's fever radiating out of her skin.

"I anoint you with oil in Jesus's name, sister," Carla began.

She asked the family to extend their hands toward Antonia. The family obediently stretched out their hands toward the weak little girl in the bed. Carla closed her eyes, raised her hands to God, and prayed a prayer with confidence far beyond her chronological years. Her prayer began by asking God to take Antonia under His mighty care, to restore her strength, and to touch her now with His healing hands as only He could do. She finished her prayer by telling God that she would give Him all the glory and praise for Antonia's healing. She thanked Him for His faithfulness and mercy. When Carla was finished praying, she opened her eyes to see the whole family weeping and wiping streams of tears away from their faces. That was the day Carla knew that she had the gift of prayer.

The next morning was the first day of the new school year. Everyone, except Antonia, gathered in the kitchen for breakfast. Sofia was making oatmeal for breakfast and was frying up green bell peppers and eggs to pack as sandwiches for the children's lunches. Everyone quietly noticed that Antonia was not down in the kitchen for breakfast, but no one said a word. They were sad to think that she was too sick to attend her first day of kindergarten. It was Vincenzo's turn to pray for the meal, and he added a short prayer for Antonia's health. They were all eating their breakfast in silence when suddenly Antonia appeared from around the corner of the kitchen.

"I'd like some peppers and eggs in my lunch too," she announced in a full, healthy voice.

Carla popped out of her chair and shouted, "Antonia!"

Gio, Vincenzo, and Mario leaped out of their chairs and joined Carla in hugging and kissing Antonia in the kitchen doorway. Sofia turned at the sound of Antonia's voice and dropped the bag lunch she was packing. Grace, still seated at the kitchen table, dropped her head in her hands and started weeping.

Gio pulled the children away from Antonia. "Antonia, if you are going to school this morning, you better hurry. It's almost time to leave. Carla, why don't you go help Antonia get ready? Sofia, pack one more lunch. Antonia is healed and going to school," Gio delegated in a cheery voice.

Everyone did their part to make it possible for Antonia to attend her first day of kindergarten.

As the children were heading out the door to begin their one-and-a-half-mile walk to school, Gio noticed Carla was hanging back from the others. Just as she reached the front door, Gio saw Carla pause.

She turned her tearstained face up to God and whispered, "Thank You, Lord, for healing my sister. I give You all the glory and honor. I will always remember Your faithfulness and will love and serve You until the day I die!"

Once Gio saw all the school-age children off to school, he returned to the kitchen. Grace and Sofia were cleaning up and talking softly when Gio entered.

"Please stop cleaning the kitchen for a minute and come and sit down with me. I have something to tell both of you," he announced.

The women put down their dishrags and dish towels and sat at the table to hear what Gio had to say. Gio looked concerned.

"Are you feeling okay, Gio?" Grace asked in a serious voice.

She could feel the communication between her and Gio dwindling. It seemed all he wanted to do was talk with his sister, Sofia. They discussed everything together, like she and Gio used to do before she came to live with them. Grace heard them talking about the vegetable garden, the animals in the barn, the bar, and the children. Seeing Gio so serious, she was worried that Gio was not well and already shared the information with Sofia and this was going to be the first she was hearing about it.

"I'm fine, Grace. This has nothing to do with my health. I need to talk to the two of you about my job," Gio confessed. "Since we decided to close the bar on Sundays, our finances have been hit hard. We are to the point now that, if we don't do something about it, we will go under, just like many others have already done," Gio said all in one breath. "This week, I was offered a job with the Works Progress Administration, WPA, as a quarry foreman in Greenville, Illinois. Since it's a government job and a foreman position, I will be making more money there than at the brick mill. If I take this job, it will make up for the bar being closed on Sunday plus more," Gio explained. "I am thinking of putting in my notice at the brick mill today. What do you two think about me making this move?" Gio asked.

Before Grace could answer, Sofia spoke. "Well, Gio, I think it's a wonderful idea," Sofia began in a bold, confirmative voice. "Greenville, Illinois, is not that far from Briarton. You will be able to do that commute easily," Sofia continued. "The job sounds like it will keep us going here without us having to reopen the bar on Sundays," she said, finally coming up for a breath.

"What about you, Grace?" Gio asked as he turned his attention to his wife. "How do you feel about this move?"

"I think it is a smart move. I don't want to go back to opening the bar on Sundays, and if this job will keep us from going under financially and keep the bar closed on Sunday so we can attend church as a family, I say take the job. Go ahead and put your notice in today," Grace said in her mild, meek voice.

"Okay, then it is settled," Gio said with a smile. "Today will be my last day at the brick mill."

Grace and Sofia watched out the window as Gio left for work that morning as a laborer at the brick mill and return that evening as a foreman running a quarry for the government. However, what Grace and Sofia were not prepared to see was Gio returning home carrying birdcages filled with twelve homing pigeons.

"What is this?" Grace asked Gio as she met him outside on the front porch.

"These are homing pigeons," he answered. "My boss heard that I lived on a farm with a barn and a lot of acreage. He asked me if I wouldn't mind keeping the homing pigeons here until he needs them for work again," explained Gio. "I told him that would be fine since we have the room in the barn," he continued.

Gio bedded down the homing pigeons and then joined the family in the kitchen for dinner.

It was Carla's turn to pray for the meal. She just finished praying, and the phone rang. It was for Sofia.

"Hello," answered Sofia.

"Hello," answered a male voice. "This is Dennis from church," he called out. "I was wondering if I could come by the farm to see you this week," he asked in a nervous voice.

"Sure," Sofia answered excitedly.

She liked Dennis. He was a nice man from church. She had not been on a date with any man since the death of her husband. She was flattered.

"I am free Tuesday evening," she said with a smile.

Dennis arrived earlier than planned on Tuesday. Sofia could tell that he was anxious to see her and for them to get to know each other. Since it was a first date, they stayed close to home. Sofia walked him around the farm acreage. She took him through the vineyard and orchard. She showed him the family vegetable garden and explained in detail how it had been a financial life-saver for them this summer. Lastly she took him through the barn, showing him all the baby goats that were born since they arrived, and naturally she showed him the homing pigeons. Dennis was especially interested in seeing them since that wasn't something that you typically see in someone's barn. The evening was quiet and good as they casually strolled around in the cool of the evening. Before they said their goodbye, Dennis asked Sofia out on a second date. Sofia accepted.

Dennis and Sofia spent the next few dates sitting on the spacious wraparound porch of the big farmhouse. They rocked on the rocking chairs and just spent time getting to know each other.

"What's your favorite food?" Sofia asked him one night.

"Probably sauerkraut and kielbasa," answered Dennis.

Sofia raised her eyebrows in shock at his answer and snickered to herself but did not say a word.

"Do you like spaghetti or any Italian food?" she casually asked.

"I get asked that a lot," Dennis answered with a smile. "I'm half-Italian. My mother is German. I guess I take after her side of the family more than my dad's because I really do not like any Italian food," he answered honestly.

"Really?" Sofia questioned with a disappointing voice. "Do you at least like the smells of Italian foods, like the smell of Italian bread baking, meatballs browning on the stove, or the smell of garlic?" she asked in a questioning voice, thinking that this question would certainly render the correct response.

"Nope, not really" was all he answered.

"What do you see yourself doing in five years?" Sofia questioned.

Without hesitation, Dennis answered, "A missionary to a faraway land."

Sofia almost fell out of her rocker at his answer. She could feel her eyes springing wide open in disbelief. How could she have gone on this many outings with this guy and not known how opposite they were?

She decided to ask one more compatibility question. "Dennis, how do you feel about children?"

"Well, since I want to be a missionary, I do not want to have children right now and, in fact, maybe never," he answered quickly and confidently.

The conversation dropped off from that point. Sofia knew from his answers that this relationship could not move forward.

She loved to cook and bake from scratch. How could she get in a relationship with a man who liked German food when she had no idea how to prepare one German dish? She knew she could never keep him happy. She was clearly not called to be a missionary's wife, and she had a four-year-old child upstairs in bed. She knotted her hands and sat in silence.

Dennis broke the silence.

"Sofia, we have seen each other outside of church several times now. I would love to see you again very soon, but I was wondering if, maybe the next time, we could leave the farm and go out to eat?" he asked in a voice filled with hope. "Also, one more thing," he said in a nervous voice, "I would like to kiss you. Would that be okay with you?"

This took Sofia by surprise. Didn't he realize that they were not compatible? Certainly he realized that his answers were all wrong for her. They could never be a match.

"Dennis, I don't think the timing is right," Sofia said, trying to let him down easily.

He looked into her eyes and saw something there that he did not see before. He was not sure if she was uncomfortable kissing him right now because it was too early in their relationship or if she never wanted to kiss him.

"Okay" was all he could squeak out.

He shook her hand and walked off the front porch. Sofia waited there until his white truck pulled away, then she walked into the house.

Gio was sitting at the kitchen table when Sofia walked into the house.

"How was your time with Dennis?" Gio asked with a smirk.

"We're definitely not a match," Sofia answered with a sigh. "He hates Italian food, wants to be a missionary, and isn't sure if he ever wants to have children," she answered in a blur.

Gio leaned back in his chair and let out a loud guffaw. "He doesn't like Italian food? What kind of man doesn't like Italian food?"

Sofia did not answer. She turned to walk out of the kitchen and up to bed but muttered loud enough for Gio to hear, "Obviously someone that's not for me."

The next few weeks were filled with phone calls from Dennis asking Sofia to have another date with him. Sofia gave the same answer each time, "Not tonight." It was uncomfortable for them to see each other in church. He wanted to sit by her and ask her out on another date, but her answer remained a solid no.

One night, when Gio and Sofia were alone in the kitchen, Sofia told Gio that she wanted nothing to do with Dennis. She told Gio that she turned him down for a date time after time but he still called and asked her out or asked her out for a date when they were in church. Gio sat and listened to Sofia's frustration with Dennis.

Gio finally said, "That's enough. I will take care of him the next time he calls."

After dinner that evening, the phone rang. Gio jumped up and announced before anyone moved that he was going to answer the phone.

"Hello," Gio answered in a stern voice, expecting to hear Dennis on the other end of the phone.

"Hello, Gio," answered Dennis. "May I please speak to Sofia?" Dennis asked.

"No, you may not," Gio replied. "Sofia has given you enough turndowns by now for you to know that she does not want to date you. Don't you get it? You two are not a match. There will be no more calling this house or asking Sofia out on a date while in church. You are friends only," Gio laid down the law.

Gio waited for Dennis to answer. Silence came from the other end of the phone. Gio waited, holding the receiver up to his ear. Finally, without a word, Dennis hung up.

Sofia was sorry that Gio had to speak in a stern tone with Dennis, but she was thankful. Dennis never called the house again. Things were strained when they saw each other at church, but at least he did not ask her out on a date again.

Two weeks later, Gio, Vincenzo, and Mario were woken up in the middle of the night by gunfire that sounded very close. Gio scurried out of bed only to meet Vincenzo and Mario on the steps going downstairs.

"Was that gunshots? Did you hear that? I think it's coming from the barn!" Vincenzo shouted to his father as he clumsily fumbled putting on his bathrobe.

"*Shh*, don't wake the others. Yes, come on. Let's get out there," Gio called as they all three flew down the steps and out to the barn.

They reached the barn just in time to see Dennis's white truck hotfooting out of the back driveway, followed by a big cloud of dust. Dennis peeled onto the main road, tires squealing. He knew he had been spotted.

"Dennis!" shouted Mario out of breath from running. "What was he doing in our barn?" Mario questioned loudly. "Oh my god, the animals!" he screamed as he took off running to the big red barn door.

Gio and Vincenzo ran close behind.

When they reached the barn, they immediately understood the situation. The barn animals were noticeably shaken from Dennis's gun being fired off in close range, but they were all safe in their stalls. However, all twelve of the homing pigeons were shot dead. They were piled up on each other in their carrier cages. They never had a chance to escape their demise, their red blood streaming down through their gray feathers, beaks sprung open.

Gio let out a muffled scream and crumbled to the floor. Vincenzo and Mario knelt down next to their father.

"We will get him, Dad," Mario said in a revengeful voice. "Dennis will be in big trouble over this when the police catch him," he continued.

"We are not reporting this to the police," Gio replied in a half-speaking, half-crying voice. "And there will be no discussion of this to the girls. Do you both understand?" Gio demanded. "I will explain things to your mother and Aunt Sofia in the morning, but not a word to your sisters." Gio got up off the barn floor, dusted himself off, and walked across the lawn to the house.

Vincenzo and Mario stayed in the barn awhile longer to make sure the barn animals were calmed down and bedded. Neither boy said a word. They had plenty of disturbing thoughts rolling around in their heads, but they remained silent. Twelve homing pigeons that were owned by their father's brand-new government job were shot to death by a man they all knew and recognized as the culprit. Why didn't their father want to report this to the police? How was their father going to explain this to his new boss? Would their father have to pay to replace the pigeons? Vincenzo and Mario stayed in the barn until they knew all was well with the animals. They carried the cages of dead pigeons around the corner to another part of the barn, closed things up, and walked back to the house.

Gio was surprised but thankful to see Grace and Sofia alone in the kitchen early in the morning. He took advantage of the adult time alone and explained to the ladies the events of the previous night. Naturally they were shocked and appalled that Dennis would do such a thing.

"Gio, what are you going to say to your boss? Do you think you will have to pay to replace the pigeons?" Sofia asked sympathetically.

"I will tell my boss first thing this morning," Gio answered Sofia's question and hung his head.

The women were his captive audience.

"If I have to pay him to replace the pigeons, I will," he said in a sad, quiet voice. He took a long breath and then started chuckling to himself. "It's funny, you know. I was going to shut down the beer and illegal moonshine sales at the bar starting this week. Since we have become born-again Christians, I have not enjoyed the bar like I used to. The thrill and excitement of the nightlife is not important to me anymore. My plan was to sell only the food and soda drinks. Even though this new job brings in good money, if I have to pay my boss back for the pigeons, I will need the extra money that beer and illegal moonshine sales bring in to help with the expense," Gio explained.

Sofia stood up and went to stand by her brother. She laid her hand tenderly on his shoulder. "Listen, Gio. I feel horribly responsible for this," she started. "Dennis was coming here to date me. We were not a match. He would not take no for an answer, and that is the only reason you got involved," she explained in a regretful voice. "If I liked him and continued dating him, this would not have happened. This is all my fault. He killed the pigeons out of revenge for me not wanting to date him anymore and for you speaking to him sternly," Sofia rationalized. "I hope you are going to report this to the authorities this morning," Sofia said.

"No, I am not going to report this," Gio answered. "I know why he did it. I probably was as much at fault as anyone for speaking to him the way I did," Gio continued.

Grace and Sofia both raised their eyebrows at Gio. They could not believe what they were hearing, but they knew better than to question or reprimand him for his logic and decision. The adults cut their conversation short when the school-age children started entering the kitchen looking for their breakfast and packed lunches as they counted down the minutes they had left before starting the long walk to school.

That evening, Gio came home from work and announced to Grace and Sofia that his boss expected to be paid back for the dead pigeons. He continued to tell his wife and sister that he had no choice but to continue the sale of 3.2 beer and illegal moonshine at the bar until that debt was paid in full. The ladies hung their head in disappointment.

True to his word, everything remained the same at the bar. Late one Saturday night, a clean-cut tall man entered the bar. Since Gio opened the bar almost one year ago now, he recognized all the customers who frequented the place. He was able to recognize whole families in the community by now and oftentimes would know their food and drink order before they even said a word. However, he did not recognize this man. It was unusual for Vincenzo and Mario to be at the bar late into the evening, but on this particular night, they were in the back party room eating dinner. They had a goat born that morning, and Vincenzo and Mario were busy caring for the new mother and baby. They barely had anything to eat since they were in the barn most of the day. Gio took a second and walked to the back room, where the boys were.

"Hey, boys, peek out into the bar and see if you recognize the tall man that just walked in," Gio said.

The boys obediently got up and peeked out into the bar. Both shook their heads in unison.

"I've never seen that man before," Vincenzo and Mario agreed.

Gio returned to the bar. He was busy since he was all alone. Sofia helped him with orders during the day but returned home to care for Vera during the later hours at the bar. Plus, Gio knew she did not care for the late bar scene. Now that his heart belonged to God, he did not care for it either. He was only continuing things this way to pay off the debt he owed his boss.

"Do you have any moonshine?" the tall man asked Gio.

"Yes, I do," answered Gio.

He reached under the bar counter and brought up a pitcher of white moonshine and poured the man a glass. Just as Gio went to return the pitcher under the bar counter, the man stood up, reached behind him, pulled out handcuffs, and handcuffed Gio's unoccupied hand.

"You, sir, are under arrest!" the stranger proclaimed loudly for all to hear. "You are in violation of the Prohibition mandate stating that all bar owners are prohibited from selling anything stronger than 3.2 beer in their establishments," he declared. "Are you aware of this mandate?" he asked as he climbed over the bar to cuff Gio's other hand.

"Yes, I am aware," Gio replied. Then, in a loud voice, Gio called out to Vincenzo and Mario, who were still eating in the back party room. "Boys, this is your cue. You know what to do!"

As fast as lightning, Vincenzo and Mario bolted out of the back room and ran to the farmhouse. They knew exactly what to do in this situation. Both boys ran down into the basement, jumping three steps at a time. They went into the secret room, where the moonshine barrels were kept, and rolled them out the walk-out basement to the open field. They opened the barrels and dumped their contents into the field, just as their father instructed them to do if he ever gave them this cue.

Grace and Sofia heard all the commotion and were yelling at Vincenzo and Mario to tell them what was going on. However, Vincenzo and Mario were on a mission to save their father any further impair. They ignored the adult women and continued on with their instructions.

Sofia had a feeling that this commotion had something to do with the bar. She had seen the people who walked in during the later bar hours and was always on guard and skeptical the few times she had to be around them. She decided to take a look out the front window.

"Grace, come quickly!" Sofia shouted to her sister-in-law. "I see lights from a police car down at the bar!" she continued.

Grace moved to the front window as fast as she could to take a look. "Oh no, something must have happened down there," Grace said in her slurred speech. "I better get down there to see if Gio is okay," she said.

"I'll go down there right now," Sofia said in a bold voice.

Not waiting for Grace to say another word, she flew out of the house without a coat and ran all the way down to the front corner of the farm property to the bar.

By the time Sofia reached the bar, the bar was empty, and the policeman was putting Gio in his squad car.

"Sofia, the bar was raided," Gio called out to his sister. "He's taking me to jail for Prohibition violations," Gio said breathlessly. "Sofia, I need my Bible. I can't go to jail without my Bible," Gio pleaded.

"Forget about your Bible. We don't have time to wait for that. I'm taking you to jail right now to be booked," the policeman said in a crude voice.

The policeman got into the front seat and was pulling out of the bar driveway when Grace reached the bar.

"Gio, Gio," she cried, "I have your Bible."

"Stop the car. That's my wife," Gio demanded of the policeman. "She has my Bible."

The policeman stopped the car and opened his window to grab the Bible from Grace. He took the Bible from Grace and threw it in the back seat at Gio.

"Grace, how did you know to bring my Bible?" Gio asked tenderly.

"Once I saw the police car and realized what was happening, I knew this would be the one thing you would want with you," she struggled to say through the tears that were flowing down her face.

"He is taking me to jail, but I will—" was all Grace could hear before the policeman rolled up the window.

Gio spent the night in jail. He was released early the next morning just in time to attend church with the family. Dennis was not in attendance that Sunday. The Rivia family never saw him again.

On Monday morning, before Gio went to work, Sofia cornered him, saying that she had something to tell him.

"Gio, I have been thinking," Sofia said. "You know that I receive a stipend from my late husband. Since I am living here rent-free, I have been able to save up some money. I have enough saved to cover the cost of the pigeons. It would make me very happy if you would take this gift of money and pay off the debt you owe your boss. Then you could stop selling beer at the bar and close the doors right after we serve dinner. What do you think?" she asked sweetly.

"Oh, Sofia, I don't know," Gio whined. "I can't take money away from you and Vera," he said.

"You are not taking money from us. I am offering it to you as a gift," she responded.

Gio took a few minutes to think it over. Finally he said, "Yes."

Sofia and Gio hugged tightly. Somehow this terrible situation made them closer in mind and spirit.

Word spread quickly through the town. Everyone was proclaiming that "the barman" was born again and would no longer sell beer or moonshine at the bar. Gio asked Sofia to make new signs for the doors of the bar indicating that they would be closed right after the dinner rush and nothing stronger than soda would be served for drinks.

With the bar closing down earlier, Gio turned his attention to some tasks he had been wanting to complete around the farm. The first job on his list was to build an outdoor brick oven. He called some men from the church and scheduled a time for them to come and help him build it, and in a few days, the Rivia family had an outdoor open-fire oven to use for baking bread and pizzas.

The new oven was a hit with the family right away. Sofia and the girls would make the homemade dough in the kitchen and then form the dough into loaves of bread or prepare it for pizza. Then they'd take it outside for baking. Even though it was early fall, the whole family enjoyed sitting outside waiting for the bread or pizza to finish baking. The smell generated in the air as it baked was every bit enjoyable as eating the finished product. Gio and Sofia agreed that the smell coming from the open fire oven was as good as any smell they ever smelled from any bakery in Italy.

While Gio continued to schedule the men of the church to come out to the farm to help him with small jobs here and there, Sofia was busy helping Carla and Antonia look more fashionable for school. One evening, when Sofia and Grace and Carla and Antonia were in the kitchen preparing for dinner, Sofia noticed that Carla seemed quiet and sad.

"What's the matter, Carla?" Sofia asked. "You seem so quiet this evening."

"Oh, nothing's really wrong, Aunt Sofia," Carla started. "I was just thinking about school."

"What's the matter at school?" Grace asked in her slurred speech.

"It's nothing with my teacher or the subjects we are studying," Carla said slowly. "It's about my hair and clothes," she said softly as if she wanted to say it out loud but didn't really want anyone to hear. "Some of the girls are mean. They tell me that my clothes are out of fashion and ugly."

The atmosphere in the kitchen got very still and quiet. Sofia recognized that both girls went off to school each day in mismatched, worn-out old clothes, with their hair hanging straight down with no style or ribbon. Sofia also knew that Grace did not have a fashion sense, so it did not bother her that her daughters went off to school dressed this way. Sofia, on the other hand, was very fashion conscious. She had always loved style and prided herself with keeping up with the latest fashion trends and colors. Sofia could say with confidence that, when Vera grew up to be school age, she would dress her in matching dresses, stockings, shoes, and bows in her hair. Grace looked at Carla with a glazed-over look on her face. Sofia could tell that Grace had no idea how to fix this concern. Finally Sofia broke the silence.

"Carla," Sofia started, "I might be able to help you and Antonia too."

Sofia looked at Grace for approval, but got nothing in return. Grace continued to have a glazed-over look on her face.

"How about if I sew you a few new dresses?" Sofia offered.

"But where would we get the fabric?" Carla asked. "I don't want Daddy to have to pay for me to get new dresses," Carla replied in a shaky voice. "I think that would make him really mad at me."

Once again, Sofia looked over at Grace. She did not move. She gave no indication that she wanted to join the conversation or help problem solve this situation regarding her daughter.

Sofia knew that Grace wore the same lack-of-fashion loose dresses every day. She also knew that Grace did not always dress this way back before children.

"I have an idea," Sofia said. "Grace, do you have a few dresses that you do not wear anymore?" Sofia asked her sister-in-law.

"Yes, I do," answered Grace.

"Do you think you could give me two or three of them so I can make some clothes for Carla and Antonia?" Sofia asked.

"Yes" was all Grace replied.

"Well, wonderful. Problem solved," Sofia said with a smile. "I will get those dresses from your mom this week, and I will start making you girls some dresses and matching hair bows," Sofia announced boldly to Carla and Antonia.

Both girls jumped with glee. They ran over to their aunt Sofia and gave her a big hug. Carla ran out of the room to go find Mario and Vincenzo to give them the news. Antonia hung back in the kitchen. She waited until Sofia left the room and walked over to where her mother was seated.

"Thank you for giving up your dresses," Antonia squeaked out.

Grace reached out and hugged her daughter. No words were exchanged.

Sofia started on making clothes right away. She was able to make three dresses each with the fabric from Grace's dresses. Both Carla and Antonia were thrilled to add these dresses to their scant wardrobe.

When Mario got wind of the girls' wardrobe update, he jumped on the bandwagon.

"Aunt Sofia told me that the girls were getting new clothes for school. I want some new clothes too," he proclaimed one evening to his father.

"The girls did not get new clothes, Mario," Gio said in a stern voice. He knew where this conversation was going with his son. "Aunt Sofia used fabric from some old dresses of your mother's to make new dresses and hair bows for the girls," he said.

"Well, I can't get new clothes made from Mother's dresses, so how can I get a new pair of trousers?" Mario asked. "The ones I have been wearing are from last school year and are much too tight. Most days, I have to wear them with the button undone," Mario confessed.

Gio thought a moment. He knew the boys needed school clothes too. He noticed how tight Mario's trousers were a few days ago, and he also noticed that Vincenzo's trousers were frayed on the bottoms of each leg.

"I've noticed that you need new school pants, and Vincenzo too," Gio started to say. "If you want new school clothes, you will have to work for them," Gio proclaimed.

Although Mario was hoping that his father would just one time graciously open his tight wallet and pay for them to get some much-needed school clothes, he was not surprised by this answer. Mario had no idea how he was going to find the time in the day to fit in extra chores. Every minute was already taken up between the long walk to school, attending school, walking the long walk home, doing homework, keeping up with all the chores in the barn, and tending to the family garden.

Mario decided to get some clarification of his father's demands.

"What do you mean when you say we will have to work for them?" Mario bravely asked his father.

"I mean you will have to do additional chores to earn the clothes. If you wash the car inside and out, rake the leaves that have fallen in the front yard, and paint the basement, we will call it done," Gio negotiated with his son.

Mario knew not to say another word for fear that his father would take back the deal completely. Instead he told his father that he and Vincenzo would agree to completing the extra chores in exchange for new school clothes. Now Mario had to find a way to tell Vincenzo that he accepted this deal without speaking to him first.

Mario and Vincenzo worked late each night to complete the jobs within the week. A few days after the extra chores were completed and Gio inspected and approved of their work, Gio followed through on his word and bought the boys two pairs of black step-in trousers for each of them and two white button-down dress shirts.

The next school day, Mario got up early to grease his hair into a fashionable style. He pulled on his new black trousers and tucked in his new starched white shirt. The shirt came with gold cuff links, and he added a bow tie. He reached into his closet and pulled out his black jacket with the wide lapel that he only wore to church. He carefully put it on. He caught a glimpse of himself in the bedroom mirror as he was heading out of his room. He stopped and took a long look at himself, paying attention to every detail of his outfit.

"I need one more thing," he whispered to himself.

He walked out of his room and down the hallway toward Aunt Sofia's room. When she moved in, she set up a small table for decoration outside of her bedroom. She had a lovely vase of fake flowers on display. Mario pulled one of the fake flowers from the vase and popped it into the buttonhole of his lapel.

"Now I am ready for school," he said to himself.

He was the last one to enter the kitchen.

"Oh, my goodness, would you look at Mario," Sofia said as he walked into the room.

Everyone turned to see what Aunt Sofia was talking about.

"Mario, why are you dressed that way?" Carla commented.

"You look like you are going to someone's funeral," Vincenzo added as he rolled his eyes at his brother.

Antonia looked at Mario and gave a giggle. "I think you look like Frank Sinatra," she said.

"That's right, Antonia." Mario laughed as he tugged at his bow tie. "I want to be a famous singer someday. If I am going to be a famous singer, I need to start dressing like one," he continued.

Vincenzo rolled his eyes again, and Carla shook her head.

"Let's go, children," Aunt Sofia called out as she stood up to begin her daily job of getting them off to school. "It's time to get going, or you're going to be late."

Sofia grabbed all the packed lunches off the kitchen counter with one swoop and handed them one at a time to each child. She couldn't help but notice how outstanding the children looked. Carla and Antonia both had on new dresses made from their mother's dresses that she did not wear anymore. Carla had her thick hair pulled back into a ponytail with a matching ribbon wrapped around it. Antonia, who had much thinner hair, had her hair combed straight down with a matching ribbon tied around her head. Their stockings matched their dresses, and their shoes were clean. Vincenzo looked handsome in his new step-in trousers and tucked-in white shirt. Vincenzo and the girls left the house together while the Frank Sinatra lookalike followed behind.

Mario's teacher pulled him aside the first chance she got. She scolded him for coming to school dressed inappropriately and for causing a distraction for the class. She wanted him to go home and come back dressed in school clothes. Mario informed her that he lived one and a half miles from school and, if he did go home to change, which he was not going to do, he simply would not return. She abruptly sat back down at her desk and told him that they would discuss this later.

The teacher was upset, but the little girls at the school were thrilled. Everyone knew where Mario was at all times. Wherever the swarm of girls was, there was Mario. The girls followed him around the schoolyard at recess, calling out his name, trying their best to get his attention. Even girls in the higher grades were calling out his name. After recess, the girl sitting behind him in class wrote her name and number on his white shirt collar. Mario lived for attention, but even this was too much for him. By the time he got home from school, he was exhausted. He couldn't wait to finish his homework, eat dinner, and relax for the evening. However, the quiet of the evening did not last long.

A few hours after dinner, a choir of little girls appeared on the Rivia front porch singing, "I love Mario. I love tea. I love him, and he loves me!"

Mario continued to dress like Frank Sinatra, boutonniere and all, to school each day. The teacher eventually came to terms with it. She conceded, as long as it did not interrupt the completion of his schoolwork, she would stop making a fuss about it. After a few days, the little girls stopped following him around the school yard at recess but never stopped whispering about him, writing him secret love notes and hoping that, one day, they would be the lucky one to steal a kiss from him.

Vincenzo could not believe the attention his little brother, Mario, received from the girls at school just because he changed the way he dressed. He shook his head at his brother. Vincenzo thought it was embarrassing. All Vincenzo wanted to do in school was learn. He was quieter than Mario and much less flamboyant. He was a deep thinker, a philosopher. Once homework and the farm chores were completed, you could find Vincenzo reading quietly in his room. He enjoyed studying. It was his favorite way to relax. It did not matter if the subject was school related or Bible related; Vincenzo loved to dig deep into it, pick it apart, and study.

One night, when Vincenzo was in his room studying from his new Bible, he felt the Lord tugging at his heart to share his findings with others. He had a deep love for God's Word and had been reading and studying it ever since he became a born-again Christian. Vincenzo knew he had a lot to share. He had filled two notebooks with notes from his research. He was confident that he wanted to share with others through preaching God's Word, but he asked the Lord for a confirmation. He did not want to do anything of this magnitude without making sure he was really hearing from God.

"Lord," Vincenzo prayed, "I feel You tugging at my heart to share what I have read and studied from Your Word. I have read and studied every day since I became a born-again Christian. I have taken careful notes. I want to share my findings with others, but I am afraid that my thinking is full of pride. I only want to preach if this idea is of You and not me. Please give me a confirmation that I am to preach," Vincenzo prayed earnestly.

The next morning at breakfast, Gio announced that he had a new idea for the family.

"I would like us to have daily devotions as a family," Gio said. "Since the morning is rushed with breakfast, packing lunches, and getting you children off to school, I would like to do devotions in the evening. We could set up chairs in the front room and have our evening devotions in there," Gio continued with his idea. "Mario, you can lead us in song since you are so interested singing. Carla, I would like you to lead us in prayer each time. It is clear to all of us that God has blessed you with the gift of prayer. Vincenzo, I would like you to preach the Word of God," Gio said as he looked around the table at his three oldest children, seeking their approval.

"Hooray!" shouted Mario. "Can I wear my bow tie and boutonniere?"

"Yes, Father," Carla answered in a humbled voice, "it would be my pleasure."

Everyone looked over at Vincenzo as they waited on his answer. Vincenzo sat at the table, head in his hands, weeping. He knew this was the confirmation he needed from God to share his findings with others. He was thrilled to start with his family, but he knew God had a much bigger group that He wanted Vincenzo to share His Word with.

Family devotions in the front room started right away. The first night was simple and basic. It was clear that this new routine was new to everyone in the family, especially Vincenzo, Carla, and Mario. It took a few family devotion times for them to feel comfortable in their newly assigned roles of leadership. Each night would begin with a few songs, led by Mario. Vincenzo preached a short sermon directly form the Word of God, and Carla ended in prayer. As the weeks progressed, the three older children became comfortable in their leadership roles. Each family devotion night got more intense as the Spirit of the Lord moved through the room. Mario's singing got more confident and robust. Vincenzo's preaching was deep and moving, with the family augmenting the sermon with amens and hallelujahs. Carla's ending prayers turned into altar calls, where the Spirit of the Lord moved down on the family.

The evening family devotions had been going on for a month or so when, one night, right there in the front room, Mario received the Holy Spirit with the evidence of speaking in a heavenly language. The family rallied around him in the makeshift altar area. Everyone knew that Mario had been seeking after the Holy Spirit, asking God to fill him to overflowing. Tonight they rejoiced that God answered his prayers.

Vincenzo continued to study God's Word and brought the findings back to the family through clear, pointed preaching. Mario chose songs that were uplifting and full of worship to the Lord. He sang loud and strong without a microphone or any accompaniment. Carla's love for praying continued to bless the family. Now every devotion ended with an altar call, with Carla circling around to lay hands on and pray for each of the family members.

One particular night, during the family devotion time, Antonia was especially moved. She started crying during Mario's song leading. Tears flowed as she raised her little hands and sang out in her young five-year-old voice to God. She lifted her voice to sing of His love and grace for her, His unending faithfulness, and how He promised to take her by the hand and be a friend. She understood Vincenzo's preaching and praised God with the other family members off and on throughout his message. When it was time for the altar call, Antonia was the first one to come forward.

"What would you like me to pray with you about, Antonia?" Carla asked as she put her arm around her little sister.

"I want to be filled with the Holy Spirit," she began. "I want to speak in a heavenly language too so I can speak to God privately without Satan listening in," she explained.

Carla chuckled to herself at her sister's innocent explanation of such an empowering thing.

"Let's pray, Antonia," Carla said. "I know God will hear and answer your prayer."

The family gathered around Antonia and started praying for God to fill her to overflowing with His Spirit.

Before Antonia walked out of the front room of the Rivia home that evening, she was filled with the Holy Spirit with the evidence of speaking in a heavenly language.

"Thank you, sister," Antonia said in a hoarse voice from crying and praying so long.

"You do not need to thank me, Antonia. It was God who heard your prayer and did all the work. You are filled with the Holy Spirit now. It will be with you forever, empowering you beyond measure at desperate times in your life that you will need Him most. Thank God, not me," Carla whispered as she hugged her little sister tenderly.

The family devotion time continued throughout the rest of the fall season and into the winter. The closer it got to Christmas, the children started asking about putting up a Christmas tree and giving Gio hints for Christmas gifts.

"We will not put up a Christmas tree," Gio said in a stern voice. "Christmas trees leave a big mess in the house and are dead before you know it. They're a waste of money," he said in a confident voice.

"I was hoping for a doll, Daddy," Antonia said in her quiet voice.

"I will help clean up the mess from the tree if you get us one, Daddy," Carla offered.

"All the other kids at school are talking about their trees. Most of them already have them put up. I thought we would be having one this year since it is our first year in this big farmhouse," said Mario.

"Well, sorry to disappoint you, children, but the answer is a firm no! Not a tree or special gifts," Gio said with a loud voice as he walked to another room of the house. The children heard him shout back into the living room, "I will allow a few decorations to be placed on the fireplace mantel!"

Christmas day came and went, and just as Gio declared, there was no tree or gifts for anyone in the Rivia home. There was no special Christmas Day dinner either. Besides giving thanks for Christ's birth before they ate, Christmas Day passed as if it was any other day of the year. Chores were completed in the house and barn, and bedtime curfew was observed.

The day after New Year's Day, school resumed, and everyone was back to the same schedule as before the holiday. Most of the children at the farmhouse school were excited to return to school to show and tell their special Christmas gifts that they found under the tree. Vincenzo, Carla, Mario, and Antonia made a vow with each other on the long walk to school to stay quiet. They did not want anyone to know about their Christmas holiday.

On the walk back home after that first day, the four children vented.

"I was never so embarrassed when Mary asked me if I got that new math game, the Path of Math," Carla cried. "She knows how much I love math and would beat everyone I played, but I had to tell her that I did not get it," Carla said with a sad voice. "I made sure I did not tell her that I didn't get anything at all. She just thinks I did not get that math game."

"I know what you mean," Mario joined in. "All my friends knew that I wanted more clothes for Christmas. They all asked me if I got a new bow tie," he said. "I did the same thing as you, Carla. I just told them that I did not get clothes, but I didn't tell them that I got nothing at all," Mario ended.

"We should just be grateful that we have a warm house and parents that love us," Vincenzo said.

No one had a response for Vincenzo's comment. They understood what he was trying to say, but no one felt like commenting.

"When I grow up and have a family, I will have a Christmas tree, gifts for my children, and make a big Christmas dinner with lots of cookies for dessert," Antonia said with a smile, dreaming of that faraway day.

Again no one made a comment, just the crunching of snow under their feet as they walked home, but they all nodded in silent agreement with Antonia.

One Saturday morning, Carla was frantically looking for Antonia. She looked everywhere she could think of but just couldn't find her. She asked her brothers and anyone else she saw if they had seen her. Everyone said that they had not seen her for a while. She looked outside in the orchard, in the barn, and all over the house, including the basement, and turned up with nothing. Finally Carla had the crazy idea to look in the laundry room. She knew it was a crazy idea, but that was the only place she didn't check. Carla opened the door, and there stood Antonia holding a mop. The mop was upright, wooden handle on the floor and rope strings up. The strings of the mop were full of hair bows, clips, and sponge rollers.

"What are you doing in here, Antonia?" Carla said with a questioning voice. "I have been looking all over for you."

Antonia stood very quiet. She did not say a word. She could only imagine how this whole thing looked to Carla. Finally

Antonia dropped the mop and ran out of the laundry room. She did not stop running until she reached her bedroom and flopped down on the bed. She was sobbing.

"What is going on? Tell me what's wrong with you," Carla said in a concerned, stern voice.

"It's the only way I can have a baby doll," Antonia sobbed. "I wanted one so badly for Christmas. My one friend at school told me that she has so much fun dressing her baby doll up in cute clothes and fixing her hair with fancy stuff," Antonia said through flowing tears running down her face. "Please don't tell Daddy or Aunt Sofia. They will take that away from me too," Antonia pleaded. "All I want is a baby doll to play with, and if I can't get one, I will use the mop," Antonia declared.

"Oh, Antonia, I will not tell Daddy or Aunt Sofia," Carla sympathized with her sister. "It will be our secret," Carla promised. "We better get back down to the laundry room and take all those hair things off the mop before you are found out," Carla said with a chuckle.

Both girls quietly walked back down to the laundry room. Carla was hoping they would not bump into anyone along the way because Antonia's eyes were as red as an apple. The girls made it to the laundry room unnoticed, but before they took all the adornments off the mop strings, Antonia convinced Carla to stay and play awhile with her and the mop. Even though playing with baby dolls or fixing hair was not a priority to Carla, she stayed anyway to appease her little sister. As they played quietly in the laundry room so no one would hear them, it was clear to Carla that her sister loved babies and loved fixing hair.

"Maybe someday you will grow up to have lots of kids and do hair, Antonia." Carla giggled.

"Maybe" was all Antonia replied.

The rest of the school year flew by without event, and before they knew it, it was summer again. By the time the summer months were upon them, everyone in the family knew Antonia's secret about the mop. She not only dressed it with towels; she created different hair fashions with the strings using rubber bands, clips, and hair bows. She even had a name for it. She would walk it around the house showing off the mop's latest clothes and hair fashions. Everyone complimented Antonia for her designs, except Aunt Sofia.

"It looks ridiculous to pretend that a mop is a person, Antonia," Aunt Sofia condemned. "I don't want to see or hear you clopping around the house with that dirty mop dressed in towels. It's not a baby doll. It's a dirty, old, smelly mop! Can't you find something else to play with that's more appropriate?"

Antonia would not say a word but sadly hang her head in shame. Maybe she was weird for wanting a baby doll so badly that she would resort to playing with a mop. She obediently returned the mop to the laundry room as she was instructed. Then she would go up to her room to hide. It hurt her feelings when Aunt Sofia spoke to her in that way. Sometimes, when Aunt Sofia had a bad day or was in a bad mood, she would lash out. And recently Aunt Sofia's bad moods were coming more frequently. Days later, when Antonia thought Aunt Sofia was in a happier mood, she would sneak back in the laundry room to play with the mop; but she would not take it out of the room.

A few weeks later, Antonia snuck in the laundry room to play with the mop. Sitting on the dryer was a brand-new baby doll still in its store package. Antonia couldn't believe her eyes. She picked up the package to examine it. It was a beautiful blond baby doll with a pink lacy dress and bonnet. The shoes were made out of velvet and had a gold clasp around the ankle. The baby was holding a purple rattle. Antonia was so excited. Maybe Aunt Sofia bought her this doll because she was tired of seeing her play with the house mop. Antonia decided to keep her finding a secret. If the doll was supposed to be surprise for her, she didn't want to ruin it by saying that she already knew about it.

Antonia waited two weeks, but no one said a word to her about the baby doll. Then, one night at dinner, it was announced that it was Vera's birthday. Aunt Sofia made a special meal of chicken and dumplings. After dinner, a big cake was carried out to the table. The cake was decorated with pink roses made out of frosting, and it had Vera's name written in the middle in purple. The cake was soft and sugary, and everyone enjoyed eating a big piece. The whole family sang happy birthday to Vera, and then Aunt Sofia popped up and walked in to the laundry room. She quickly returned, carrying a gift. The box looked suspiciously the same size as the baby doll package Antonia had been admiring for weeks. Vera torn into the gift wrap, and there was the blond-haired baby doll with the pink dress that Antonia thought was bought for her.

Vera ripped the baby doll from the cardboard package and hugged it tightly. Everyone made a comment about the beautiful doll, except Carla and Antonia. Carla stayed quiet because she knew how much Antonia wanted a baby doll, and Antonia said nothing because she knew she would burst into tears and then scream.

The summer months were difficult. Antonia had to be home every day to watch Vera play with her beautiful new baby doll while she snuck in the laundry room to play with the dirty mop. Since Vincenzo and Mario were getting bigger and stronger, Gio delegated more physical jobs for them to tackle in the barn as well as around the farm. Aunt Sofia spent her days sequestered in her room designing and sewing outfits for Vera to wear for her upcoming first year in school.

But even though no one spoke of it, the most difficult part of the summer for the family was watching Grace's health decline. Her left leg dragged more than it had previously. It took great effort on her part to lift it off the ground. She now needed help getting up and down the stairs. Her left arm was getting progressively weaker, and she often called on Carla and Antonia to help her put on her stockings, shoes, and help comb her hair. It took most of the morning for the girls to help undress Grace from her sleeping clothes and get her dressed and ready for the day. Most mornings, they did not get down to the kitchen to eat breakfast until ten o'clock.

One day, when Carla and Antonia were alone, Carla asked the question that everyone was ignoring.

"Antonia, who is going to help dress Mommy when we go back to school?" Carla asked sincerely. "We will never get down to breakfast on time to leave for school. Mommy is much weaker than she was last summer. Do you think Aunt Sofia will help us in the mornings?" Carla questioned.

"I don't think Aunt Sofia is going to help at all. I think she will make us get up earlier to help Mommy since we are her children and she is just an in-law," Antonia reasoned.

"I think you are right," Carla replied in a soft, worried voice. "I think, if Mommy continues to get weaker, Aunt Sofia will have less and less to do with her," Carla said.

Antonia did not say a word in response. She simply looked her older sister directly in the eye and shook her head in agreement.

One morning, after helping Grace get ready for the day, Carla and Antonia walked into the kitchen to eat their breakfast. Aunt Sofia and Gio were sitting around the kitchen table, deep in conversation.

Gio looked up as the girls entered the room.

"Just the girl I wanted to talk to this morning," Gio said, zeroing in on Antonia.

Antonia's eyes grew wide with fear. What had she done now? What new job was going to be added to the summer list of things she had to accomplish? She had no idea what her dad would have to say to her. Maybe Aunt Sofia told him how upset she was with her playing with the mop. Antonia froze in the spot she was standing and waited.

"Aunt Sofia and I were just discussing how thin your hair is," Gio began. "She has noticed, and so have I, that your hair is not growing like the other children. It's much thinner than Carla's hair and even little Virginia's hair," Gio continued. "Aunt Sofia has an idea on how to make your hair grow in thicker, and summertime is the best time to do it. The idea is to shave your head bald. That will cause the hair to grow in thicker," Gio explained.

Antonia's eyes grew wide, and she stood up a little straighter. Without making eye contact with her sister, Carla slowly reached over and grabbed her sister's hand.

"What do you think, Antonia? Don't you want to go to first grade with thicker hair? Such thick hair that it will actually hold a bow or ribbon in place? Aunt Sofia has agreed to sew you some new hair bands to wear, but your hair needs to be thicker first," Gio said in a convincing voice, trying to sell his daughter on the idea.

"Maybe we should ask Mommy first" was all Antonia could squeak out.

"Nonsense!" Aunt Sofia shouted as she stood up, making the wooded kitchen chair almost flip backward. "Your mother knows nothing of style, nor does she care," Aunt Sofia announced. "I have read about this hair-thickening technique in the latest fashion magazines, and I know what I am talking about," she said with authority. "It is summer. This is the best time to shave your head. It will make you cooler, and it will be grown out some before you return to school for first grade," she proclaimed.

Antonia knew the decision had already been made for her. There was no debate, no discussion, or asking anyone else's opinion. She sat on the chair as instructed. At the sound of the clipper turning on, Carla left the room. There was no way she could stay and watch this humiliating process. Within a minute or two, Antonia was completely bald. She walked out of the kitchen rubbing her newly shaved head. She walked into the living room to show her mother. Grace looked up at Antonia as she walked across the room. Grace remained silent but closed her eyes and shook her head. Carla cried.

After a few weeks of looking at Antonia with a bald head, the family became accustomed to it. There came a time when they didn't even notice, and they all went on with their summer. The months flew by without event. Vincenzo and Mario stayed busy with chores in the barn and cutting acres of grass around the farm; and Carla and Antonia, and sometimes even young Virginia, helped Gio and Aunt Sofia tend to the garden and orchards. One day, when Aunt Sofia was in the kitchen washing fruits and vegetables that were to be canned for winter, Carla got brave enough to ask why Vera was never called to help them in the garden or with the canning of the harvest or why she was never required to help them clean the big farmhouse.

"She's too delicate, Carla," Aunt Sofia explained. "She's too fragile and ladylike for any chores that require getting your hands dirty. Plus, she's had a difficult start in life, you know, losing a father and all. I can't ask her to help with chores. This is the one way I can repay her for not having a daddy," Sofia said in a melancholy tone.

Carla staired at her aunt. She did not like what she saw in her eyes. She saw something that she had never seen before. Aunt Sofia held Carla's gaze and stubbornly stared right back. Then she gave Carla a smirk and winked, as if to say "There is your answer, Carla. Don't ever ask me that again. My daughter is more important and worth more than you."

Once Sofia read in Carla's eyes that she understood her non-verbal body language, she turned and walked back out to the garden for another bushel full of fruits and vegetables to wash for canning. Carla stood stunned but not surprised. Carla was intuitive, observant, and smart for her young age. She understood what was ahead. She knew that, the older Vera got, eventually she would be Aunt Sofia's only concern and that she and her siblings, along with their sickly mother, would fade in the background. Carla closed her eyes and said a silent prayer that, with each day forward, God's grace would make them strong in their weakness.

Before long, the summer months melted away, and the first day of school was upon them. Carla and Antonia got up earlier than needed to help with their mother. Once Grace was downstairs and made comfortable, they went back upstairs to get themselves ready.

Carla and Antonia found the kitchen buzzing with excitement. Vincenzo and Mario were eating their breakfast excitedly in anticipation of the first day of the school year. Virginia was awake already and running around the kitchen. Aunt Sofia was bagging the last of the school lunches, and Gio was sitting at the table supervising. Vera stood off to the side dressed in a yellow dress that was covered in ruffles. She had her hair curled and pulled back with a matching ribbon. Aunt Sofia gave her strict instructions to stand there and not to move. She did not want any of her ruffles wrinkled or flattened before she arrived at her first day of school.

"There you two are," Gio said as Carla and Antonia walked into the kitchen. "We have been waiting for you to get down here," he calmly said as if he forgot the added early morning chore that had to be completed before they could come down for breakfast. "I have an announcement for all of you before you head off to school," Gio said with excitement in his voice. "We are going to open up our nightly devotion time to the community. Several neighbors have heard of Vincenzo's preaching and Mario's singing and would like to join us in the front room for devotions. We will begin the community devotions this evening," he announced.

There was no time left for excitement or discussion. It was time to head out the door for the long walk to school. Aunt Sofia stood by the opened front door with lunches piled in her arms. The older children were the first ones past Aunt Sofia and were handed a brown paper sack lunch. Vera was the last one out the door and Aunt Sofia handed her a handmade cloth lunch bag. She bent down and squeezed her daughter tightly and covered her face with kisses. Tears flowed down Aunt Sofia's face as she unclenched her daughter and sent her on her way to her first day of school.

All five children were exhausted when they returned home from the first day of their school year. They knew that it would take them a week or two to get back into the swing of the school year routine. Gio ignored their tired faces at the dinner table. He announced for the second time that family devotions, now open to the community, would begin tonight in the prayer room. The children helped clear and wash the dinner dishes, headed upstairs to complete any schoolwork, and were back downstairs for devotions.

Everyone was surprised to see how many people of the community showed up on that first night. They had thirty people on chairs in the prayer room. Gio made a note to set out more chairs the next night. Mario led the group in singing, Vincenzo preached, and Carla led the altar call time. Many neighbors came forward for prayer—some praying for healing, some for unsaved loved ones, and some for God to help them with their financial needs. Carla asked others to surround the neighbor as she prayed urgently for each need. The community devotion continued every day of the week, leaving the weekends for neighbors to attend their individual churches.

The colorful fall months came and went. Community devotions continued, increasing in number each week. By winter, Gio and the boys were setting up forty chairs each night in the prayer room. Antonia and Virginia greeted the people coming in. Mario was learning new songs each month to teach to the group. Vincenzo continued to read and study God's Word, asking for His guidance on what to preach, and Carla prayed over the people. Gio, Grace, Aunt Sofia, and Vera were part of the audience with the other neighbors.

Before anyone knew it, spring was in the air. The barn had three nanny goats that delivered their baby kids. One nanny had twins, one had a single kid, and one had a stillborn kid. Vincenzo and Mario asked Gio if they could bring the baby kids to the community devotion if they brought them one at the time. They knew that the spring air was too cold for the babies, and the heaters in the barn could not keep it warm enough. Gio agreed, and the first baby kid was brought to the community devotion that evening. All the neighbors were excited and laughed and pet the new barn baby. After devotions were over, Vincenzo and Mario showed the neighbors how they fed the kids with a bottle and spoon. It was a real treat for everyone.

Later that evening, Aunt Sofia saw water on the floor in the prayer room.

"Gio!" she shouted. "You are going to have to stop letting the boys bring the baby kids into the prayer room during community devotions. I saw water on the floor, and I am sure it was from the animals," she said in a loud, upset voice. "Just one more thing for me to clean up!" she mumbled to herself.

"Well, we can't have that," Gio quickly agreed, recognizing that Sofia was upset. "I'll tell the boys in the morning to keep the kids in the barn."

Carla and Antonia could hear Aunt Sofia's loud, angry voice all the way upstairs. They were sorry that the baby kids had to stay out in the barn from now on, not only because it would be cold, but because they knew the baby kids were not responsible for the water on the floor. Grace was.

"I am so sorry, girls. I didn't even realize I was relieving myself," Grace confessed in a shaky voice. "I have noticed recently that I sometimes do not have the feeling of a full bladder," she said slowly and apologetically. "The feeling comes and goes. It's not always this way, so I am asking you girls to not tell your father, please. I am enough of a burden to him as it is," she said, head down, almost in a whisper.

"Let's get you changed into your night clothes, Mommy," Carla said.

Antonia shook her head in agreement as she helped her older sister change their mother's wet clothes.

Carla and Antonia moved quickly to get their mother washed up, changed, and in bed before anyone knew what had happened. The girls talked privately and decided that they would add helping their mother get to the bathroom as frequently as possible to their list of care needs for her. Deciding what to do about this situation while they were in school was more challenging, but after much discussion, they came up with a plan so that they did not have to share this private and embarrassing information with anyone else.

The school year zoomed by with a few outstanding accomplishments from the children. Vincenzo was placed on the honor roll, Carla won an award for outstanding math student of the year, and Antonia won the school spelling bee. The children were excited to share their achievements with the family, but the only recognition they received was from Grace. She gave them a thumbs-up!

Summer months at the big farm were a repeat of the last— chores all day long and community devotions in the evening. Carla and Antonia continued to work together on a care plan for their mother. They worked together well and were able to keep the truth about their mother's needs private between the two of them.

When the hot, humid Illinois summer turned to fall and another school year was about to begin, everyone was excited. It was Virginia's turn to go to school. Finally all the children would be out of the house during the daytime hours. Routinely Aunt Sofia stood by the front door and handed out the bag lunches. Virginia received her brown school lunch bag with pride. She had spent years watching this procedure happen with her older brothers and sisters, and now it was her turn.

With all the children out of the house, Sofia could take long naps in the afternoon. She decided that, since all the children were school age now, they were old enough to do for themselves. She stopped washing clothes for the whole family. She only washed clothes for her and Vera. She stopped doing most of the gardening, saving a good portion of the chores for the children to do after school. It had been almost four years since she moved in with her brother and his children. During those years, she had picked up most of the responsibility as the woman of the home, and now she was tired and wanted a break.

Early one October afternoon, Gio had the opportunity to leave work early. He walked in on Sofia taking an afternoon nap. He found her sprawled out on the couch, feet out from under a blanket, snoring.

"What in the world is going on here?" Gio said in a loud voice, waking Sofia up from a sound sleep.

Sofia jerked awake at the sudden break in the dead quiet of the house and came to attention in one fell swoop. She was sound asleep one moment; and the next, she was standing face-to-face with her brother, who apparently was not happy that she was resting in the middle of the day. She rubbed her neck. Getting off the couch with such a start made her twist her neck.

"What are you doing home so early?" Sofia asked her brother.

"What's the matter? Am I not permitted to come home to my own house early?" he said in a sarcastic tone.

"Well, sure you are. It's just not like you to come home in the afternoon," she continued.

"Maybe I should come home early more often. Then I could see how lazy you are for napping in the afternoon instead of getting the laundry done, doing some of the ironing, or starting dinner," he said straight to her face.

"All I have done for the past four years is work my fingers to the bone in this big farmhouse. I take care of your children. I take care of your house. I take care of the family garden, and now apparently I have to take care of your wife too!" Sofia shouted in a sarcastic voice, with sarcastic body language to match, as she held back no words.

"What are you talking about? What do you mean you are taking care of my wife?" Gio questioned in a surprised voice.

Sofia did not know if she should reveal her discovery to Gio. She had secretly known for a few weeks now that Grace was not able to hold her bladder and that Carla and Antonia were taking care of the situation. Sofia was not going to complain; she was very happy that they were handling their mother's issue because she certainly was not willing to deal with it. She thought her brother should know the extent that Grace's health had declined. Sofia could tell by Gio's reaction that he did not know anything about it. Sofia explained the situation to Gio in detail.

"What are we going to do?" Gio asked his sister quietly. He did not want Grace to hear him speaking with Sofia.

"Obviously moving to this big farmhouse has not been the answer to Grace's health concerns like you originally thought. Before I even moved here, you told me that the one reason why you wanted to move to the country was for Grace's health to improve. The quiet, the fresh air, the fresh garden vegetables and eggs, and fresh fruit right off the tree. Well"—Sofia let out a sarcastic giggle—"she has not improved. In fact, she has declined. She still has headaches that send her to bed with a tightly wrapped head. She drags her left leg, and her left arm has barely any strength. When are you going to wake up and see that this move to the country has not helped, Gio?" Sofia sternly accounted to her brother.

Gio stood silent before his sister's critical eyes.

"Yes, I know," Gio whispered. "I had such great hopes of her improving, but after four years, nothing," Gio said with sadness in his voice.

"I am tired, Gio. This place is a lot of work. Your five children, my Vera, the huge inside, all the acreage, the gas station, and now Grace to take care of too? It's too much," Sofia confessed. "You either make a decision with me in mind, or Vera and I are out of here," Sofia said straightforward.

Again Gio stood silent before his sister's threat.

"We will move back to the city," Gio announced. "I know someone at the quarry that is looking to move to the country. I will start asking tomorrow," Gio promised.

Sofia smiled at her brother. That was the answer she wanted to hear.

Western Avenue House

Briarton, Illinois
1936–1947

GIO FOUND A BUDDY AT work who was looking to rent some farm-
land. When his buddy heard that the fourteen acres came with
a big farmhouse, barn, animals, vineyard, two orchards, and an
established garden, it was a done deal. Gio sold the gas station and
bar at the front corner of the farmhouse lot as a separate piece of
real estate.

Within weeks, Gio and the family moved back to the city. Gio
found a big two-story house that had a big porch, which became the
piano room; a fully finished attic including an equipped kitchen;
and enough bedrooms and baths to comfortably accommodate the
whole family. On the day they moved in, Gio stood in the hallway and announced room assignments. Gio and Grace were in the
first room, Antonia and Virginia in the second, and Vincenzo and
Mario in the third. Sofia, Vera, and Carla had their own rooms.

Since the move took place during the school year, Gio had
to go enroll the children. On the ride to the school, Gio could
not help remembering that, the last time the family moved, Grace
enrolled the children. He silently realized how much her health
declined in the past four years.

Gio was able to enroll Virginia in first grade, Vera in second
grade, Antonia in third grade, Mario in seventh grade, Carla in
eighth grade, and Vincenzo in tenth grade. However, the school

administrators brought to Gio's attention that Mario was not in the correct grade for his young age. Gio did not explain to them why Mario was a year ahead of his peers. He remained silent as they explained that Mario would not be permitted to pass to middle school at the end of the year due to his age. He would have to repeat seventh grade in order to catch up with the correct-aged peers. Gio agreed to the school's plan. He would deal with explaining this to Mario later.

Mario was not upset when he heard the news. He told his father that, during the year he had to repeat, he would ditch school as much as he could and hang out at work with him. Mario reasoned that, since the repeated year would be redundant curriculum anyway, he would not be missing out. Gio agreed. He loved having Mario at the construction site with him. Gio thought he was an excellent worker and natural leader and enjoyed his company too. Gio's chest puffed with pride to hear Mario talk about wanting to grow up to be just like him someday. Mario's ambition was to become a supervisor of a construction site, just like his father.

Gio encouraged Vincenzo to do the same, but Vincenzo was not interested. He loved going to school and learning too much. Vincenzo enjoyed reading, researching, and investigation. It was difficult for Vincenzo to understand Mario's rationale. Vincenzo would never entertain the idea of missing school unless he was ill. Plus, he did not enjoy going to work with his father. He did not have the same dreams as his brother, Mario.

Carla held on to her dream of going to college and becoming a math teacher. Even though she was only in eighth grade, she shared her dreams with her teachers. They all supported Carla and her dream. They made it clear that she was on the correct path for achieving her goal.

Ever since Antonia had her head shaved as a young girl, she proclaimed that she wanted to become a beautician. She knew that she could work with any head of hair, thin or thick or long or short, in order to make her client feel beautiful. She promised herself to never shave a client's head bald in order for them to gain thicker hair. She often shared her dreams with her teachers, but she did not receive the same support that Carla received from her teachers.

"Antonia, you will never become a beautician unless you work harder," her teachers would say.

Shy, quiet Antonia would hang her head and walk away. This response discouraged her. She felt defeated and lost without direction or guidance and often gave up on her dreams. With a quiet, sickly mother at home, an aunt that was only interested in housework, and a father that was not interested in her schooling, it was easier to just give up. It was difficult for her to see a successful future ahead. From birth, Antonia suffered with upper-respiratory flare-ups. It was not uncommon for her to miss a week's worth of school each month due to illness. Her poor attendance did not help convince teachers that she was taking her future dreams seriously.

Vera and Virginia were only in first and second grade when the family moved to the new city school. They had not yet zeroed in on future goals. But even at that young age, it was clear that Vera loved attention, and Virginia loved the Lord.

The first summer at the new home was exciting for the children. Their chores were greatly decreased now that they did not have to take care of the demands of the big farm, barn, and corner-lot gas station and bar. The houses were closer together in the city, so they were able to walk to neighbors' homes and make friends. They had sidewalks and streetlights in the city too. So they played sidewalk and street games with neighbor friends until it got dark. The children seemed healthier and noticeably happier that summer living in the city. The same could not be said about the adults. The older children were very aware of the loud constant fighting between Gio and his sister, Sofia. Their arguing became more frequent with the move to the city, and the trigger was always the same—Grace.

"If you think for one minute that I am going to stay in this house and take care of your wife all day long, you are crazy, Gio," the children heard her shout at their father one evening.

"Lower your voice, Sofia. The children might hear you," Gio said in a quiet voice.

"I don't care who hears me," Sofia continued. "You need to hire someone because there is no way that I am going to clean up after her once the children go back to school in the fall. She needs help getting in and out of bed, getting in the bathroom on time, dressing, combing her hair, and bathing. No way, Gio. I am not doing this. You either hire someone soon to take care of her, or Vera and I are moving to the attic. And if we do that, you and the children are on your own to take care of everything in the house, including Grace!" Sofia shouted.

"I know it's going to be a lot of work once the children are in school and aren't home to help. I'll look into hiring someone before the week is out," Gio promised.

When the week came and went and no home-care nurse was hired, Sofia kept her word and moved to the attic with Vera. She did not leave the attic. All responsibility of the house and Grace fell on Gio and the children. The older girls cooked, cleaned, and did laundry. Virginia picked up the books and toys. The boys helped with the lawn care and washing the cars.

After two weeks of living in the attic with Vera, Sofia cooled off and weaned her way back down into the house with Gio and the family. She apologized to all, and things returned to normal.

The children returned to school, and Sofia was faced with another school year of being alone all day long tending to the house chores, as well as Grace's needs. The school year dragged on, and Sofia became weary of her duties. She approached Gio again about her concerns.

"Gio, I am not going to have this conversation with you again. Please hire someone to care for Grace," Sofia demanded. "I am not going to care for her all day and keep your house in order too," she said.

"I know, Sofia," Gio replied. "I am working on hiring a care nurse to come to the house," Gio said.

"You have said that before," Sofia said, raising her voice. "I mean it, Gio. I'm moving back into the attic with Vera again. You can handle the house and Grace with your children!" she shouted.

True to her warning, Sofia moved into the finished attic with the complete kitchen to show Gio that she meant business. However, Gio did not follow through with hiring home nursing care for Grace. Sofia stayed in the attic with Vera for three weeks this time. Caring for the house and Grace with the children in school for the second school year at the new house was challenging for all. The children had less time to complete schoolwork and less time to relax and play outside. The atmosphere in the house was tense.

Grace kept hearing Sofia talking up in the attic and could hear Vera running about up there. One evening, when Gio came to bed, she asked him what was going on.

"Sofia agreed to move here from New York to help me out with the children, but now after all this time, she's tired," Gio tried to explain to Grace without telling her Sofia's change in heart had to do with the added burden of taking care of her.

Even though Gio left out the details, Grace clearly got the message. She understood all too clearly. Just because she was quiet and did not verbalize her thoughts to anyone, she was very aware of the sacrifice the family was making in order to care for her daily needs. She was also aware that, in her state of health, it was difficult for her to be the wife she once was to her husband. Just the thought of it embarrassed her. She diverted her eyes from Gio. Without saying a word, she hung her head and let out a deep sigh.

By the time the second summer in the Western Avenue home rolled around and no health-care nurse had been hired, Sofia approached Gio again.

"Look, Gio. I need some help getting Grace in and out of the bathtub. With not being able to control her bladder, she needs to soak in a tub. You need to hire someone to at least bathe her," Sofia pleaded with her brother.

"I am tired of having this conversation with you," Gio half shouted. "I am not hiring a health-care nurse to come into the home to do anything with Grace when I have you and the girls to help out," Gio said with a determined voice.

"Fine, I am more than tired of having this conversation with you too," Sofia snapped back at her brother. "Here's the deal, Gio. You either hire someone to at least come in and bathe her, or I am calling a nursing home and having someone come out to evaluate her," Sofia demanded.

Gio knew by the look in Sofia's eyes that she meant every word of her threat. They spent several seconds staring into each other's stubborn eyes. Finally Sofia broke the stare down.

"If you want to let me know the answer to your decision, you can find Vera and me in the attic apartment. We will be there until you either hire someone or sign her over to a nursing home. Your choice, Gio," Sofia spoke out forcefully. "This time, if you don't give the answer I want to hear, we will be moving back to New York. So last chance to make a good decision, Gio, or there will be life-altering consequences for you and the children," she said abruptly.

The next day, Gio hired a health-care nurse to come to the house three times each week specifically to bathe Grace. Sofia lived up in the attic apartment with Vera for the first month after the nurse was hired just to make sure that Gio did not discontinue her services.

It was clear to Gio that hiring the health-care nurse was a smart move for everyone involved. Having her come to the home reduced the tension between him and Sofia. It took that demand off young Carla and Antonia, and he noticed an improvement in Grace's demeanor. Each time the nurse came to bathe Grace, she would play relaxing music for her and would use two different types of bath sponges to gently wash Grace's broken body from head to toe. Then she would lean her back in the tub and take her time washing and massaging her head using wonderful-smelling shampoo and cream rinses. After a long hot soak in the tub, she would pat Grace dry and style her hair. The nurse asked Grace if she had any pretty nightgowns.

"I have a few tucked away in the back of my lingerie drawer," Grace answered. "Gio ordered them for me years ago from New

York. I haven't thought about them or worn them for a very long time," Grace mumbled.

"Well, we're going to pull them out tonight," the health-care nurse responded.

Grace showed the nurse where to find the nightgowns. To the nurse's surprise, they were much more detailed and delicate than expected. She picked out a pale-pink negligee made of satin and chiffon, with a delicate underlay of lace at the shoulders, waist, and hem. The nurse thought the pale pink would stand out against Grace's dark hair and skin tone. As she helped Grace into the negligee, she told her that the soft, rich fabrics would feel refreshing against her skin. Once dressed, Grace agreed. She had forgotten what it felt like to go to bed feeling clean, elegant, and ladylike.

One evening in early August, Gio came to bed late. He stayed up later than usual to work on some projects he was working on out in the garage. It was a hot, humid evening, and he was dripping with sweat from working outside. He decided to take a shower before getting in bed. The bedroom was dark. Grace was already asleep. The cool water of the shower felt invigorating as it rolled down his hot skin. He dried off and headed for the bedroom.

As he opened the bedroom door, the night-light Grace used on her side of the bed cast a soft sheen over her face, hair, and body. Gio stood in the bedroom doorway and loved what he saw. She was dressed in a light-blue negligee that he remembered buying for her years ago. She was sound asleep with her left arm up over her head, her dark hair loose and tousled over her pillow. She had kicked off half of her bed coverings, and the chic blue negligee was exposed. The wife he saw lying on the bed brought flashbacks of a wife he once knew and desired. Gio gently shut the bedroom door, climbed into bed, and woke Grace up with a soft kiss.

The next morning, Gio helped Grace down the stairs to the kitchen. He wanted her by his side at the kitchen table. He made them some hot coffee as they sat and talked without Sofia or Vera interfering in their conversation. It felt good. It felt like old times. Grace secretly hoped that Sofia and her daughter would stay in the attic apartment a few more weeks.

Eventually the boys came down for breakfast. Carla and Antonia entered together with confused looks on their faces.

"There you are, Mommy," Carla said. "Antonia and I went to your bedroom to help you out of bed, but you were not there," Carla said with a questioning look.

"Daddy decided to help me down the stairs this morning," Grace said with a glow on her face.

She glanced over at Gio with a smile. Her hair was still loose, just the way Gio liked it. Gio smiled at his wife.

Gio waited for Virginia to enter the kitchen and start eating her breakfast before he announced that it was time to find a church in the area.

"We have been at this house almost two years now and have not decided on a church to call home," Gio began. "I would like to decide on a church we all can enjoy and start attending regularly this week," Gio declared.

Everyone spoke at once, giving their opinion of where they wanted to worship. Gio and Grace listened to all of their suggestions and comments. Finally they decided on a church that they thought the whole family would be comfortable attending.

On Sunday, everyone got ready for church. Sofia and Vera stayed up in the attic apartment and did not attend with the rest of the family. Once at church, everyone split up to attend their age group of activities. Vincenzo, Mario, and Carla headed off to the youth room. Antonia and Virginia headed off to the children's church, and Grace and Gio headed off to the adult worship. Everyone was warm and welcoming to the newcomers. Gio saw a few coworkers. The girls recognized and went over to sit with some friends from school. Grace exchanged phone numbers with a few new lady friends, and Mario met Julia.

With all the end-of-summer fun activities that their new church organized, the remaining weeks of summer flew by. Before they knew it, it was time once more to start thinking of new clothes, shoes, and school supplies for the new school year. Money was tight, but they managed to each get a few new things to start the year.

Everyone fell back into the school year schedule quickly. Sofia, who eventually moved back down into the house from the attic apartment, stood at her post at the front door handing out lunches as the children marched out the door off to school; and Gio stood by with his hot cup of coffee in hand. Grace was not downstairs. She told Carla and Antonia that she would not need their help getting down to the kitchen and that she wanted to stay in bed awhile longer. They thought this was unusual but agreed to let her rest. On the way to school, the girls talked.

"What do you think was wrong with Mommy this morning?" Antonia asked her sister.

"I don't know," responded Carla with a worried look on her face. "I heard her crying earlier. I hope her head is not hurting this morning. I know how bad her headaches can get."

"We can ask her when we get home," Antonia suggested.

The girls walked the rest of the way to school in silence, both deep in thought about their mother's health. Virginia and Vera were running and laughing together ahead of them, and Vincenzo and Mario were in the rear having a discussion about Mario's new position as youth group leader at church.

"What are the new lessons and activities coming up, Mario?" Vincenzo was asking.

"The next lesson is about the Holy Spirit," Mario said. "That topic covers three lessons. It should be a good one," he continued. "There are so many fun activities coming up I can't remember them all," he said with a chuckle. "I can check with Julia after school. She will know all of them. She is the editor of the *Youth in Action* newsletter," Mario said with a smile as he thought of Julia.

"What's that smile for?" Vincenzo teased his little brother. "Are you sweet on her?"

"She's a great girl, Vincenzo. She comes from a good family, and she loves the Lord," Mario said with a straight face.

"She's pretty cute too, don't you think?" Vincenzo said, wanting to know where his brother stood in this situation.

"Yes, she's striking," Mario replied. "But I made a decision. I am not moving forward with any girl until I hear from God. I told

God to let me know who my bride will be. Until I get that signal from God, I am not moving forward with any girl," Mario said emphatically. "We're supposed to meet at her house this week to stamp the church's address on some church pamphlets. She said that she'd make cocoa for us to drink," Mario informed his brother.

Vincenzo smiled. He could not help but think that Julia was interested in Mario. He did not say anything more to his younger brother. He knew Mario wanted God to lead him to the right woman. He also knew that his brother was filling out personality surveys that were found in magazines in order to reveal whom he would be compatible with. Vincenzo did not say a word but shook his head as he continued walking to school. He was amazed at how different he was from his brother.

When the children got home from school, they saw that their mother finally made it downstairs for the day. She was sitting in the kitchen talking on the phone. They did not know whom she was talking to, nor did they understand most of the conversation. But something was upsetting her because she was crying. As soon as she realized that the children were home from school, she abruptly cut the conversation off and hung up the phone.

"What's the matter, Mommy?" Carla asked.

"It's nothing, Carla," Grace answered quickly. "You guys must be hungry from school. Go ahead and make yourselves a snack and be sure to clean up and turn off the lights when you are finished," she said as she slowly walked out of the room.

The children obeyed their mother. When they were finished eating and cleaning up and turned the kitchen light off, they went upstairs to complete their after-school chores and schoolwork. At dinner, their mother was absent from the table. No one asked where she was. The next morning, Grace told Carla and Antonia to go ahead downstairs for breakfast. She was going to stay in bed a little longer. As soon as the girls closed Grace's bedroom door, they heard her praying out to God. Carla and Antonia stood outside the door listening. They could not make out their mother's words, but they could hear an urgency in her voice. They know something was very wrong.

When the children returned home from school, Grace was sitting at the kitchen table. Her eyes were puffy and red. She had her head wrapped tightly in a scarf. She did not look well.

"What's the matter, Mommy?" Carla asked.

Grace did not speak; she just closed her eyes and shook her head.

"Who helped you down the stairs this morning, Mommy?" Antonia asked.

Grace answered her daughter without opening her eyes, "I had a visitor come to the house this morning. She helped me get to the kitchen."

The children helped themselves to an after-school snack. They talked among themselves about their school day and joked around with one another. Grace remained silent. She sat at the kitchen table, held her tightly wrapped head in her hands, and never looked up. They assumed she had another one of her bad headaches and decided not to ask any more questions. Eventually they finished eating, cleaned up their mess, and made their way out of the room and on to their after-school chores and activities.

Later that evening, when the children filtered into the kitchen for dinner, they found their parents whispering, deep in conversation. Grace was still sitting at the table, but this time, she was openly crying. Gio was sitting next to her, rubbing his head with both hands. He had a look on his face that none of the children had ever seen. It was sadness, worry, and shock all rolled into a wide-eyed glare of disbelief. Vincenzo was the first one to speak.

"What is going on?" he said in a firm questioning voice that came out more like a demand to know. "Things have been weird around here lately, especially with Mom, and we all want to know what is going on," he continued.

"We will wait for Sofia and Vera to come down for dinner first," Gio replied in a stern tone. "We will tell everyone the news at one time."

Everyone was curious to hear, but no one was prepared for the announcement.

"Mom called an old friend to come over to see her this morning," Gio started. "Only she didn't come over just to visit Mom. She came over to give Mom a test, a pregnancy test. The test showed that Mommy is going to have a baby around the end of your school year," Gio announced.

There was complete silence in the room. Gio took a quick glance around the table. Everyone sat frozen in time. Vincenzo had his head dropped in his hands. Mario was frozen in a cold stare, trying to process what was just said. Carla's eyes were open as wide as saucers, and she had her hand clenched over her mouth as if to command her mouth to be silent. Antonia's and Virginia's faces were lit up with excitement, and they both had a huge toothy smile plastered on their face. Vera sat clueless, and Sofia sat at the end of the table with squinted eyes and a scowl of disbelief on her face.

Antonia was the first to break the silence. "We're going to have a new baby in the house?" she burst out with excitement as she hopped off her chair and skipped over to her mother. "We're going to have a real live baby doll in the house." She giggled with glee.

Grace was not celebrating. Instead, at the words of her innocent nine-year-old daughter, she put her head down on the table and sobbed.

Carla felt like she was going to explode if she didn't say something. She popped up out of her chair, pointed at her dad at the end of the table, and shouted, "How could you do this to Mom? Do you not see how fragile and broken she is? Maybe you don't since you don't take care of her like Antonia and I do. How is she going to have a baby in her state of health? Honestly, Dad, this is not good." Carla spit it out without thinking of the ramifications from her dad.

"You will not speak to me that way in my house, Carla!" Gio shouted as he, too, popped up from his seat. "You can take your mouth to your room, right now!" he continued to shout as he sharply pointed at the kitchen door for her to leave.

Vincenzo popped up next. "What about me? Did anyone think how weird this will be for me? I am fifteen, and I'm going to have a little brother or sister? Don't worry, Dad. You don't have to kick me out of the kitchen like Carla. I'm gone!" Vincenzo shouted as he exited the kitchen and ran up to his room.

Although it was a quiet dinner, the rest of the family stayed to eat. Everyone was lost in their own thoughts. Antonia and Virginia did not understand why Vincenzo and Carla were so upset at the news. A new baby sounded fun and exciting to them. Mario was twelve. He was not worried about being embarrassed to have a baby sister or brother arrive in the spring, but he was worried about his mom. Even at his young age, he understood the complications involving her health. Vera had no idea what was going on and could care less. Gio and Sofia exchanged fire-hot glares at each other throughout the rest of the meal, giving the nonverbal message that they would take up this subject later in private. Grace barely ate two bites of the food on her plate. Although she was silent, her mind was engaged.

The next morning, Carla could not get her mother down the stairs to the kitchen fast enough. She was starving. Neither she nor Vincenzo came back down to the kitchen after their father's announcement at dinner. When Carla got to the kitchen, Vincenzo was already there eating his breakfast. Carla could tell by the way he was shoveling in his food that he was as hungry as she was. Soon all the other children piled in the kitchen, ate their breakfast, and were off to school. The morning was unfolding like any other school day, but to Grace, it felt like it was moving in slow motion. As soon as she heard the front door close and could hear Sofia climbing the steps to her bedroom, Grace picked up the phone.

She dialed Ethel, the neighbor across the street. Grace told her about the pregnancy test. Ethel was shocked and worried at the news. After they talked for a few minutes, it was clear to Ethel that Grace did not want to proceed with the pregnancy. Ethel told Grace about a relative of hers that got pregnant out of wedlock. She did not want to tell her parents; so she took unbearably hot baths, jumped down steps, and pushed on her stomach with her balled-up fists while she was lying down on her bed. She ended up miscarrying the baby in her first trimester.

Grace hung up the phone and contemplated the information she just heard. She knew it was wrong before the Lord to think this way, but she also knew that her body could not take delivering another baby. If she did go through with the pregnancy, how would she take care of a newborn baby in her condition? She couldn't even bathe herself, let alone a newborn. She thought back to when she was pregnant and had her first children. It made her tear up to think of how her body and mind had changed. She did not want to share these thoughts with anyone in the family. She would take care of losing this baby on her own. If she was successful with following her neighbor's plan, everyone would think that she lost the baby because of her poor health. Grace couldn't see any other way but to abort this baby.

That same day, Grace started in on following her neighbor's instructions. When she was alone in her room at night, she would push as hard as she could on her stomach. She would push so hard it brought tears to her eyes. When the health-care nurse came to bathe her, she asked her to make the water hotter than usual. The nurse was reluctant, but Grace insisted. If the water was not unbearably hot, Grace would wait until the nurse left the room to add scalding-hot water to the tub. Her skin would be as red as an apple when she emerged from the tub.

Grace did not know how she was going to jump down the steps since Carla and Antonia were usually with her, so she had to modify the plan. Grace decided that, after the children left for school and Sofia was back upstairs in her room, she would climb just one step up by herself and then jump the step back down. Grace followed her neighbor's instructions for three weeks. She did not have any signs of distress with the pregnancy.

Grace knew that, if she was going to end this pregnancy, time was of the essence. If Ethel's ideas for naturally aborting a baby did not work, she had to move on to a new plan. After mulling over her options all day, she decided to reach out to a doctor that was a relative on her mother's side of the family. He promptly made a house call that afternoon.

It took a while to gather history and complete an exam. Then he offered his opinion.

"Grace, if I were you, I'd abort this baby. You're in no health to deliver. In fact, it may cause your death. Even if you do deliver this baby and live, how are you going to care for an infant? Yes, Sofia will help, but even with her help, how are you going to take care of a newborn with five other children that still need your attention?" the doctor asked.

"These are all questions I have been asking myself for a month now. The one thing that is stopping me is I know that aborting this baby is wrong before the Lord," Grace replied.

"I heard that you and the family are now born-again Christians. I understand what you are saying, but…," the doctor said, leaving the sentence hanging right there. He looked Grace directly in the eyes and handed her his business card. "Call my office and set up an appointment," he whispered. "The sooner the better."

Grace collected herself, then picked up the phone with shaking hands. She slowly dialed the number on the card.

Her voice was barely a whisper as she spoke into the receiver, "I would like to schedule an appointment for an abortion."

Grace could hear the children coming in from school. She did not want them to hear what she was contemplating about their little brother or sister. She hung up the phone and turned around, but it was too late. Carla was standing at the kitchen door with a look of horror on her face.

"Who were you talking to, Mom?" Carla said in a shaky voice.

Grace felt her stomach do a flip, and she thought she was going to faint. She never wanted anyone to know what she was thinking or planning. She slowly walked over to one of the kitchen chairs and sat down.

"I know you will not understand this, Carla, but I don't think I can go on with this pregnancy," Grace started. "I am not in good-enough health to carry and deliver this baby. I met with a doctor earlier today. He told me that I could possibly die during delivery.

Even if everything goes okay, how am I going to care for it?" she continued.

"You can call that midwife that delivered all of us. She will help you. What about Aunt Sofia? She will help while we are in school," Carla tried to reason with her mom.

"It's not that simple, Carla. There is a lot that goes with having a baby. I got pregnant by mistake. It was one night of careless thinking. I can't do this a sixth time. I am not strong enough, Carla. I could die. Please understand," Grace pleaded.

"Who did I hear you talking to on the phone?" Carla asked a second time.

"A doctor that is on my mother's side of the family," Grace answered, hoping that Carla did not hear the part of the conversation requesting an appointment.

"I heard you make an appointment. What for?" Carla continued. "You already confirmed that you are pregnant."

Grace knew that she was cornered. She decided to tell her oldest daughter the truth. She just hoped that the rest of the children did not come into the kitchen looking for their after-school snack just yet.

"I made an appointment for him to perform an abortion," Grace said in a soft, weak voice.

Carla doubled over, and tears flowed freely. She held on to the back of one of the kitchen chairs for support.

"Where is your faith in God? How can you do this?" she questioned in horror. "Don't you know that God does not want us to abort babies? The Bible says that He knew us before we were even shaped in our mother's dark womb. He not only knew us before we came out and saw light, but He had specific plans for us before we were even born. That tells me that God already knows this baby, and I don't mean whether it's a boy or girl. I mean God knows all about it. He knows its beginning and end. He has great plans for this baby to prosper," Carla confidently proclaimed to her mother.

Just as Carla finished saying her last word, the other children came into the kitchen. They were hungry to get their after-school snack. Grace remained seated, but Carla slipped out.

The next morning was a Saturday. Carla woke up early and went down to the kitchen, where Grace kept her phone directory. Carla wasted no time. She looked up three of her mother's closest friends from church. She called each one and explained the situation in detail. All three understood the urgency of the matter. They agreed to come to the house to pray for Grace. Carla did not tell her mother that they were coming. She decided to deal with any consequences later.

True to their word, all three ladies came to pray for Grace. They went up to her bedroom, surrounded her bed, and joined hands. One of the ladies anointed her head with oil. They agreed and prayed in Jesus's name that God would give her the physical strength she needed to continue carrying the baby to full term. Next they prayed for her mental health, that worry and fear of her death during the delivery would vanish, and that the delivery would be smooth and easy. The ladies prayed that the baby would be healthy in all ways. One lady specifically prayed that the baby would come to know Christ at an early age and that his life would become a testimony of God's mercy and grace for all to hear. They prayed for the support of family and friends to surround Grace once the baby was born and that she would choose grace to give this child a chance at life.

The abortion was scheduled for Monday at the home. She filled Sofia in on her plans and asked her to be by her side during the abortion. Gio did not know that she had an appointment the next day to abort their baby. Grace went to church on Sunday and emptied her heart and mind before the Lord. The rest of the day was a blur. It was a long night; she barely slept. Finally the sun came up on Monday morning. Grace pretended that it was a normal Monday morning, following the typical school-day routine.

However, at ten, the day was anything but typical. The doctor and his nurse entered Grace's bedroom to prepare the bed for the procedure. The nurse set out all of the needed sterile instruments. The doctor double-checked the nurse's work. Grace changed into the sterile clothing as she was instructed. The nurse helped Grace onto the prepared bed. Sofia sat on a chair by her side. The doctor and the nurse were at the foot of the bed.

"Okay, Grace, we are ready to begin," the doctor announced.

"*Wait!*" Grace cried out. "There will be no abortion today."

At the end of the school day, Carla came running into the house ahead of her brothers and sisters. She bypassed the kitchen and flew up the stairs as fast as her feet would carry her. She slowly entered her mother's bedroom expecting to see her in bed recovering from her ten o'clock appointment. Carla was confused. The bedroom was empty. The bed was neatly made, and there was no sign anywhere in the room that a doctor and his nurse performed a procedure there. She went back downstairs to look for her mother. She found her in the kitchen helping the children get their after-school snack. Grace looked up as Carla walked into the kitchen.

"Hello, Mom," Carla said slowly. "How was your day?"

"My day was uneventful, Carla," she mumbled with a half smile. "I think I will have a peanut butter and Graham cracker too," she said, looking directly at Carla. "This baby inside of me is telling me that it's hungry."

Grace gave the children the okay to tell friends from church and at school that the family was expecting another child sometime in May. Vincenzo and Carla did not tell anyone. Mario told those who asked. Antonia and Virginia told anyone who would listen. Vera did not care one way or another. She just wanted to make sure that the new baby did not interrupt her lifestyle in any way.

"Momma," Vera called to her mother one evening, "will things change for me once Aunt Grace has the baby?"

"What would make you think that, Vera?" Sofia asked in return.

"I'm afraid that another baby in the house will make things change too much. My friend Sarah's mother just had a baby a few weeks ago. Sarah told me how much work it is to have a new baby in the house. She said it cries all night long and her mother has to get up to take care of it. She's too tired to spend much time with Sarah anymore. You will be really busy helping with the new baby.

Who will design and sew my school clothes and matching hair bows? Who will shine my shoes? Will you have time to pack me a special lunch for me like you do now? Will you promise that, once the baby comes, you will not forget about me?"

Sofia closed her eyes and drew in a deep breath. "Vera, I promise that I will not forget about you once the baby arrives. Even though I will be helping Aunt Grace with the new baby, you will always be my number one concern, and don't you ever forget about that," Sofia said tenderly to her young daughter.

Although Sofia was able to help settle Vera's mind, her mind was racing. The more she thought about it, the more she knew that Vera's thinking was correct. There was no doubt that the new baby would bring change to the household. Sofia was used to having quiet during the day. That would be the first thing to change. She started thinking about all the added responsibility she would have since Grace's help with the baby would be limited.

Sofia could not get the conversation with Vera out of her mind. She tossed and turned all night and hardly got any sleep. In order to turn her mind off, she decided she needed to talk to her brother about this first thing in the morning. She also decided that she was going to prove to Vera that the new baby would not change things between the two of them. Sofia decided not to wait in order to prove that to her daughter. She would start giving Vera added attention starting tomorrow.

Sofia was up bright and early. The first thing she did was pack a special lunch for Vera. She made her a meat loaf sandwich on homemade bread, celery filled with some pimento cheese, and two homemade cookies. She added two notes of encouragement to the homemade cloth bag for Vera to read once she got to her lunch break. She quickly fried up some green peppers and eggs for the other children's paper-bag lunches.

For dinner that evening, Sofia fried four thick pork chops for the adults and Vera. She added some mashed potatoes and pork gravy to the plates. The other children had hamburger and fried potatoes. The adults drank coffee, the Rivia children drank water, and Vera drank Ovaltine.

The children noticed the favoritism that their cousin was receiving but said nothing. They did not understand what caused this action but were too afraid to question the change. They sat at the kitchen table eating in silence but spoke nonverbal volumes to one another through their eyes from across the table. The ongoing favoritism of Vera ate at their hearts. They felt confused and rejected.

One night after dinner, when the children were cleaning up the kitchen, they heard music coming from the ice-cream truck.

"Vera, hurry," Aunt Sofia called out with a giggle in her throat. "I hear the ice-cream truck coming down the road. Take these coins and go buy yourself a treat."

The rest of the children stood at the front window watching as Vera ran down the driveway to buy herself an ice cream. They watched as she unwrapped the treat in the driveway and ate it outside on the lawn. Later that evening, she gathered her cousins together.

"I did not use all of my ice-cream money tonight. I want to share it with you so that, next time the ice cream truck comes by, we all can buy a treat," she said in a tender voice.

Vera gave each of her cousins a few coins. Two days later, the ice-cream truck returned. All six of the children ran to the street to buy a treat. They all thanked Vera. It was a simple gesture they would never forget.

Everyone stayed busy over the next few months of the school year. Vincenzo was always preparing for special church events that he was asked to speak at. Mario was busy with Julia working on the *Youth in Action* paper, and Carla was digging deep into schoolwork. She was almost at the end of her tenth-grade year, and she was more driven than ever to get good-enough grades to attend college to become a math teacher. The younger girls stayed busy completing their household chores and homework. Even though everyone was busy, they couldn't help but notice Grace's growing belly. There was no question that the baby was coming soon.

When Grace reached the eighth month of her pregnancy, midwife Marino announced that she did not feel competent to deliver this baby at home. She strongly suggested that, with Grace's health issues, she deliver this baby at the hospital with a doctor. Gio did not want to hear this news. He had many heated conversations with the midwife. She stood her ground, and in the end, the midwife won. She helped Grace schedule with a doctor at the hospital. As she had all five babies in the comfort of her home, the thought of having this baby at the hospital provoked unimaginable fear. As the time for delivery approached, Grace's coping mechanism was to withdraw. The reality that a newborn was going to be in the house soon overwhelmed her. She was not ready, mentally or physically. She was nervous about the delivery and even more nervous about how she was going to care for a newborn.

During her last month of pregnancy, her headaches became more and more frequent. She became depressed and withdrew from the family completely. She stayed upstairs in bed the majority of the day. All meals were brought up to her. The only time she left the bed was when the nurse came to bathe her and intermittent times when she realized her bladder was full.

In April, the children could feel the home atmosphere becoming increasingly tense. They noticed that Gio and Sofia spent more and more time in secret conversations. As soon as anyone walked into the room, they stopped whispering. The children did not know what all the private conversations were about, but they did recognize that they involved something very serious. One night, when the children were alone in the kitchen, they discussed their observations.

"I'm sure it has something to do with Mom being so close to having the baby," Vincenzo rationalized.

"Maybe something is wrong with Mom and the baby that no one is telling us," Carla guessed.

"No, I don't think that is the problem," Mario interjected. "I think the deep conversations have to do with who is going to take care of the baby once it is born. Mom is going to need a lot of help. We are all in school, so we can't help during the day. That means that the biggest part of the responsibility is going to fall on Aunt Sofia. I don't think she wants that to happen," Mario reported.

"Why do you think that?" Carla asked her younger brother.

"I overheard a conversation one day between Aunt Sofia and Dad," Mario said. "Aunt Sofia was telling Dad that she would leave with Vera and go back to New York if he put all that responsibility on her. She was afraid of what the added responsibility would do to her relationship with Vera. She did not think that Vera would do well with time away from her while she took care of a new baby," Mario blurted out.

The children listened with wide eyes to what Mario overheard, and then they got still and quiet. Each were lost in their own solution to the problem. Maybe Gio would hire in help for Grace and the newborn. Maybe Aunt Sofia needed to take on the responsibilities of the baby during the day, and then they would shoulder the responsibility once they returned from school.

Before the tension in the house got better, it got much worse. The closer it got to the delivery of the baby, Gio and Sofia all but isolated themselves. They seemed to be in constant private conversation with one another. It was obvious when they agreed and disagreed on the matter. Sometimes they were smiling and nodding their heads in agreement; and other times, they were on their feet, arms flailing, beet red in the face, and loud. Just when the children thought they could not take any more of the secrecy and tension, Gio and Sofia gathered them together in the living room for a family announcement.

"All of you know that it will not be long now until the new baby arrives," Gio began. "You also know that Mom is in poor health and that delivering this baby will be a challenge, let alone caring for the newborn once it comes home. Therefore, Aunt Sofia and I have made a decision." Gio paused to take in a deep breath. "We have decided that Carla will quit school to stay home to take care of the baby," Gio announced.

All at once, the room got completely silent, and then it got loud with sighs and gasps of surprise.

"*What!*" Carla cried out as she jumped to her feet.

Her eyes were wide and glassy. Her dark complexion was quickly filled with red blotches.

"What did you just say?" she bluntly asked, half questioning in disbelief. "Did you say I have to quit school to take care of the baby? There is no way. I am only in tenth grade. I have two more years to go. I can't get into a college without a high school degree. I'm going to be a math teacher, remember?" she cried out in a choked-up voice.

"Sit down and calm down, Carla," Gio demanded with authority. He stood up as Carla obediently sat down. Gio continued in a voice and mannerism that was minus compassion or interest in her opinion. "Mom needs help with the baby. Mario, Antonia, and Virginia are too young to quit school. Vincenzo is too close to graduating to quit. It only makes sense that you would be the one to stay home to help out," Gio reasoned.

"Aunt Sofia and I decided that we are going to set up the crib in your room. You will have the responsibility to care for the baby through the night. You will take your end-of-year exams for tenth grade and not return in the fall," Gio affirmed. "Aunt Sofia will watch the baby for your last few days of school, then the baby will be your full responsibility. This decision is not up for discussion or debate. This is the order of events once the baby comes home from the hospital," Gio said in closing. After his last declaration, he turned and walked out of the room.

Carla turned and looked at Aunt Sofia. "Did my mother have any say in this decision? Does she even know that this is going to be the plan?" Carla asked her aunt.

Sofia's answer was curt. "This decision was made by your dad and I. Grace is in no frame of mind to make a decision of this importance," Sofia said with a smirk on her face.

She did not want to answer any more questions from Carla, so she quietly got up and walked out of the room to join her brother.

In early May, Gio and Sofia set up a crib and a shelf stocked with baby needs in Carla's room. The timing couldn't have been more perfect since Grace went into labor that evening. Gio drove her to the hospital, where the doctor and midwife Marino were waiting. The delivery was fast and easy, and Gio called home to tell the family that the baby was a boy. He named the baby Gio

Jr. Grace remained in the hospital a week for continued observation. Junior was healthy and released from the hospital before his mother.

When Gio carried his newborn son into the house, everyone gathered around to take a look.

"I want to hold him first," Antonia cried out.

"You are too young to hold an infant," Gio said.

Vincenzo and Mario thought he was very small and cute. They each took turns holding him, counting his fingers and toes, and rubbing their hands over his soft newborn hair. Antonia and Virginia claimed him as their live, personal baby doll. They were upset with their dad for not letting them hold or feed him like their older brothers.

Carla sat across the room, quietly staring, deep in her own thoughts. Her heart and mind were full of questions, anger, and bitterness. She wished she had an interest in this baby like Antonia and Virginia did. She was fourteen, about to finish year-end exams for tenth grade. What did she know about caring for a baby? This live baby was not a baby doll to her. He was the reason she was told she had to quit school. As far as she was concerned, all her hard work to maintain excellent grades and all her dreams of college and becoming a teacher evaporated with one simple statement: "You will quit school after your exams and will not return in the fall."

That first night having Junior in the crib beside her bed was unnerving. Carla was awake most of the night listening for sounds of him breathing and waiting for him to cry for a bottle or diaper change. He never did. He slept peacefully through the first night. Carla was used to getting up earlier than she needed to for school because she and Antonia had to care for their mother. However, Grace was still in the hospital recovering from Junior's birth. Once she realized that she really did not need to get up that early, she sat back down on the bed. She was tired from not getting any sleep. Today was exam day. Her last day of school—forever. She would go to school, take her exams, and come home. From her bed, she peeked into the crib at her tiny newborn brother. He was awake but content. Carla stood up and lifted him out of the crib. She changed his diaper and made him a bottle. She walked over to a rocker that her father and Aunt Sofia added to her room, sat down, and started feeding the baby.

"Junior," she whispered to the tiny baby in her arms. "I am angry and bitter in my heart that I had to quit school to take care of you. Mom is ill, and I have to help. Even though I was not too excited to have another child brought into this home, here you are. You are our miracle baby. Mom chose life for you, and I am so thankful for that," Carla said in a choked-up voice, remembering all too well the day she overheard her mother on the phone setting up an appointment to abort him.

"Anyway," she continued, wiping her eyes, "you will probably find this out real soon, but I know nothing about babies. I never even played with baby dolls when I was younger. So you will have to help me learn how to take care of you, okay?"

She switched the baby to her other arm, and he gave a little stir.

"I know, if Mom was home, she'd speak into your life. I listened to her do that with the others when they were first born. Mom is not home from the hospital yet, so you are stuck with me, Junior," she said with a giggle. She shifted the baby to her lap this time so she could look him straight in the face. "Junior, even though it hurts to give up my dreams and quit school to take care of you, I promise to do my best to love and care for you as your big sister. In return, you grow up and become someone important, you hear? You get your full education, marry a sweet girl, and live your life for the Lord. Your accomplishments will be my reward," Carla spoke into the tiny newborn's soul.

She was not sure if a baby this young was able to react with a smile yet; but she was positive that, when she said those words, his tiny eyes lit up, he kicked his legs, and he gave her a smile.

Carla laughed out loud at his response. "Okay then, Junior, let's get on with life."

Carla just finished feeding Junior his last bottle of the day and put him down for the night when she heard the doorbell ring.

She couldn't imagine who would be coming to the house at this late hour. The closer she got to the front door, she heard a familiar voice. She skipped down the stairs to the living room; and there stood Mr. Janson, the high school truant officer, speaking to Gio.

"I am sorry to come to your home so late, Mr. Rivia, but I got detained making other house calls," Mr. Janson said. "I am here to speak to you about your daughter Carla quitting high school," he continued. "I have spoken to all of her teachers, and they all agree that Carla should not quit her academic plan. She is a bright student and is on track to attend college," Mr. Janson went on but quickly realized that his request was falling on deaf ears.

"You can stop right there, Mr. Janson," Gio spoke up. He raised his head and squared his shoulders and spoke right into the truant officer's face. "Carla is my daughter, not yours, and I will choose whatever I need to choose for her," Gio said in a demeaning voice. He turned and put his hand on Mr. Janson's arm and led him back to the front door. "Here, let me show you out," Gio said as he escorted the visitor out the door.

Carla turned around and went back up to her room. That was all the confirmation she needed to hear. Her teachers were fighting for her to continue high school and go on to college, but her father was the dead end to her dreams.

Everyone was busy all summer. Between having a new baby in the house, Grace needing almost-round-the-clock care, and Gio and Sofia fighting off and on causing her to retreat with Vera to the attic apartment, it was a whirlwind. On the weeks Sofia moved to the attic, all the household chores fell on the children. Cleaning the house, including the windows and floors; laundry and ironing; and cooking were just a few. Gio expected the house to run as usual even though Grace and Sofia were not contributing.

Soon summer was gone, and the children started their next school year, minus Carla. It was awkward to watch them all leave for school and her stay home. It hurt to watch Vincenzo return home with schoolbooks and schoolwork while she sat feeding and burping Junior. Of all the children, watching Vincenzo affected Carla the most. He was going to graduate soon, and Carla knew that she would have been next. She could feel bitterness and resentment building in her heart and mind toward Vincenzo. She envied that he was a boy. If he was a girl and she was a boy, he would have been the one to quit school, not her. Carla could feel the jealousy, bitterness, and envy building so strong inside her that she turned to the Lord to help her gain peace over this turmoil.

The next Sunday, the pastor spoke from the book of Matthew in the Bible. The point of his sermon was, What good is money, fame, an important job, or power if you lose your soul? If you have all of these things in your earthly life but die when your heart is not right with God, you end up losing your soul for eternity to hell. Something clicked within Carla as she listened to the pastor. She felt like the message was specifically meant for her. She knew this scripture, but hearing it that day brought peace to her heart and mind.

Her dream was to go to college and gain prominence in the world of mathematics. Carla knew she excelled in math. She had since she was a young child. Her big ambition in life was to build a career to the highest level in math. Maybe if that happened, she'd get so caught up with gaining power that she'd lose her soul. Maybe it was God's will for her to stay home with Junior to feed into his life. Carla knew that her mother was too ill to do that, and recently she noticed that Aunt Sofia's character was questionable. That sermon was a turning point in her life. She decided that day to stop harboring bitterness and jealously toward Vincenzo and start cheering him on. She was at peace with staying home raising Junior.

In the fall, the truant officer from the high school returned to the Rivia home one more time. He put forth a gallant effort one more time, hoping Gio would have softened a little since the last visit. He was not there long before he realized this was a waste of time. Gio had his mind made up that Carla was the one to stay home to raise the new baby. Mr. Janson left the Rivia home for the second time, feeling defeated. All of Carla's teachers wanted her to return to school. He felt bad to have to go back to report she was signed out of school forever.

Every day since Carla quit school was the same. Her days consisted of taking care of all of Junior's needs, all the household chores, and cooking. Once the others were off to school, Aunt Sofia disappeared into her bedroom. Grace spent the majority of the day in her bed. Carla was left alone with all the household jobs and Junior.

One day, Carla was not feeling well. She went up to Aunt Sofia's bedroom and quietly knocked on the door.

"What do you want?" she heard Aunt Sofia call out from inside.

"I am not feeling well today, Aunt Sofia. Do you think you can come out and help me get my jobs completed?" Carla asked in a kind voice.

"What's the matter with you?" Aunt Sofia called back from within her room.

"It's that time of month for me, and I am in a lot of pain from cramping," she explained through the door.

"Just keep moving around, Carla," Aunt Sofia answered. "You'll feel better in no time."

Carla could not believe her answer. She slowly sat down on the floor right outside of Aunt Sofia's room. She put her head in her hands and cried. Her cramps were so bad that one of her legs was going numb. She sat there for a while, then picked herself up to continue her chores. She knew, if she didn't finish all of the jobs in the day, she would have to finish them in the evening. That would make it more difficult with caring for Junior.

She decided to start with the more involved jobs first just to get them over with. She carried three heavy tubs of water to the washing machine, scrubbed the kitchen floor on her hands and knees, and then climbed into the bathtub and scrubbed the tile from top to bottom. Next she completed the easier jobs. She ironed three baskets of shirts, set out the afternoon snacks for the children, and dusted the living room. By the time all of her chores were finished, she was shaking. Her cramps were so painful she threw herself on her bed, buried her head in her hands, and wept openly. Eventually she fell asleep from exhaustion.

An hour later, Carla was awakened by Aunt Sofia calling out her name.

"Carla, the mail is here, and you got a letter!" Aunt Sofia shouted up to Carla's room.

"A letter?" Carla questioned.

She slipped her shoes on and ran down the stairs. She had never received a letter in the mail before. Maybe it was from the school. Maybe they decided to contact her directly instead of sending the truant officer out again.

Sofia handed Carla the letter. She examined it for a clue of who sent it. There was no return address, just the letters *EG* written in the corner. It was a mystery to Carla. She brought the letter back upstairs with her to open and read in private. To her surprise, it was from a boy that she met in the church youth group. His name was Enzo. He recently joined the Civilian Conservation Corps (CCC). He was away for six months cutting down trees, making trails for electric lines. In the letter, he asked Carla if she wanted to be in correspondence with him while he was away. Carla did not hesitate. She wrote Enzo back that same evening, and the letters continued to be reciprocated well into the spring.

By the time Enzo fulfilled his duties with the CCC, Junior was almost one year old. Carla was proud to show her little brother off to Enzo. Almost every letter she sent him had something written in it about Junior. Enzo was excited to meet the little guy Carla talked so much about. Once he had the chance to meet him, he understood. Enzo thought Junior was special. He also thought the same thing about Carla. That night, he told her so, and she agreed to date him.

One evening, when Enzo came over to date Carla, she was in the middle of feeding Junior. Enzo waited patiently for her to finish feeding him and then carry him upstairs to put him down for the evening. The couple decided to visit for a while longer. They sat on the couch in the living room and talked about the past and the future. It was getting late, and Carla knew she would have to be up early the next morning with the baby. She said goodbye to Enzo at the front door and made her way upstairs to bed. As she passed Aunt Sofia's room, she heard a man's voice inside. Carla stopped and listened closer. The man's voice sounded like her father's voice. Carla decided to walk down the hallway to her parents' bedroom. The door was ajar. She peeked inside. Her mother was sound asleep on her side of the bed, but her father's side was empty.

The next morning, Carla waited until Aunt Sofia was busy downstairs getting the children ready for school before she went to speak to her mother. Carla tapped lightly on the bedroom door.

"Come on in," Grace responded in her mumbled speech.

Carla found her mother sitting up in bed.

"Good morning, Mom," Carla began.

Grace returned a weak smile.

"Last night, after Enzo left, I heard Dad in Aunt Sofia's room," Carla said, not wasting any time to get right to the point. "I wanted to be sure it was Dad, so I peeked into your room, and he was not in bed. His side of the bed was empty," Carla continued.

She waited for a response from her mother. She could tell by her face that she was not telling her something that she didn't already know. Finally Grace spoke.

"Your father has been leaving our bed to go to her room since I came home from the hospital after having Junior," Grace began.

"But," Carla interrupted her mother, "that's almost a year now." "You've known all along?" she asked her mother.

"At first, I wasn't sure where he was going. I would call out to him when I heard him getting up, but he would ignore me. When this first started happening, he would only leave our bed once in a while, and he would only be gone a few hours. Now he leaves our bed almost every night, and most of the time, he is gone until early morning. He sneaks back into bed about an hour before he has to get up for work. He has no idea I know. He thinks I am sound asleep," Grace explained to her oldest daughter.

"How did you figure he was going to Aunt Sofia's room?" Carla asked next for clarification.

"One night, Sofia came to our room seeking him out. She walked into our bedroom and went to Dad's side of the bed. She thought I was asleep, so she was whispering, but I could hear her. She whispered to him that she was ready for him now and invited him to her room," Grace said in a choked-up voice.

She put her hands over her eyes as if, if she covered them, she wouldn't be able to see images of what was happening in her head. She started to tear up. Carla did not ask any more questions until her mother regained her composure.

Carla refused to watch her father and Aunt Sofia add this emotional pain to her mother's life. After all the physical challenges she had to endure, there was no way she was going to sit back and have her mother endure this additional pain. Carla abruptly stood up.

"I am going downstairs right now to speak to her and tell her how sorry I am that she ever came to our home," Carla said in a determined voice.

"Wait, please wait, Carla," Grace called out to her. "Please don't go confront Sofia," Grace insisted. "This is not your battle to fight. Let it go," Grace continued. "I might not be able to walk or talk right anymore. I might not be young and strong like I used to be. But one thing I can do is pray," Grace said as she stopped and put her head in her hands and started tearing up again.

"What do you think I do up here in this bedroom all day long? I'm praying for my six children downstairs. I call each of you out by name before the Lord, and I pray that God will have mercy on all of you for not having a healthy mother. I pray God's grace covers each of you and rewards you with an adult life filled with love, joy, and prosperity, an adult life so richly deserved after growing up in this house with an invalid mother and deceptive father and aunt," Grace said, looking straight into Carla's dark eyes.

When she continued talking, she diverted her eyes and said, "I pray for your father and Sofia too. God reminded me that, what you sow, you reap," Grace got quiet and took a long, slow breath. "The battle is the Lord's, Carla. They are sowing something wrong. You let the Lord take care of the reaping."

It was difficult for Carla to remain quiet and not say anything the next time she bumped into Aunt Sofia, but out of respect for her mother, she remained silent. She went about her business taking care of Junior and checking off household chores from her list of duties. The day passed without event, and soon Gio returned from work. He waited for everyone to be seated at the dinner table before he announced that he was looking to buy a summer home at Lake Carlyle. All the children shouted with glee. Their summers would be filled with swimming, boating, water skiing, and fishing.

"If everything goes as planned, I should be the owner of the property by next month. That means that, when you children get out of school for the summer, we will have a summer home," Gio said with a smile.

This news brought another round of celebration. Everyone was shouting and laughing and imagining all the summer fun they would be having at the lake. To Gio's expectations, the deal went through, and the whole family enjoyed all the summer fun Lake Carlyle had to offer. The children learned how to swim. Mario learned how to run a motorboat, and Virginia learned how to fish.

As the years went by, the older children stopped going to the lake during the summers. Vincenzo graduated high school and joined the US Navy. Carla took advantage of the break from watching Junior and doing housework with everyone gone. Plus, she didn't want to leave Enzo since they were now engaged to be married. And Mario was involved in church activities with Julia.

One evening in early June, Gio, Grace, Sofia, and the younger children returned from the lake. Carla was in the kitchen fixing herself some dinner. She heard the front door open and saw Aunt Sofia and Gio carrying in beach bags full of wet swimsuits and towels. Virginia was carrying in the fishing poles, with Junior close behind trying to help her, while Antonia helped Grace get up the stairs. Carla stayed quiet in the kitchen, where no one could see her, eager to give herself a few more minutes of relaxation before having to help them sort out all the beach gear. She was just about to start eating her soup and sandwich when she saw Aunt Sofia motion Gio to meet her in the laundry room. That was all Carla needed to see. She immediately lost her appetite. She didn't care if she promised her mother or not; she couldn't stay silent any longer. She decided to confront her aunt tonight.

Carla strategically waited for the right time. She knew that Aunt Sofia would not go to Gio's room to get him until she thought Grace was sound asleep. As soon as Aunt Sofia was in her bedroom for the night, Carla tapped on her door.

"Who is it?" Sofia called out.

"Carla" was all she said.

Sofia came to the door. "What do you need, Carla?" Sofia asked.

"I need you to leave my father alone," Carla said, jumping right into the conversation. "I know what you are doing with my father, and so does my mother. You think, just because my mother is not well, that she is dumb. Well, guess what? She is smarter than you will ever be," Carla said with distain. "I wish you never came to our house. You came to help my father out when we were little children, but you outstayed your welcome," Carla proclaimed.

At first, Sofia just stared at Carla and did not say a word. Then she started in. "Who do you think you are to speak to an adult this way?" she began. "You wait until your father hears about this disrespect. You wait until he hears how you are speaking to me after all that I have done for you and this family. If it wasn't for me, you'd still be wearing those green-brown stockings you were wearing when I first arrived," Sofia said with a condescending smirk on her face.

"You were supposed to come here to help us out, not help yourself to our father," Carla said in a staccato voice.

With that, Sofia reached out and grabbed her by the arm. She ushered Carla out of her bedroom. She was happy to leave. She said what was needed to be said.

The next morning, the family was surprised to see four suitcases packed and waiting at the front door. Overnight Aunt Sofia and Vera decided to go back to New York for a short while. When asked why she was making the visit, Sofia informed the family that she was invited to visit New York as a missionary on assignment to the streets of the city. Everyone stood confused at the sudden decision to leave, but they congratulated her anyway—everyone but Carla. She was the only one who knew the real reason why she was making the move in haste.

Carla and Enzo saw Aunt Sofia's sudden visit to New York as a window of opportunity to get married. Neither one of them wanted Sofia to attend their wedding. Enzo approached Gio, asking for his blessing.

"You have my blessing, Enzo," Gio began. "But be sure Carla understands one thing. If she leaves, there's no returning," he clarified in a stern voice.

Enzo and Carla got married in late June. It was a simple ceremony held in front of the brick fireplace in the living room of the house on Chicago Avenue. Before the wedding began, Carla went to her mother's bedroom to show her the dress and flowers Enzo bought for her.

"You look lovely, Carla," Grace said in her slurred speech. "My prayer for you is that you and Enzo stay close to the Lord all the days of your life together. God will help you through any trials. This has been my prayer for you as I lay here in this bed each day," Grace continued.

Carla bend down and thanked her mother for her well-wishes. She gave her a kiss on the cheek and told her that she loved her.

Grace remained upstairs in her bedroom during the ceremony. Enzo and Carla promised their love to one another until the day the Lord took them home. They held hands, and Enzo kissed the bride in front of family and a few friends. They had no honeymoon, but that didn't matter to either of them, especially Carla. She couldn't wait to get out of the house and away from Aunt Sofia.

The newlywed couple moved into a small converted apartment on the upper floor of someone's home. It had a bedroom, living room, bathroom, and a makeshift kitchen. The kitchen had a stove and refrigerator but no sink. Carla set up a card table in the middle of the room to use for a kitchen table. After using the table to eat their meals, Carla used it as her sink top. She would carry tubs of water from the bathtub to the kitchen, then set the tub on the card table to wash dishes. She and Enzo had many laughs about their new lifestyle. They told everyone that their new lifestyle was called camping!

The day after the wedding, Carla returned to her family home to gather a few more things and to visit with her mother, sisters, and brothers. When she entered the house, Aunt Sofia was sitting on the couch in the living room.

"Well, your trip as a missionary to the streets of New York sure was short," Carla said with a chuckle in her throat.

Aunt Sofia ignored her sarcastic comment and threw one right back at her. "I heard you got married here last night. I can't help but notice your swollen belly. Did you have to get married, Carla? It sure looks that way to me," Aunt Sofia said with a serious face.

Carla quickly gathered the items she came after and left the house. She was so upset she did not go to her mother's room to say hello, and she did not see her sisters and brothers. She couldn't get out of the house fast enough. When she got back to her little apartment, Enzo could see that Carla was upset. She stormed into the house and passed by Enzo as if he was invisible. She stomped her way to their bedroom and dumped the big armload of items she was carrying on their bed. He could hear her mumbling to herself but could not understand what she was saying. He thought it best to not ask. He decided to go sit in the living room to wait for her to calm down. He was making his way to the couch when he heard her call out to him in an unrecognizable, stern voice.

"I didn't want to have children for a very long time."

Confused as to where this statement was coming from, Enzo made a puzzling look but stayed quiet. "Okay" was all he responded. He knew eventually Carla would tell him the story.

Carla finally calmed down and told Enzo the whole story. He was as upset as she was when he heard that Aunt Sofia accused Carla of being pregnant and having to get married. Now Enzo understood why Carla said what she said about waiting to have children. She felt waiting years would prove Aunt Sofia wrong.

Carla was thankful that Enzo understood and agreed to the plan for their future.

The weekend was productive. Carla and Enzo went to church for the first time as a married couple. She was able to find a place in the small apartment for all the items she brought over from her family home, and she hung some pictures here and there to add character to the small space. It was a beautiful Monday. Carla decided to pull back all the draperies and open all the windows in the apartment to enjoy the fresh June day. She was almost done opening the windows when the phone rang.

"Hello," Carla answered.

"Carla," she heard Mario's shaking voice on the other end of the line. "There's been an accident. Dad and the family were on their way to the summer home in Lake Carlyle when they got in a crash," Mario cried out. "Mom is really in bad shape," he said.

Carla held the phone to her ear but did not speak. She was processing all that Mario just said to her.

Finally she responded, "What happened?"

"Apparently the driver in the car in front of them stopped abruptly. To avoid hitting the car, Dad swerved to the left, into oncoming traffic, and another car hit them head-on. All the doors flew open at the impact. Dad, Antonia, and Junior remained in the car, but everyone else flew out. Dad is okay. Antonia was in the back seat with Junior on her lap. They both passed out, and Junior remained knocked out all the way to the hospital in the ambulance. Antonia has a pretty bad gash on her shoulder from broken glass, but Junior was protected by Antonia's body covering him.

"Aunt Sofia and Vera were in the front seat with Dad. They flew out and ended up in the middle of the street. Aunt Sofia has broken ribs, and Vera is shaken but only has some small cuts and bruises. Virginia flew out too but is okay. Mom got the worst of the injuries. She flew out, tumbled on the road several times, and landed under a parked car. She has broken ribs, a broken leg, and cuts on her head. The doctors want to keep Aunt Sofia overnight in the hospital," Mario reported to his sister. "Mom will have to stay a much longer period of time."

"Oh, Mario, I need to go help until things are better," Carla said with a choked-up voice.

"Yes, we will all help out in any way we can," Mario said in a sad, loyal voice.

Carla and Mario were there to help the day Aunt Sofia came home from the hospital. She was moving slowly but was in good spirits, and they knew she would recover quickly. Grace was hospitalized for one month. Her recovery process was much different. She had a cast on her leg, which limited her mobility even more than usual. She was noticeably more withdrawn. She never joined in any conversation, and she never smiled. She remained silent as if she was in her own world—far, far away in thought.

Antonia would periodically bring happy little Junior up to her room, thinking that might cheer her up. It didn't. She remained stonewalled. She was not interested in anything. It was clear to the whole family that she was in a state of depression. They thought she may still have been shaken from the trauma of the accident, but as time progressed, they realized it was more than that. She was both physically and mentally not improving.

At the sixth-week doctor's visit after the accident, Grace had the cast removed from her leg. Everyone was excited to see the cast come off in the hope that she would regain some mobility and snap out of her depression. However, when the doctor asked her to stand, she was not able to weight bear. This appointment led to several other appointments with various specialists and physical therapists all evaluating Grace's issue. The more appointments she was scheduled for, the more depressed she became. After allotting Grace a reasonable amount of time to improve, the doctor reviewed the notes from his colleagues, conducted a final examination himself, and determined that, with the particular way the cast had to be put on her broken leg, nerves were pulled. He declared Grace's leg as being permanently damaged with no hope of rejuvenation. The doctor marked her file invalid, and Grace was put in a wheelchair. From that point on, she lost all independence. She had to be lifted in and out of the bathtub, off and on the toilet and bed, and in and out of the car. With these new demands put on the family, Sofia kept suggesting that Grace go to a nursing home.

"Gio, now that Carla is married and out of the house, how am I going to take care of Grace by myself all day long? I can barely lift her," Sofia said, confronting her brother one day.

"I will not put her in a nursing home. I will figure out something else," Gio replied in a stern voice.

Sofia backed off for a while and stopped asking Gio to put Grace in a nursing home. She did not want him to be upset with her, and she did not want to go back up to the attic apartment with Vera either. She knew he would think of something; he always did.

The family had a short break from all the depressing and stressful situations at home when Vincenzo announced he was getting married. He was in his twenties now and out of the service and met a sweet girl at church. Her name was Bianca, and when he asked her to marry him, she said yes.

"Vincenzo, what a coincidence that we would be married in the same year," Carla said to him when she found out about his proposal.

"Yes, I guess we'll never forget each other's anniversary," Vincenzo replied with a smile and chuckle.

The wedding was simple but sweet. Colorful, fragrant flowers were strategically placed around the room. Happy music filled the air, making people laugh, dance, and catch up with old friends they hadn't seen in a long time. The homemade food was delicious, and the cake was mouthwatering. Friends and family agreed that the light, carefree day was a much-needed oasis in the midst of illness, depression, frustration, and stress.

At the end of that year, the war broke out, and Mario enlisted in the 882nd Airborne Engineer Aviation Battalion. His job was to go to airstrips to prepare for planes to come in. He was sad to say goodbye to family and friends and especially Julia. He knew that, if God wanted him to end up with her someday, God would work out all the details. In the meantime, even with going away on assignment and all, Mario continued to diligently pray that God would reveal to him his bride.

A few days before Mario had to leave Briarton, he decided to spend some time alone with Junior. It did not bother Mario that Junior was more than a decade younger than him; he loved him. He didn't just want to tell him that he loved him. He wanted to show him through some sort of action. Mario thought Junior was adorable and funny too. He decided to take him for a ride in his car to get some ice cream. Junior loved ice cream and was more than willing to get away from all of his sisters to go with his older brother.

Mario had Junior sit in the back seat as he drove. They reached the ice-cream parlor. Mario told Junior to pick out any flavored ice cream he wanted, and they ate it right there in the shop. Again Mario got Junior situated in the back seat of his car and started driving home. They were almost back home when Mario heard the back seat door open. The outside air rushed into the car from the wide-open space that the door once covered. He jerked his neck around to see what was going on. Junior was not in the back seat. He yanked the steering wheel to the right and parked the car in the grass along the road.

"Junior!" Mario shouted as he ejected his body out from behind the wheel.

He looked back down the road and saw him sitting among some tall grass.

"What in the world happened, Junior?" Mario asked as he trotted back to where the small boy was sitting.

He reached down and drew his brother up in his shaking arms. Then he lowered him back down in the tall grass and sat next to him.

"Are you okay?"

"Yes, Mario, I'm okay. I wanted to come up in the front seat to sit by you," Junior explained.

The brothers sat in the tall grass for a long time. Mario tried explaining to Junior that he was going away to serve his country in the war. He cried as he tried to make this big life-altering experience sound unimportant and simple so that his little brother could understand. Mario promised to write to Junior to check up on him; but he knew, even with corresponding regularly, when he returned home, things would be different. His little brother would be much older. Being away, he would miss many firsts of his brother's young life. And he would return a grown man.

Mario frequently received mail from home. He was writing to Julia and three other ladies. All came from good families and wrote very well. He enjoyed receiving their letters. He promptly wrote back so that, before long, he would receive another letter. He continued praying that God would direct his path ahead and show him which one would be his bride.

He also received letters from family too. One day, he received a letter from Vincenzo announcing that he and Bianca were expecting their first baby. With all the talk of war around him, he was excited to receive some happy news. He wrote his older brother back, congratulating them on the baby.

However, around the time Mario was expecting to hear of the birth of the baby, tragic news arrived. Bianca had complications during the baby's birth and died in childbirth. Their little baby girl died too. Bianca and the baby were buried together in the same casket. He could hear the anguish in his brother's letter, and it was difficult to console him from far away. Mario was heartbroken for Vincenzo and all the family involved. He sent his brother a letter of sympathy but encouragement too. He reminded Vincenzo that God promised to be a strong tower for anyone that ran to Him. In Vincenzo's sorrow, it sounded like he wanted to run from God. Mario reminded him that, in this tragic time filled with hurt, confusion, and fear, God would be his strong tower of safety if he would only run to Him.

Mario could barely keep his mind on his duties for thinking of the pain going on at home. It was so difficult to be this far away when everything felt like it was falling apart. He hated feeling helpless. To make matters worse, he received a letter from Carla informing him that their mother's health was progressively getting worse. Aunt Sofia was getting more and more frustrated with taking care of Grace, and she was taking out her frustration on anyone around her. She was unbearable to live with. Carla reported that

BRENDA HELTON

their dad was doing everything he could think of to keep Aunt Sofia happy. Now that their mother was an invalid and bedridden, he needed her to stay to help out.

Back home, Gio finally felt that he had the solution to the problem. He wanted to run his idea past Sofia before he made his announcement to the family. He called Sofia into the kitchen late one evening to share his plan with her. His plan sounded wonderful to her. She was relieved and excited. They decided to share the solution with the children after they came home from school the next day. Both Gio and Sofia rested well that evening. The solution to the problem was made and agreed upon.

The next afternoon, Gio came home from work early. He wanted to be home when the children arrived to make the big announcement. Gio and Sofia watched out the front window for the children. Once they were in sight, Gio noticed three boys circling around Antonia. She was talking and laughing with them. Virginia and Vera were walking beside her. Once she reached the front door, Aunt Sofia reached out and slapped Antonia across the face.

"Now I know why your grades are so bad in school," she started without any explanation. "You are only interested in the boys. Your father and I watched you walking home with three of them. You sure looked like you were enjoying yourself with them," she accused shy, timid Antonia.

"Those boys are our friends," Antonia began. "They are not my boyfriends. They live down the street. That's why they were walking with us," Antonia continued.

"Sit down, all of you," Gio demanded. "This is the perfect time to make the family announcement Aunt Sofia and I have been waiting to make," Gio said, clearing his throat. "Next week is your last week of school for the year. After next week"—Gio paused and looked directly at Antonia—"you, Antonia, will not be returning to school. Aunt Sofia and I agreed on a solution to the situation involving your mom. You have had enough schooling to quit. You will finish ninth grade, and then you will stay home to help take care of Junior and any care Mom would need. You have

190

missed a lot of school anyway due to your respiratory problems. Your grades are not good, and all you are interested in is boys, as you just proved to us," Gio said all in one breath.

Antonia sat at the end of the couch in a fetal position. Her eyes were wide, and she held her hand over the red spot on her cheek where Aunt Sofia slapped her. She could not believe her ears. First, Carla; now her? It was important for Vincenzo and Mario to complete school but not Carla and her? She was glad no one could see how badly she was shaking. She felt like she had a hurricane going on inside of her gut. She decided to stay quiet. She learned from Carla that her rebuttal would make the decision worse. When her father and Aunt Sofia were finished with their announcement, she calmly walked to her room, closed the door, and wept.

The next day at school, Antonia told her teacher that she would not be returning to school for tenth grade. She explained the situation at home with her mother and little brother that was not yet school age.

"Antonia, I am so sorry to hear this news. I know how badly you wanted to complete school to be a beautician," the teacher said with sad eyes.

She noticed Antonia dropped her chin down to her chest in defeat and embarrassment. The teacher gently lifted Antonia's chin up so that they were eye to eye.

"You make sure that you are here at school on the very last day, okay? We will be taking a group picture. I want you to be in that final school picture, Antonia," the teacher said with tenderness in her voice. Then she bent down and gently whispered in her ear, "I want you standing right next to me."

The truant officer came to the house to encourage her father to change his mind. The following week, he came again. Antonia's classroom teacher called her home to explain to Gio that Antonia had a dream for her future and she deserved to see it fulfilled. Even Carla tried to convince her father that Antonia needed school more than any of them. All opinions fell on deaf ears. Gio made up his mind that completing ninth grade was enough schooling for his daughter. End of discussion.

Antonia did not feel the magnitude of change in her newly assigned lifestyle until fall rolled around and Virginia and Vera returned to school. On the morning of their first day back, Antonia sat quietly on the upstairs steps watching. Aunt Sofia stood in her usual position at the front door handing out school lunches as the children said goodbye on their way out the door. Antonia felt a twinge of jealously and bitterness spear her heart. She should be heading out the door to school with them. This was supposed to be her first day of high school. This should have been an exciting big day for her. Instead she was stuck home doing housework and caring for her four-year-old brother and her bedridden mother.

She closed her eyes and drew in a long, deep breath. She knew what she was harboring in her heart was wrong. She wanted to stop these thoughts and feelings before they festered and got out of control. She folded her hands, bowed her head, and started to pray.

"Lord, this is a tough day. I should be going to my first day of high school. Instead I am stuck here. I choose not to be jealous of my school friends that have that opportunity this morning. I choose not to be bitter in my heart. I choose to be thankful because I have You in my life to fill my heart's emptiness. Please be my closest friend. Please take these jealous and bitter thoughts away and fill those spots with Your love and grace," Antonia prayed as tears ran down her face. "God, cover me with Your grace as I begin this new lifestyle today. I promise to always be faithful to You, Lord. And I know You, in return, will be faithful to me all the days of my life. Amen."

She took a few minutes to collect herself before reaching in her pocket to review the list of jobs Aunt Sofia wrote down for her to complete by the end of the day.

"First things first," she said to herself as she stood up and walked to the kitchen to prepare breakfast for her mother.

When she got there, she saw that Aunt Sofia was already in the kitchen feeding Junior.

"When you carry up the breakfast tray to your mom, be sure to stay up there and finish all of the jobs I listed on the paper before coming back down to complete the jobs down here," Aunt Sofia directed.

"Yes, I will," answered Antonia.

"And," Aunt Sofia added, "make sure that, when you wash the metal blinds on the windows of the main floor today, you wash each slat separately. I will check your work this evening."

Antonia looked at the long list of jobs listed on the paper. She knew that she better get busy right away in order to be finished by the time Virginia and Vera got home from school. Aunt Sofia demanded that, if she didn't get the list of jobs done by afternoon, she'd have to complete them after dinner hours until every job was checked off. Tomorrow she would get a new list of chores. Aunt Sofia warned her not to get behind.

She carried up her mother's breakfast tray and, hearing Aunt Sofia's instructions ringing in her ears, stayed upstairs until all the jobs were completed. She reached for her list and quickly checked off "feed Mom," "empty bedpan," "sponge bathe Mom," "strip bed of soiled sheets," "put clean sheets on bed," and "dress Mom for the day." On her way back downstairs, she walked by Aunt Sofia's bedroom door and could hear her moving about in her room.

She went downstairs to complete her chores on the main floor. She started with feeding Junior his lunch. After she was finished, she put him down for his nap. While he slept, she got busy completing the downstairs chores. Several hours later, Antonia pulled the list back out of her pocket and checked off "dust and vacuum the whole downstairs," "scrub the bathroom and kitchen floors," "wash laundry and sheets," "wash the metal blinds on the downstairs windows," and "get dinner started."

As she checked off the list, she noticed blood smearing on the paper. She looked closely at her hand and realized that the sharp metal of the blinds must have cut her fingers when she was washing them. She was too tired to search for ointment or Band-Aids. She decided to drag herself upstairs to wash up a bit and maybe relax for a few minutes before Virginia and Vera came home from school.

Antonia took her time washing up at the bathroom sink, letting the cool water and sweet-smelling soap run down her face and arms. She gently patted herself dry, relishing the few minutes she had to pamper herself. She quietly walked to her bedroom and was about to lie down for a few minutes when she heard Junior waking up from his nap. By the time she got him settled and happy playing with toys, the girls came home looking for their after-school snack. Even though she was exhausted, she jumped right in to take care of the girls.

After all, Antonia thought to herself, *this is my new lifestyle. I might as well get used to it.*

Every day after that first day was a repeat of the last for Antonia: wash, scrub, dust, cook, watch over Junior, and care for her mother's needs. Aunt Sofia's daily routine was to hand out the school lunches at the front door each morning and feed Junior his breakfast. After that, she would head back upstairs, where she would close herself in her bedroom for the rest of the day. She came back out for dinner. Antonia's jobs ended for the day after she fed everyone their dinner and the kitchen was sparkling clean, ready for the next day.

Each day was loaded with daily jobs that needed completed. Antonia was so busy that the following days and months ticked by quickly. Her priorities were her mother and Junior. With the exception of some bedsores that had to be tended to by a visiting nurse, Grace was stable. Junior was happy and well taken care of. Antonia observed that he was much taller than any of the children his age in the neighborhood. He had thick dark hair, a big smile, and a contagious laugh. Antonia thought he was adorable. His presence brought joy to her heart and a smile to her face. Before long, it was time to enroll Junior in school.

"Antonia," Aunt Sofia called out one morning, "would you take Junior to the doctor for his enrollment physical and shots?"

"Yes, Aunt Sofia, I'll do that for you," Antonia obediently answered.

After his appointment, she walked him to the school to enroll him for kindergarten. The night before Junior's first day of school, Antonia could barely sleep. She peeked in on Junior as he was sleeping. He seemed to be doing fine. No signs of anxiety or unrest. Why was she so nervous? She tried falling asleep, but soon the room was filled with the signs of dawn. She gave up on rest. Antonia walked to Junior's room and woke the sleepy kindergartener up.

"Time for your first day of school, Junior," Antonia announced in a cheery voice.

Junior tumbled out of bed. Antonia had his outfit pressed and sitting out on the dresser. She dressed him in a stylish outfit, helped him tie his polished black shoes, greased his hair back, and proudly walked him to school.

When she returned home, Aunt Sofia was already upstairs in her bedroom. Antonia went to check in on her mother. She was sound asleep in her bed. She sat on the bottom step of the main stairway leading to the upstairs and pulled her daily chore list out of her pocket—vacuum, dust, scrub the bathroom floor, wipe down the metal blinds in every room of the house, and wash the walls in the kitchen. She was exhausted just reading the list. She was sad that Junior was not home to brighten her day. His smile and funny expressions interrupted her dull lifestyle.

Aunt Sofia and her mother were upstairs in their bedrooms. Her older siblings were grown and out of the house, and the younger ones were at school. She had no one to talk to. She had nothing in common with the kids her age; they were all in high school. Antonia quickly turned off those thoughts running through her head. She stood up and reminded herself that, if she didn't get started on all these chores, she'd be completing them well into the evening hours. She quickly went to the supply closet and pulled out a bucket and some rags.

"Just another boring day," she whispered to herself as she turned on the vacuum cleaner.

A few months into the school year, Antonia received a call from Junior's kindergarten teacher.

"May I speak to your mother, please?" requested the teacher.

"May I ask what this is about? My mother is not able to come to the phone," Antonia responded.

"I am calling to inform you that Junior is having difficulty following directions in school. He refuses to take his midday nap because he is assigned a mat next to a girl. Therefore, he is disruptive during nap time, and the others are not able to rest," the teacher explained.

"I am so sorry to hear this," Antonia said. "I will be sure to speak to him."

"There is one more issue," the teacher continued. "It is a requirement at the kindergarten level that all students drink prune juice with their snack. Students are not permitted to get milk until first grade. Junior gets quite upset when handed his prune juice. He wants milk. He acts out and becomes quite verbal about this. His actions disrupt the class," the teacher reported.

"I will speak to him about these matters today," Antonia said in a sweet voice. "I will also pass this information on to my mother.

Later that day, Junior was questioned about this report. He confessed that all was true. He promised to cooperate with the teacher and the school rules for kindergarten. However, a few weeks later, the teacher called the house again. This time, Aunt Sofia spoke to Junior about his offenses. Again he promised to correct his ways. A few weeks later, Junior walked into the house early from school.

"What are you doing home so early, Junior?" Antonia asked her little brother.

"I quit!" he responded, making an ugly, scrunched-up face.

"Quit? What do you mean you quit?" Antonia asked Junior.

"I don't like school, and I'm not going back!" Junior shouted as he ran out of the room.

That evening, after dinner, Gio and Aunt Sofia spoke with Junior and decided to keep him home for the rest of the year. After all, it was only kindergarten, Gio poorly reasoned.

Antonia was happy to have Junior home. He was company for her as she completed all of her household chores. Junior would play on the steps or go up into the finished attic area and play with his toys all by himself. Oftentimes Antonia would hear him playing ball or see him sitting at the kitchen table drawing with his imaginary friends. This concerned her, but when she asked her father if Junior could have some neighbor friends over to play with him during the day, the idea was shot down. Gio did not want neighborhood friends in the house.

"Let him continue to play with his imaginary friends. They'll keep the house cleaner," Gio answered with a chuckle.

Christmas was approaching fast, and all the kids were excited. Gio and Sofia promised them gifts this year if they were good. The anticipation of Christmas gifts was too much for Junior to handle. He decided to go snooping around in Aunt Sofia's room while she was busy downstairs in the kitchen. He was sure he saw her sneak into her room with shopping bags a while ago. He entered quietly even though he knew she was nowhere around. First he checked her closet. Nothing. Next he checked under her bed. Nothing again. Finally he checked her drawer. There he found a colorful box. He slowly lifted off the lid and found a red-and-black Mickey Mouse watch. He jumped up and down and covered his mouth with his hand to be sure that no sound escaped. He quietly replaced the lid and carefully put it back in her drawer.

"Vincenzo, Mario, guess what!" Junior shouted with glee to his brothers. "I'm getting a red-and-black Mickey Mouse watch for Christmas. I saw it in Aunt Sofia's room," Junior reported.

Junior could not wait for Christmas morning. The days leading up to the holiday felt like years for the young boy. Finally Christmas morning arrived. Junior was handed his gift. The wrapped box was the same size as the box he found in Aunt Sofia's room days ago. He knew it was his Mickey watch. As he unwrapped his gift, he silently reminded himself to act surprised when he lifted the lid. He didn't want anyone to know that he had snooped and already knew his gift. However, he soon realized he didn't need to act. He lifted the lid of the small box to see the contents filled with coal. His jaw dropped to his chest, and he looked up at his dad.

"That's what you get for snooping," Gio said. "You will not receive a gift this year."

Junior hung his head. Tears filled his eyes.

"Don't you cry like a girl now, Junior," Gio said.

He knew he was bad.

Having Junior home during the rest of his kindergarten year made the days go by faster for Antonia. Every chance she had, she sent Junior outside to play with a neighborhood girl. She'd watch from the window as the little girl taught Junior to roller-skate and share her scooter with him. She noticed that, once Junior was interacting with the neighbor girl, his imaginary friends slowly disappeared.

By the time Junior entered first grade, Antonia was ready to have him in school all day. However, it was not long into the school year before calls from the teacher and principal started ringing into the house. Several of the calls from the teacher were in regard to Junior not being adequately prepared for first grade. He missed too much of his kindergarten year and was academically behind his peers. He didn't know all his alphabet, numbers, colors, or shapes. He was disruptive in class and had difficulty following directions. Then, one day, the principal called. Aunt Sofia took the call.

"I am calling to report that Junior punched another first grader today for fighting over a coat hook in the cloakroom. He declared the coat hook was his when it really belonged to the other boy. Junior punched him in the face, and the teacher sent him to see me in the office," the principal reported.

"Oh my, is the little boy, okay?" Sofia responded.

"Yes, he had a bloody nose, but I think he will be fine," the principal told Sofia. "I wanted you to know that, as a punishment, I had Junior bend over the table in my office, and I paddled him two times," the principal continued to report. "I'm sure you realize that his sister Virginia was a student in my elementary school a while ago. I remember her well. She was a lovely, sweet young lady. We never had an issue with her. I am sad to report that Junior is not as easy as Virginia," the principal said in a disgusted tone.

"I am sorry to hear all the trouble Junior is having in school," Sofia said. "We will do better at home to help him catch up and to help him understand the importance of behaving in school," Sofia exclaimed in a confident voice.

Antonia was listening to the conversation from another room. She was happy to hear that Aunt Sofia realized how much attention Junior needed in order to be successful in school and that she was willing to help him catch up to his peers. However, Antonia soon realized that it was all talk. Junior never was told that the principal called the home. He never received any help from an adult with his homework, reading, spelling, or math in order to catch up. No adult ever attended a parent conference.

Junior was aware that no adult cared about his schooling, so why should he? He barely made it through first grade, and besides having a pretty young teacher for second grade, it was a repeat of first. Junior failed third grade. A combination of no support or interest in his schooling from the adults at home and attention-seeking, mischievous behavior in class—from untying the teacher's shoes from under her desk to shooting spit wads—led to a sad, confused little boy. He was told he was dumb and a crybaby and would never amount to anything so often he started to believe what he was told.

All summers between school years were spent at the lake. The family would leave for Lake Carlyle in the afternoon on the last day of school and return a few days before school began in the fall. Grace was totally bedridden by that summer, so Gio decided to buy an old trailer and park it next to the cottage. During the evening hours, Gio would wheel Grace over to the trailer, get her settle in her bed, and return to the cottage, where he slept. Grace slept in the trailer by herself. She wondered if Gio was sleeping alone in the cottage.

In the fall, Grace had to spend a few weeks out of each month in a nursing home for medical staff to tend to her bedsores. Due to her silent mothering, Junior saw Aunt Sofia as his mother. He called her Sitzie. Gio continued retreating to Aunt Sofia's bedroom from time to time to maintain an adult lifestyle. Vincenzo met a wonderful new woman named Ada and was planning to marry her. Carla was happily married to Enzo. They finally moved from the tiny upstairs apartment and into a home. After four years of marriage, they finally decided to start a family.

Mario finally made his decision on a wife. After writing to four women during his years in the service, Mario felt God was telling him that Julia was to be his wife. When he arrived home from the service and saw that she decorated the whole front yard of her home with welcome-home signs, banners, and streamers just for him, that sealed the deal. He asked her to marry him. Virginia was doing well in high school. She was planning on attending college once she graduated. Antonia was now seventeen. It should have been her senior year. Instead she completed chores from a list drawn up by her aunt while her aunt relaxed in her bedroom all day.

In December, Antonia got a call from her cousin Camilla.

"Antonia, would you and Virginia like to attend a Christmas party this Saturday night?" Camilla asked. "Vera is going with Andrew Ricci, and I asked his brother, Lewis, to go with me. Lewis just returned from the army. It will be fun. There will be music, wine, and dancing. Would you like to come?" Camilla continued.

It did not take Antonia long to decide. She had such a dull, boring life it sounded like a lot of upbeat fun.

"Sure, Camilla, we'd love to attend," Antonia answered.

Antonia took a look in her closet and decided to wear a black velvet skirt with a white lace blouse. She added a thin red sash to her waist for a more festive look. She decided to wear her black velvet heels and a black velvet clutch purse. She looked in the mirror and approved of what she saw. Virginia wore a green party dress with silver shoes and purse. She added a hair bow and some simple jewelry. Even though Vera and Camilla had dates, Antonia and Virginia were very excited to attend. They were happy that Camilla thought to invite them.

The party was booming when they arrived. The music was loud, and the whiskey and wine were flowing. Antonia and Virginia took a seat at a table by themselves. Most of the guests were dancing on the big wooden dance floor or standing around drinking. Antonia looked around the room for Camilla and Vera.

"There they are, Antonia!" Virginia shouted to her sister over the loud music. "Looks like Vera and Camilla have had too much to drink already," Virginia continued.

Antonia looked in the direction that Virginia pointed. Just as she spotted them, she caught eyes with Lewis, Camilla's date. He nodded his head at Antonia and gave a big smile. She returned the smile. She hadn't seen Lewis since he went into the army. He was eight years older than her, so that made her only thirteen when he enlisted. So much had happened to her between thirteen and seventeen. She had so many adult responsibilities now and had matured beyond measure. Lewis thought so too.

It wasn't long before Lewis approached her.

"Why don't you come over here and sit on my lap, Antonia?" Lewis invited.

"Camilla is your date. Won't that be rude?" Antonia asked with a timid voice and a blushed red face.

"She won't mind. She's drunk. I'm not interested in that kind of girl," Lewis spoke from his heart. "When I saw you come into the room, you looked like an angel. I would like to get to know you better," Lewis said.

While Antonia and Lewis sat together for the rest of the party, Camilla kept herself busy flirting and dancing. She was loud and animated. Every once in a while, she'd let out an obnoxious laugh that almost sounded like a scream. Every time she passed by where they were sitting, she had a fresh drink in her hand. Before long, she stopped and got very quiet, and her eyes got as big as saucers. Her face seemed to be turning green, and then she ran to the closest trash can and loudly vomited the full content of her stomach in front of all the guests. Vera got drunk too, but Andrew drove her home before she got sick. Then he returned to the party to pick up his brother.

Lewis could not wait until morning to tell his parents that he spent the party talking to Antonia Rivia. His father was thrilled that he connected with her, but his mother was concerned that she was too young for him.

"She's eight years younger than you, Lewis. You're a grown man and have been in the army for four years. She's still in her parent's house," Lewis's mother presented her case.

In return, Antonia couldn't wait for morning to tell her father that she reconnected with Lewis Ricci at the Christmas party last evening.

Gio threw his head back and laughed a deep, belly-shaking laugh. "Lewis Ricci?" he started. "His father is a poor, ignorant Italian man. He didn't even finish elementary school," Gio said in a half-laughing voice.

Antonia's joy in telling her father about Lewis left her heart, and she walked out of the room without saying a word.

Lewis called Antonia the next morning and asked her out on a date. He had just returned from the army and had to borrow his father's car, or they had to take the bus. But Antonia did not mind. With each date, she fell more in love with him, and she knew he felt the same. He had all the qualities she wanted in a man. He was respectful and kind, but most of all, he loved God. He would pick her up for church, would take her out for dinner, and would call her every day until, one day, it all came to a stop.

"Why are you sitting around the house, Antonia?" Aunt Sofia asked her one evening. "I thought you were dating Lewis Ricci."

"I thought I was dating him too," Antonia said in a choked-up voice. "He was calling me every day but, for some reason, just stopped," she continued.

"That's strange," Aunt Sofia replied, pausing a moment to think. "Have you called him to ask him why he stopped calling you?"

"No," Antonia said, too shy to even imagine following through with that but caring enough for him to try.

"I think you should call. Try it. You'll feel better afterward because then you will have an answer," Aunt Sofia suggested.

Antonia decided to give Lewis one more evening to call her. If he didn't call, she'd call him. The evening went by without a call.

In the morning, Antonia got up her nerve to call Lewis's house. She quickly understood why the calls and dates ended.

"I heard that your father is not happy with me dating you because he thinks my father is a stupid, poor Italian," Lewis said bluntly. "My father is a kind, generous man. He is a man of his word who keeps promises made. He is a man of integrity and a respected pastor of a church. It is true that he is not highly educated nor wealthy monetarily, but no one can dispute that he has riches untold in the Lord's eyes. I am sorry that your father does not see that, but I do not feel a need to explain or prove my father to him. I am sorry, Antonia. I thought we could have something special, but I cannot be involved with a woman whose family does not respect my father."

"I am so sorry you heard this, Lewis," Antonia spoke softly. "Please accept my apology for my father's rude comments and behavior. I cannot control my father's thinking, but I can guarantee that I do not think or feel that way toward your father or any of your family," Antonia said, waiting to hear Lewis's response.

The silence on the other end of the phone was deafening.

"I am glad to hear that, Antonia," Lewis finally spoke, breaking the silence. "I'm sorry for not calling to explain this to you and for cutting off all communication so abruptly."

Six months later, Lewis asked Antonia to marry him. Lewis wanted them to get married in identical navy-blue tailored suits. Antonia agreed. Instead of an engagement ring, Lewis gave Antonia a watch. They got married in the fall, just two months after Mario and Julia. Lewis and Antonia got married in the Western Avenue home under an arch in the piano room. Before the wedding started, Antonia went upstairs to see her mother.

"Mom, it's my wedding day. I'm marrying Lewis today," Antonia said as she reached for her mother's hand.

"I am so happy for you, Antonia," Grace whispered in her slurred speech. "You look beautiful, my daughter," she continued. "I have been up in this bed praying that God would bring a wonderful man your way, a godly man that would be the spiritual leader of your home, be a good husband, and be a good father to your children someday. You deserve all the blessings of God for giving up your youth to take care of me." Grace paused to catch her breath and wipe her tears. "I am so happy for you on your special day," Grace whispered as she closed her eyes and put her head back down on her pillow.

Antonia reached over the bed and gave her mother a kiss on the cheek.

"You rest now, Mom," Antonia mouthed.

The wedding was simple but lovely. Exchanging of the rings was not permitted to be part of the wedding ceremony, so Lewis and Antonia exchanged wedding rings in the kitchen of the home. They went back out to the living room, where sandwiches, punch, and cake were waiting.

"Do you see all those sandwiches?" Junior asked Virginia with eyes as wide as saucers. "I bet that tray is stacked four feet high with them," he commented with glee.

Virginia just smiled and laughed.

While everyone was eating and mingling, Sofia pulled Antonia aside to speak with her.

"Even though you are married and moving out of the house, I am asking that you come back at least two times a week to wash your mother's bedding and clothes," Sofia instructed.

"I was planning on getting a job, Aunt Sofia," Antonia answered.

"That's fine. You don't need to come in the day. You can come during the evening to do the washing. Just make sure you return to take care of that job," Sofia said, a bit more demanding.

"I will," Antonia replied.

With the four older children out of the home, Sofia was left to care for sixteen-year-old Virginia, nine-year-old Junior, and, of course, her daughter, Vera, who was now seventeen. Without Carla or Antonia in the home to care for Junior, Sofia developed a bond with him. Junior grew to love his aunt Sofia and regarded her as his mother. After all, he barely knew his real mother. She was never downstairs to play with him or care for him. She never called him upstairs to visit or talk to her. He understood that she was ill and needed to rest, but whenever he got brave enough to peek into her room, all he was able to see was her covered up in bed with only her head and hands visible. Her fingers were bony and snarly, and the few times she did call out to him, her voice sounded scary. Every once in a while, she would be aware that he was in the hallway or at her door, and she would tell him to get five cents out of her top dresser for the ice-cream truck.

At the beginning of the next school year, Sofia noticed a severe decline in Grace. She spent more time in and out of the nursing home than in previous years. It used to be that she would only be transported to the nursing home to care for bedsores, but now it involved many more health issues. A few days later, Sofia broached the subject with Gio.

"I see a decline in Grace lately. Don't you?" Sofia asked.

"Yes, I do. I don't think she is going to live much longer," Gio replied.

"I have been thinking," Sofia began. "When Grace dies, Vera and I will move back to New York."

"I understand" was all that Gio replied.

It was a dreary February afternoon. It was the kind of dreary that you felt all the way down to your bones. The sky was gray, and the spitting rain was annoying. It was too light to use an umbrella but enough to mist your face and hair if you did not use one. Junior hated this kind of weather. He pulled his wool coat closer to his body and walked as fast as his legs would carry him just to reach home and get dried off. As he turned the corner onto Western Avenue, he noticed a lot of cars parked in his driveway and at the curb in front of his home. Antonia and Virginia were sitting on the front porch waiting for him. As Junior approached, they jumped up to meet him.

"What's going on?" Junior asked as he observed his sisters' red eyes.

They looked like they had been crying for hours.

"It's Mom, Junior. She's dying," Virginia said in a choked-up voice.

"We need to go up to her bedroom to say our goodbyes," Antonia added in a quiet, calm voice.

"Do we have to?" asked Junior in a reluctant voice.

"Yes, of course we do," answered his older sisters in unison.

"This may be the last day we see her alive," Virginia explained.

Junior slowly and reluctantly followed his sisters up the stairs to their mother's bedroom. He could think of a hundred better things to do than go see his dying mother. He walked into the room but hung back toward the door. There she lay in her bed. Her face was skin and bones, with her long, bony fingers curling out over the edge of her blanket. Her fingers were scary to Junior. She did not look like she was in distress. In fact, she looked like she was sleeping. Everyone in the room was crying into their hand- kerchiefs. All the adults took turns rotating around her bed saying their goodbyes, reaching out to pat her hand or stroke her head. Some bent down to give her a kiss, and some whispered, "We'll see you again in heaven, Grace."

Just as slowly as Junior entered the room, he quietly exited. He trotted back down the stairs all the way to the basement. He first strapped on his skates, then switched back to his gym shoes and started shooting hoops. He was just about to shoot his third hoop from the imaginary foul line when he saw Mario appear out of nowhere. From the look on his face, he knew he was in trouble.

"Would you like to tell me what you are doing in this base- ment playing when our mother is upstairs taking her last breath?" Mario asked in an interrogating voice.

"I don't know" was all Junior could answer. "What's the big deal? We don't have to feed her anymore. The girls don't have to carry her to the bathroom or change her sheets. Poor woman, she's probably happier dying, don't you think?" Junior said in a noncha- lant, neutral tone.

It only took Mario one giant leap to reach his little brother, where he was standing at his imaginary foul line. Mario raised his foot that was wearing a size 11 cowboy boot and swiftly and inten- tionally booted Junior in his hindside, causing Junior to squeal out in pain.

"Now you get your sore tailbone upstairs right now, little brother. You will stand with all of us as our mother passes to heaven."

Junior managed to follow his brother out of the basement and all the way to their mother's room holding his aching backside. When they reached her bedroom, Grace had already passed to her eternal home.

The Monday after Grace's funeral, Sofia and Vera packed up their belongings and left for New York. Sofia felt like her time helping her brother came to an end. All the older children were grown, married, and out of the house. Virginia was a senior and was starting Bible college in Pennsylvania in the fall. That only left Junior for Gio to raise. She hugged everyone goodbye and walked out the door without turning around.

Junior was confused. He watched his mother die just a few days before. Now Sitzie, the only real mother he had, was walking out the door. Who decided this? Where was she going, and how could she walk out on him so easily? He knew his father was in charge of the family, but Sitzie added the structure and some love too. Without her around and with Virginia going away to college, Junior was sad, alone, and concerned for his future.

The Pawn Years

1947–1953

JUST BEFORE THE END OF the school year, Gio gathered Virginia and Junior for an announcement.

"I bought a run-down hotel on Crest's Beach in Lake Carlyle that I am going to renovate. It sits on an abandoned golf course across the lake from our Lake Carlyle cottage. I already have all the cable roof torn down and the top floor. When I am finished, it will be a two-floor hotel with a flat roof. It has two common bathrooms on each floor and kitchen and dining room for the guests. We will use that as our kitchen and place to eat. I figure I will sleep in one room, Junior will take another, and we will fit Virginia in somewhere for the next few months until she heads off to college," Gio explained to his stunned listeners.

Virginia and Junior knew better than to question their father. It was best to just pretend to go along with his plan and save the peace. They both stood in silence, nodded their heads when he was finished, and saved their concerns and comments for later when they were alone.

"What am I going to do without you here, Virginia?" Junior asked his sister that evening.

"I know it's going to be different and even difficult sometimes being alone with Dad, Junior, but know that I will be praying for you every day and night when I go to college, just like I do now," Virginia said as she reached out to hug her little brother. "God will protect you and make a way for you, Junior. I promise to keep in touch with you as much as I can," Virginia reassured him.

Junior buried his head in her neck and cried openly. He knew his sister was his best friend and the only sibling left to watch over him. He did not want to live alone with his father.

Whether Junior was prepared for his new lifestyle or not, it was here. Shortly after Virginia went off to college, Gio and Junior settled into the hotel and called it their home. Gio jumped right in and bought a TV for the hotel kitchen, served drinks at the hotel bar, cooked meals for the guests, and got close to the hotel staff and guests in a short amount of time.

Junior was busy trying to adapt to his new lifestyle and adjust to attending a country school. Junior had to wake himself up, go down to the hotel kitchen to eat cereal, and then walk through the abandoned golf course to catch the school bus. He never saw his father in the morning. He was never in his room, and he never saw him on the hotel grounds before it was time for him to walk to school. Junior felt very alone.

When Junior got home from school, he saw his father laughing and talking to a lady in the hotel kitchen. Gio caught Junior's eye and motioned for him to come over and join them.

"Junior, I want you to meet my lady friend, Erma. She's one of the cooks here at the hotel, and this is her daughter, Betty," Gio said with a happy voice and a smile on his face. "I think Betty is just about your age too," Gio continued.

"Hello," Junior said in a shy voice as he extended his hand for Erma to shake. "Nice to meet you and Betty too," he said in a mannerly voice.

"Nice to meet you too, Junior," Erma exchanged. "Your dad invited us out to dinner with you this evening," Erma said with a twinkle in her eye.

Junior looked up at Gio for confirmation. Gio shook his head yes to confirm.

"I thought we'd take Erma and Betty across the lake to that little Italian restaurant we like so much. What do you think, Junior?" Gio asked.

"That's fine with me," Junior responded.

Dinner felt awkward. Junior could tell by the way Gio was talking and laughing that he really liked this lady. Occasionally Gio would reach out and pat Erma on the hand or give her shoulder a squeeze to emphasize a point. Junior and Betty remained quiet for most of the dinner. They sat back, ate their meal, and tried to tolerate the time together.

Over the next few weeks, Junior noticed that his dad was up and out of bed before he left for school. Gio wasn't in his bedroom. He wasn't in the kitchen when Junior went down to eat breakfast, and his car was not in the parking lot when he left for school. Junior decided to ask him where he was so early in the morning, but days and weeks went by before he had a chance to ask him.

"I have been looking for you before school every morning for a few weeks now, Dad," Junior began. "I've gone in your room to say goodbye, but you're not in there. And I've looked for you in the kitchen too, and you're not in there either. Lots of mornings, I don't even see your car in the parking lot. Where are you?" Junior asked with an innocent voice. He was not ready for his father's gruff response.

"Not that it is any of your business, but I might as well tell you before you hear it from someone else at the hotel. Erma and I are in a relationship. We spend our nights at the cottage across the lake," Gio answered in a sarcastic voice.

"You leave the hotel after I go to sleep?" Junior whispered aloud in shock. "Is a parent allowed to do that? I'm only ten years old. Isn't that abandoning your child?" Junior asked, using the same innocent tone of voice.

"You know what you are? You are a snotty-nosed brat that is a complication in my life. If I didn't have you like a ball and chain around my leg, I would be free. All your sisters and brothers are grown and out doing their own thing. Even Sofia left to do her own thing, and here I am, stuck with a ten-year-old who is acting like a baby because he needs his 'daddy' to be with him in the evenings," Gio unloaded on his son.

Junior remained silent. He knew it was no good to confront his father; he would never truly be heard. He quietly walked back to his own room and cried himself to sleep on his bed.

Later that week, when Virginia called Junior for her regular monthly checkup call to see how things were going, he told her about their dad and Erma. He also told her about the prostitutes that were using the hotel to turn their tricks, how they'd leave their door ajar, and all that he witnessed. He told Virginia about the men that would call him aside wanting to share their pornography magazines with him. He went on to tell her that his friends from school found out where he was living.

"Now everyone knows that I live in a sleazy hotel with a bunch of prostitutes, Virginia," Junior explained to his sister. "I am teased and made fun of in school."

Virginia was heartbroken for her young brother. She cried with him and prayed for him over the phone. They were closer than sister and brother; they were best buddies. She was all he had in his life that offered him encouragement and an uplifting word.

Virginia called her dad as soon as she got off the phone with Junior. She was not afraid of Gio. She made her demands known on behalf of her little brother. Before the conversation ended, Gio agreed to have the hotel grounds keeper and his wife check in on Junior when he was away with Erma.

As Junior turned eleven, he got more daring. He'd go down into the hotel kitchen each evening and make himself double cheeseburgers and fries and would pour himself two large glasses of soda. He grabbed bags of snacks that were meant for the lobby vending machines and would take them back to his room with him to eat during the evening hours. Needless to say, Junior was eating anything and everything he wanted and was gaining weight out of control.

Outsmarting the old grounds keeper and his wife, he started stealing cigarettes from the hotel machines and selling them at school. He was making quite a profit from his sales. One afternoon after school, Gio saw the wad of money in Junior's book bag.

"Where did you get all that money?" Gio asked in stern voice.

"Not that it's any of your business," Junior started to say in a sarcastic voice, mocking his dad.

That was all Junior was able to get out before his dad grabbed a large butcher knife off the kitchen rack and started chasing him through the back hallway.

"You can run now, Junior, but watch out. I will get you later!" Gio shouted in a loud, out-of-breath voice as he smacked Junior as hard as he could on the back using the large blade as a paddle.

Junior stayed away from the hotel until dark set in. Later that evening, when he was getting ready for bed, Junior turned toward the mirror and saw a perfect outline of the large kitchen butcher knife imprinted in the middle of his back.

In November, Gio and Erma got married at the justice of the peace in Lake Carlyle. Junior stayed at the hotel alone while they went on a honeymoon. When they returned, Junior and Betty were told that they were moving into the cottage across the lake.

"Are you going to let everyone in the family know that you got married?" Junior asked his father one day.

"You don't worry about that. I'll take care of it," Gio sharply responded to his son. "Anyway, you have enough to worry about without worrying about my business. I drove by the hotel and saw that you didn't finish picking up the trash in the empty lot or cutting the grass in the field. What about your job of scraping and painting the handrails like I asked you to do? Don't you need to get over there to finish your chores?" Gio spoke in a demanding voice.

"Yes, I do" was all Junior answered.

He knew it was worthless to try to ask his dad anything or try to hold a civil conversation with him. He quickly hopped on his bike and rode over to the hotel to finish his chores. He knew, as soon as these jobs were completed, he'd get more added on. There was always something to do at the hotel, and if all the jobs ever happened to all be completed, Gio would create more chores or a project just to keep Junior busy and out of his and Erma's hair.

It was a few days later when Junior found out from Virginia that Gio and Erma drove into Briarton to announce their marriage to each of the married children.

"This is my wife!" Gio announced in a curt, no-nonsense manner to each of his older children.

All were shocked to hear the news and immediately thought it was an enormous mistake. Vincenzo and Mario questioned her about being a bartender at the hotel and how quickly Gio married her after their mother's death. Antonia didn't like Erma's response when asked about having their young eleven-year-old brother living with them. And Carla cringed in her chair at Erma's answer to the questions "What church do you attend?" and "Where is your heart with the Lord?"

"What do you mean by where is my heart with the Lord? I don't understand that question," Erma answered. "I really never went to church."

"Dad"—Carla turned to look at her father—"you've stopped going to church? Does that mean Junior doesn't go either?" Carla asked in a serious voice.

"No. All that started slowing down when your mother was bedridden. I just never returned. Now the hotel renovation takes up most of my time. Plus, Erma is not Italian and wouldn't want to attend the small Italian church," Gio pleaded his case.

"There are other churches to attend. You don't have to go to the Italian church if Erma has issues with that. You know how important it is to be involved in a church, and Junior needs that," Carla said even though she knew her opinion was falling on deaf ears.

The visit was over once church and the Lord were mentioned. Tension was thick in the room, so Gio and Erma walked out.

The only free time Junior had was late at night. He and Betty would roller-skate to the corner and back and up and down the driveway of the cottage. Neither one of them were good skaters. They spent more time on the ground than they were upright, but it was fun to get outside and to have someone close to his age to talk to. They would skate and talk about school and anything else that was on their minds.

"What's your favorite subject in school, Junior?" Betty asked him one night.

"Probably math. I like history too," Junior answered, thinking how nice it was to have someone show enough interest in him to ask.

"I like gym class," Betty said. "I especially love running track."

Junior started laughing. "Gym is my least favorite thing. I'm too big to play games or run track. I get all out of breath and sweat like crazy," Junior answered truthfully.

Betty just smiled at Junior. She was too kind to comment, but she had quietly noticed that he was getting heavier. She had seen all the food he cooked for himself for dinner at the hotel, not to mention all the snacks from the vending machine. She knew, without an adult to supervise, a kid would choose to eat that way.

"Want to know a secret?" Betty asked Junior.

"Sure," Junior replied.

"This is my last week here. I overheard my mother talking to your dad, and she told him that she asked her sister, who lives in Chicago, Illinois, if she would take me in," Betty said in a choked-up voice.

Junior could tell that she was holding back tears.

"Oh no, Betty, that's awful. I will miss having you around to talk to and skate with," Junior responded. "Why would your mother ask her sister to take you away?" Junior asked in a curious voice.

Betty scrunched her shoulders. "I guess she wants to be alone with her new husband. I think I'm a burden to her," Betty cried out, unable to hold back her tears any longer.

Junior gave her a hug and whispered in her ear, "That's okay. I'm a burden to my dad too."

The next morning, Junior was awakened by Erma's loud shouting.

"What in the world did you and Betty do last night when you were out roller-skating?" she shouted. "Your shirt is all dirty. I just washed that a few days ago," she continued in her loud voice. "Well, I'll tell you what, young man. You will only get one shirt to wear per day. If you dirty it, too bad, I am absolutely not going to be washing and ironing like crazy for you," she declared. As she turned to walk out of the room, she shouted over her shoulder, "And if you think I am kidding, just try me!"

Junior knew that he was not wanted. He felt he was an interruption in his father's life, and being married to Erma did not help matters. She didn't want her own daughter living in the cottage with them, let alone a stepson.

After Betty left for Chicago, Illinois, Junior learned to do his chores faster and would disappear out of sight down by the lake before his father could find him and assign more chores and projects. It was the time he spent down by the lake alone that he felt peace and a connection to God. Sometimes he'd reminisce about Aunt Sofia. He'd see her in his mind's eye ironing his shirts and singing songs of the church. He'd try to remember the tunes and the words of the songs she would sing and try to sing them to himself as he sat on the grassy lakeshore. He'd remember her telling him Bible stories and how Jesus knew him and loved him from his mother's womb. Junior would sit at the lake reminiscing, and before long, he'd be talking to the Lord. He always hated to leave. He didn't want the peaceful feeling to go away.

"If you like going down by the lakeshore so much, you'll love sitting by the ocean, Junior," Gio said to his son one afternoon. "Erma and I are going to head down to Alabama for a short vacation, and you are going with us."

"But, Dad, I can't just leave for a week during the school year," Junior explained.

"There you go not appreciating what I am doing for you again," Gio said in a disgusted voice. "I see how much you like sitting on the lakeshore here at Lake Carlyle, and I offer to take you to see the ocean, and you tell me no. There is just no pleasing you," Gio grumbled.

"I would love to go to Alabama to see the ocean, but what about school? I am so far behind from years past I don't think I will ever catch up," Junior explained.

"It will only be for one week, Junior," Gio responded. "School will just have to wait."

Gio, Erma, and Junior packed up the car and headed to Alabama for a one-week vacation. However, one week turned into two, and Junior was getting nervous about catching up with his schoolwork. When he approached his father about his concerns, Gio laughed and told him to relax.

"I told you school can wait" was Gio's quick, inconsiderate response.

When news reached Carla that Gio and Erma were taking sporadic vacations to Alabama every few months during the school year, Carla immediately called her father.

"I am hearing from Virginia that you and Erma are taking Junior to Alabama on vacation every few months for a week or two at a time. This can't happen, Dad. Junior is already behind his peers in school," Carla spoke sternly to her father. "Elementary school is important. He needs these basic years to have something to build on later when he reaches junior high and high school," Carla explained in a stern voice. "Enzo and I have been discussing this situation. If you continue to put Erma and your new life before Junior's needs, we want him to come and live with us in Hickory next year for his sixth-grade year. Robert is five and would love for his uncle Junior to come and live with us."

Carla could not see her father's face over the phone, but it lit up like a Christmas tree. Junior to go live with Enzo and Carla? Gio could not contain himself. He covered the mouthpiece of the phone so Carla could not hear his squeals of glee. This arrangement was what he was hoping for ever since Grace died; he just didn't want to be the one to raise the question "Who wants Junior?"

When Junior heard the news, he was excited. He loved Carla and Enzo, and he was thrilled to spend the year with his five-year-old nephew, Robert. He realized years ago that his father did not want to raise him alone. Then, when Erma entered the family, Junior quickly knew that neither of them wanted to raise him. Perhaps his oldest sister, Carla, did. Deep in his heart, he wondered if anyone really and truly wanted him. He felt like a pawn piece being moved around on a chessboard.

During the year he spent with Enzo and Carla, he prospered. Not only was he doing better in school, but he started attending church. It was at Carla and Enzo's church that he reconnected with all the Bible stories he heard from Aunt Sofia and all the hymns she sang while she stood ironing his shirts. Shortly after he started going to church, he accepted Christ as his Savior and became a born-again, spirit-filled Christian, with the evidence of speaking in a heavenly language. He knew his year at Enzo and Carla's house was coming to a close, but if for no other reason, he was glad he came just to hear about God and His love for him. Junior recognized the year spent with his oldest sister and her husband as a changing point in his life.

Junior returned to Gio and Erma's care to attend seventh grade. While he was living in Hickory, they moved from Lake Carlyle to North Richmond, Illinois. This time, they were renting a small farmhouse. However, in January, Gio announced that they were moving to Orlando, Alabama. Junior attended that school for approximately four months, and Gio announced that they were moving back to North Richmond, Illinois. Junior was yo-yoed back and forth so many times his mind was scrambled. He wasn't in one place long enough to establish friends, build rapport with teachers, or learn anything.

When Junior was enrolled in North Richmond schools for the second time during his seventh-grade year, his class was learning Latin. He panicked. He felt like he couldn't breathe. How was he going to learn this when there was less than a month left of seventh grade? He knew he couldn't complain or make a fuss about this to his father. That would start a war. He decided to talk to God instead. He remembered everything he learned from Carla and Enzo's church. He knew God's grace would help him through this mess.

After the summer months, Gio and Erma packed up once more and returned to Alabama. This time, they found a home in Red River Lake. Junior's brain felt like scrambled eggs, but he decided to make the best of his eighth-grade year. He was thirteen now and realized that he had nothing in comparison to others his age. He had no friends, no positive memories of school, and no adult that cared enough to guide him. He was a young boy living with an old man and a stepmother that was all talk.

To Junior's surprise, his father and Erma decided to stay the whole school year in Red River Lake, Alabama. One night at dinner, Junior found enough courage to asked his father about going to church.

"Dad, if I found a church around here to attend, would you permit me to go?" Junior asked with fear and trepidation.

He wanted so badly to ask his dad what happened to him going to church. He knew from his brothers and sisters that there was a time long ago when his dad was the spiritual leader of their home and openly read his Bible and loved the Lord. Junior even heard that his father was instrumental in his family having a community prayer group in their home. Junior silently wondered about this time in his father's life and wanted to understand what happened to his love and dedication to the Lord but didn't dare ask such a pointed question. He knew to stay silent.

"That's fine, but don't expect me to attend with you. I'll drop you off and pick you up. That's all," Gio answered.

That was good enough for Junior to hear. He started looking for a church right after dinner.

Junior was hungry to find a church. He missed attending church regularly like he did when he lived with Carla and Enzo. He found a church that was close to their home. Gio dropped Junior off without saying goodbye. Junior didn't care. He entered the church alone and immediately got lost in the worship music. He sang the songs and sincerely worshiped the Lord from that very first Sunday as if he'd attended there all his life. The pastor delivered a down-to-earth message in a down-to-earth manner, and Junior understood every point of the sermon.

He returned the next week and joined the youth group. The youth pastor connected with him on his first visit and took him under his wing. The youth pastor was a good listener and, over time, mentored Junior in the Lord. It wasn't long before Junior realized that the pastor and the teens in the youth group liked him for who he was. He didn't feel stupid around them or like he was annoying or a pain. He felt accepted and wanted. Surprisingly none of his past mattered to this group of church people. He had friends and was liked for the first time.

Junior was excited to begin ninth grade. This was his second year attending school in Red River Lake. It had been a long time since he was in a school for two consecutive years. When he went to the school at the end of the summer to pick up his schedule, the principal pulled him aside.

"I had to make a small change on your schedule," the principal started. "I changed your social studies teacher from Mr. Miller to Ms. Clark, Junior," the principal declared. "We had a student move out of state over the summer, and that created a space in her class. Mr. Miller's class was already too full, so by making the switch, both teachers' classes are an equal," Principal Jackson said.

"That's fine with me, Principal Jackson."

Junior took the schedule that was handed to him by the principal and went to find his locker.

That ninth-grade year, Junior spent a lot of time people watching. He inconspicuously spent a lot of time observing and listening to his peers. He looked at their style of clothes, hair, and glasses. In the lunchroom, he watched what they ate and observed their body types. He watched their actions and reactions to things, and he listened when they shared their dreams and life goals. After doing this for a few weeks, Junior decided he wanted to change. One day after school, he retreated to his bedroom and shut the door. He took a long look at himself in the mirror.

"I see a dumb fat slob with outdated style that is going to amount to absolutely nothing, just like his father and stepmother say, unless he stops, turns around, and takes a step in the right direction, *fast!*" Junior whispered to the hated image he saw staring back at him in the mirror. "Today, Gio Rivia Jr., you make that turn and step in the right direction."

A second later, Junior was facedown on the floor.

He cried out to God, "God, please help me. I don't want to be the person I see in the mirror anymore. Help me to turn and take a step in the right direction. Then order my steps from this day forward, Lord. I need Your help. Help me to get my mind and body in shape. Change my actions and attitudes. Mold me into the person I need to be to bring glory and honor to Your name. I will love and serve You all the days of my life."

Junior stayed flat on the floor thanking and worshipping God for the courage he knew he would receive from the Lord to make that turn.

That night while he was sleeping, he heard the Lord's gentle voice saying, "Everything is going to turn out okay. Obey Me, serve Me, and all the rest will come." Junior woke up with tears in his eyes and a damp pillow case. He knew the Lord heard his prayer.

He started the day in a good mood. He focused in school, participated in class, and ate a healthy lunch. After school, he stepped into the boy's locker room and changed his clothes. He trotted over to the track behind the school and ran a mile. He felt like he was going to die several times around the track, but kept going. He was winded and sweating through his clothes but felt good about his accomplishment. He decided to repeat this routine tomorrow.

When he got home that afternoon, he saw a small motorboat out on the lake behind his home.

"Whose boat is that?" Junior asked his dad.

"Yours," Gio responded. "I know how much you enjoyed sitting on the lakeshore at Lake Carlisle, I thought you'd enjoy going out on this lake with a small motorboat."

Junior was in shock. His father actually did something nice for him.

"Thanks, Dad," Junior said with a smile, "I'll take good care of it."

That evening, Junior took the small motorboat out on the lake with a book bag full of his schoolbooks. He practiced reading paperback books aloud to the fish circling around the boat. Next he'd complete his homework. He'd draw, and then he prayed. He sang and worshiped the Lord out on the water. He cried out to the Lord and thanked Him for His faithfulness, mercy, and grace.

It was when Junior was out on his little boat that he decided he needed to get a job. He was tired of begging his father for money. He felt he was old enough to earn his own. First he got a job bagging groceries at a neighborhood corner store. He'd made a point to help the elderly customers get home safely with their groceries. Next he got a job at a chicken restaurant. When Gio gave him a bike to ride back and forth to his jobs, the owner of the bike shop asked him to come work for him fixing and washing bikes in the back of the shop. Before long, Junior had enough money to buy a camera. He loved visualizing and setting up creative shots behind the camera. He'd take his time preparing for the specific colors, angles, and lighting he wanted to capture. When the film was developed, he was pleased with his work.

Toward the end of Junior's ninth-grade year, his social studies teacher assigned a project. The class was to research and write a paper on what they wanted to be as an adult. Junior decided to talk to his father about his project.

"Well, what do you think you'd be interested in?" Gio asked his son.

"I think I'd like to build," Junior responded. "Maybe an engineer."

"That would be a structural engineer," Gio interjected.

"But I love to draw. I like to design, you know, be by myself and think, create," Junior added.

"What kind of job would you get drawing? That makes no sense to me." Gio laughed.

"Do you have any house plans from any of your building jobs?" Junior questioned.

"Let me go look," Gio answered and went into his study to look around for something to satisfy his son.

Gio returned with a plan of an old house. Together they cut strips out of plywood and used Elmer's glue to frame the house to scale. When Gio thought the project was completed, he went to bed. Junior stayed up and added one final touch to the house. He added a small sign to the front of the house that read "Gio Rivia

Jr., Architect." Ms. Clark smiled when Junior turned in his project. She loved his work and gave him an A.

That grade fueled his tank. He was so excited. He had never, in all of his school career, received a grade like that. He started to work harder, and before long, he was earning Bs on his report cards. He continued running track. The one mile he barely ran on the first day turned into three. He was eating smart and was dropping all the pounds he gained cooking for himself at the hotel.

One day, during the last week of ninth grade, Gio and Junior got into a disagreement. The disagreement led to Erma interjecting her thoughts. That made the disagreement, which possibly could have been defused, escalate. One thing led to another, and the disagreement became physical.

"Oh, no, you're not," Junior snapped at his father, raising his fist.

"Don't you ever raise your fist at me," Gio responded and punched his son in the chest.

"Well, I guess I just graduated from here. I'm out. It's over. This is the end. You'll never hit me again, and I'll never return to this house!" Junior shouted back to his father.

Junior immediately called Virginia. He explained the situation to his sister and did not leave out the part about how he was not returning to Alabama to live with their father and Erma ever again. Virginia understood the seriousness of the situation. Between Carla, Enzo, and Virginia, they put their heads together and made a way for Junior to get on a bus in Alabama and travel to Illinois to stay with them. Even though Virginia attended college in Pennsylvania, she used Carla's house in Illinois as her home base during the summer months when the college was closed.

That particular summer, she and her friend Barb were traveling around to various churches on the East Coast organizing and leading vacation Bible schools for elementary-aged children. When Virginia's traveling commitments ended, she worked on a plan for Junior. They heard her make phone calls to various people, raising her voice on occasion to the person on the other end of the line. They watched as she took notes on legal pads that she kept hidden in a file folder. Everyone could hear and see that she was actively working on a plan for her little brother, but when asked about her progress, she clammed up, saying she would not be sharing any of the plan until everything was confirmed.

In the meantime, Enzo hired Junior to help him do odd jobs around his workplace. Junior was careful to save every penny he made. He did not know what the future held for him and wanted to make sure that, wherever he landed, he'd have some cash in his wallet.

Just when Junior thought no plan was ever going to work out for him and convinced himself that he would probably have to return to Alabama and live with his father and Erma two more years, Virginia called them all together to reveal her plan.

"I know it has taken quite a while to get all this together, but we're finally set with a solid plan for you, Junior," Virginia announced with a big smile on her face.

Everyone froze in place. No one even took a breath. Carla and Enzo sat up at attention as if that action would improve their attention and hearing. Junior methodically scooted to the end of his chair in anticipation.

"I found a Christian school in Middleton, New Mexico, that has an opening for Junior. It's just south of Robertson. It has three schools on the campus, Middleton Christian School, Christ Junior College, and a Bible institute. The three groups of students share the same dorm. When I asked what the tuition was, I immediately knew that I could not cover it with the little bit of money I make being a seamstress on campus and my vacation Bible school earnings. So I called Dad," Virginia said in a voice just above a whisper.

Carla let out a gasp, and Junior shot up out of his seat with a look of horror on his face.

"Everyone, calm down and let me finish," Virginia instructed, waving her hands out in front of her for everyone to be seated. "It's good news. Dad has agreed to pay for your first year's tuition in full. He wants you to return home to Alabama, gather the few things you have there, and he and Erma will drive you to New Mexico. You begin at the beginning of September," Virginia said.

"Thank you so much for gathering all of this information, Virginia. I will never be able to thank you enough for all of this," Junior said as he hugged his sister in thanks.

"You are my little brother. I don't want you to repay me anything. I love you and believe in you. I know that God created that opening this late in the summer just for you," Virginia said to Junior in her typical uplifting voice.

Virginia stayed and answered a few other questions Carla and Enzo had about Junior's transition, and everyone was starting to exit the room when Junior popped up with one more question.

"Wait, I just thought of something. I have no clothes to wear. I have lost so much weight that nothing fits right. Dad refused to buy me better-fitting clothes. I have barely anything to bring with me," Junior said in a panicked voice.

"I forgot to tell you that part. I already thought of that, and I have that covered too," Virginia said with a giggle. "I called Vincenzo in New York. I guess Vincenzo owes Dad some money. Vincenzo called Dad and told him that instead of sending him the money he owes him, he'd just use the money on getting you some new clothes for New Mexico," Virginia said.

At that news, the whole room filled with laughter. Between Virginia finding a school for Junior away from his dad, tuition paid in full, and getting some appropriate clothes, it felt like a huge burden was lifted from everyone's shoulders. It was a day to celebrate, and everyone celebrated big.

That next week, Junior went to New York to visit his oldest brother, Vincenzo, and his new wife, Ada. Vincenzo took Gio to Robert Hall Clothier and bought him underclothes, button-down shirts, trousers, shoes, and jackets. The money Gio made all summer from working with Enzo covered his bedding and enough toiletries to get him started. Junior traveled back to Alabama by bus. He was at his dad's house for two days; and then Gio and Erma drove Junior to Middleton, New Mexico, to begin his tenth-grade year of high school. Gio pulled up to the front door of the school, got out of the car to help Junior empty the trunk, waved, and drove away. Junior thought he never saw such a beautiful sight as the red taillights of his dad's car driving away.

Middleton Christian School

Middleton, New Mexico
1953–1955

JUNIOR WAS TOLD THAT HIS dorm room was up on the top floor and that his roommate arrived the day before and was waiting to meet him. He grabbed his suitcases filled with all his new clothes, shoes, and jackets; threw two plastic bags carrying his linens across his back; and headed up the stairs to the top floor. The dorm was old and dated, but Junior didn't care. He was far away from his dad and Erma in Alabama. He spent most of that first day unpacking his suitcase, hanging up clothes, setting out his toiletries, and making his bed. Junior thought the dark-green bedspread he picked out looked super on his bed. He was excited to start school and see where God ordered his steps.

He soon figured out that his roommate was very nice but quiet and shy. They didn't have much in common with him but thought he was fine to room with. However, Junior met a second-year college student that lived across the hall from him. His name was George. Junior and George hit it off from almost the first day they met. They had a lot in common, enjoyed talking and laughing together, and spent most every evening together eating dinner and studying.

One evening, shortly after Junior arrived at the Christian school, a group of guys from the dorm asked him if he wanted to go into town. Junior had finished all his schoolwork and had no plans for the evening, so he agreed to go.

"Hey, George, are you busy tonight?" Junior asked his best friend. "A group of guys from the dorm are heading into town. Would you like to come along?"

"I think I'm going to pass, Junior. I have a big test coming up next week and want to get a head start on studying for it," George replied.

Junior did not know the guys he was heading into town with very well. They were older students that did not live on his floor at the dorm. But he had nothing better to do that evening, so he tagged along. However, as soon as they got into town, Junior realized these were not the guys he wanted to hang out with. The first thing they did was find a bar. One guy bought a round of beers for his friends and told them that there was more where that came from. Junior declined on the beer. This made the guys roar with laughter. Then they happened upon a group of college girls who agreed to entertain them by putting on a little show. Junior saw enough of that living at the hotel. He was not interested and quickly refused to take part in any of it.

"Junior won't, but we will," the guys chanted over and over, increasing in volume.

He knew that it was a minimum of four miles back to the dorm, but he didn't care. Junior took off on foot at ten o'clock in the evening. He finally reached the dorm at midnight. He was thirsty and exhausted, but he made it back. He decided to knock on George's door. He figured that he would still be up studying. Junior told George all about his trip into town with the older guys.

"I don't understand," started Junior. "I thought this was a Christian school. Why did I just experience what I experienced if I am at a supposedly Christian school?"

"I used to ask myself the same thing when I first started here. I think it's because many parents think that sending their way-ward child to a Christian school will straighten them out," George answered.

"I want nothing to do with any of that," Junior said.

"Me either," George agreed. "That's why we need to stick together, buddy."

The fall weather was moving in, and Junior heard of a job opening at a cotton gin. It paid 50¢ an hour. After listening to the job description, he thought it would be a job he could handle. He and another boy were hired to turn bales of hay using large hooks. Working together as a team, they turned hundreds of bales. Junior saved as much money as he could. He learned to do that many years ago when he had to resort to begging his father for a dime. He knew to save his money because he never knew what was around the next corner.

Junior and George started taking the bus to church on Sundays. One Sunday evening in October, while the pastor was at the pulpit preaching, an usher approached him with a written message. The pastor paused his message to make an announcement.

"Any students here this evening from Middleton Christian School in Middleton, please step to the lobby for an announcement," the pastor read to the congregation with a shaky voice.

Immediately about twenty students stood up and walked to the lobby of the church. Once all the students were gathered around, the head administrator of the school made his announcement.

"It is with a sad heart that I come here to announce that your dorm on campus caught on fire approximately two hours ago, and it is in full blaze of fire as we speak. I have arranged for a bus to take you back to the school, where we will make further announcements for sleeping arrangements and for your care. We will help you through this unfortunate event and will make sure you are well taken care of along the way," the administrator said as he pointed to the bus waiting in the parking lot.

It took a while and some coaching from the administrator for all to exit the lobby and board the waiting bus. No one could process what a blazing dorm filled with all their clothes, books, notes, and personal belongings would look like. They all felt like time was moving in slow motion. When the bus pulled up to the dorm, they each found a spot on the curb across the street and sang worship songs as they watched their school home burn to the ground.

News of the burning school spread through the community quickly. Several prominent families stepped up to house the students while displaced. Junior and George were assigned to the Daniels family. Junior had no idea where his roommate ended up. Each student of the school was given $15 for toiletries and $25 for clothes. That was enough to get them started, but Junior knew that would not be enough. He called his father in the morning to explain the situation and to ask him for money. Gio eventually sent some money, but Junior never stopped hearing about the sacrifice it was to send it his way. After repeatedly hearing about his sacrifice, Junior wished he never would have asked for his help.

Due to the fire, the administration felt a need to do something for student morale. They felt bad that students had to split up in housing all around the community, losing touch with friends from the dorm. After much deliberation, they decided to hold a special social event held on campus at the student union. Students could come and exchange phone numbers, talk about how they were doing, and catch up with their friends in a casual, fun way. The administration would supply food and drinks for all.

"Hey, Junior, want to go over to the student union?" George asked his best friend after they were finished working on their homework assignments. "Tonight is the night that the administration is hosting that social event for the students in the student union. I walked by there today and saw them setting up the tables. It looks like it's going to be a big deal. Want to go see what it's all about?"

"Sure," Junior answered back. "Give me five more minutes to finish my assignment."

The administration did an outstanding job of setting up food tables around the room filled with various sandwiches, crackers and cheese, and dips and spreads, along with mouthwatering desserts. The student union was filled to capacity with excited students hugging and greeting one another warmly, lots of talking about their temporary living space, and a healthy dose of laughter all mixed together. However, with all the noise enveloping the large room, Junior zeroed in on one particular laugh. It was more of a girly giggle than a laugh, but it was contagious.

Hearing the giggle made him start giggling too even though he was way across the room. He was compelled to find out where this cute, girly giggle was coming from. Junior strained his neck around tall and short and thin and wide people to identify the giggle. Finally the crowded room of people shifted, and he found himself looking across the room at the loveliest sight he had ever seen. Junior had never seen her before in classes on campus or at his church, so he had no idea who she was. But he had to find out. He couldn't stop staring at her.

It wasn't long before George observed his friend's strange behavior.

"What in the world are you doing, Junior?" George asked.

When Junior did not respond, he asked again and added a sharp nudge to Junior's side.

"What—Ouch, what did you do that for? You almost made me drop my plate of food," Junior replied.

"I was wondering what you are doing. You look like you're going to end up at a chiropractor this evening for the way you're twisting and bending to see all the way to the other side of the room," George said.

"Oh, sorry. I was looking at that tall, thin, amazingly beautiful young lady over there. She's standing with three other girls. Do you see the one I'm talking about? She's holding a soda in her hand like she's a hired model for the soda company. See her perfect smile?" Junior continued. "And hear her laugh? It's contagious," Junior said with starstruck eyes.

"Whoa, slow down, brother! You've really got it bad," George said. "I see her, but you better stop gawking at her before she and her friends comes over here and take you out!" George said, giving his friend a light punch in the shoulder while letting out a laugh.

"Seriously, George, I have been praying for a wife, and I think she's the one," Junior said in a confident voice.

"Oh, come on, Junior. You can't be serious. You are way too young to be thinking something like that."

Junior stood and talked to George and some of his other friends for a few more minutes, all the while trying to build up courage to walk over to the other side of the room to introduce himself to the lovely girl with the cute giggle.

"Hi, ladies," Junior began, "how are you doing at your temporary housing?"

All four girls answered fine in unison.

One of the girls asked Junior where he was assigned.

"I was housed with my buddy George at the Daniel's house," Junior answered.

At that comment, the pretty girl with the cute giggle gave a gasp.

"The Daniel's house? Well, that's my uncle Bob," she said with a beautiful big smile. "My name is Suzanna. What's your name?" she asked him in her sweet New Mexico accent.

"Jun—" he started to answer but then thought how stupid that name sounded. "Actually my name is Gio Rivia Jr. Everyone calls me Junior since Gio is also my father's name. Just reduces confusion, you know."

The longer they talked together, Junior noticed that, one by one, the other girls walked off to talk, eat, or leave the student union. Junior found out that Suzanna went to a church that was closer to the school than the one he attended. He asked her if it would be all right if he attended church with her on Sunday and maybe take her out for ice cream afterward. Suzanna shook her head yes.

Suzanna's church was great, but it couldn't end fast enough on that Sunday. All that was on Junior's mind was to have some time alone with Suzanna walking to the ice-cream parlor. He only had a little bit of money in his pocket but felt confident that it would be enough to cover ice cream. After all, how much could Suzanna eat? He decided that he would only get a small cone. That way, no matter what she ordered, he would have enough money.

Once they reached the ice-cream shop, Junior asked Suzanna to order first. To his surprise, she ordered a hamburger, fries, a milkshake, and a small cone. He could feel his face turning red. He felt sick to his stomach. What was he going to do? He definitely did not have enough money to cover that much food. He was too embarrassed to tell her that he did not have enough money to pay, so he decided to tell her that he didn't bring enough money with him and would have to run back to the dorm to get more.

Junior knew full well that he had no other money back at the dorm. He planned on running back to the dorm to beg his buddies for any money they could spare. Suzanna was smart enough to understand what was happening. When she asked him how much money he actually had on him, she changed her order to a small cone. In spite of the initial mishap, they had a wonderful time talking and laughing.

When he walked her home, she asked him to come inside so she could introduce him to her family. Gio sheepishly stepped inside. He didn't know what to expect. He had never done anything like this before. Junior and Suzanna had just sat down on the couch when her mother and father came out to meet Junior.

"Well, hello, Junior," Suzanna's mother said, opening the conversation. "I have heard a lot about you from my brother. Do you know that my brother is Mr. Daniels, the man who is providing your temporary housing until the dorm is rebuilt?"

"Yes, ma'am, I do," Junior said, feeling more relaxed.

He couldn't believe how friendly Suzanna's mother was for just meeting him. The conversation flowed like water. No awkward silence or uncomfortable moments. Junior had never met such loving, kind, open, positive people. He was astounded at their love. Not only did they show love one to another; but they called each other loving words like dear, honey, and sweety. Junior never heard or felt this much love in all his life.

As he sat on the couch with Suzanna, he silently spoke to the Lord, *God, thank You for leading me to meet Suzanna and her family. I hope something develops between us, but even if it doesn't, thank You for giving me the opportunity to experience a normal family, a godly family filled with encouragement, love, and kindness. This is the way You want us to build a family. This is the way I want to build a family when the time comes.*

Junior stayed a while longer, then excused himself.

By the next month, Junior and Suzanna were going steady.

During the months that the students were living in temporary housing, a great revival came to campus. It was during this revival that God called Junior to be an architect.

God spoke directly to Junior, *Be a businessman that lives My standards and principles even in the face of the worst situations. Be a businessman of integrity, honesty, and wisdom.*

Junior answered the Lord, *It's a done deal.*

Junior and George spent one full year living at the Daniel's home. During that time, the burnt-down dorm was cleared away, and a brand-new dorm was being built in its place. Junior continued to date Suzanna throughout his first year at Middleton Christian School.

When summer came around, the students were promised that they would have a new dorm to move into when they returned to school in the fall. Most of the students traveled home to family. Carla invited Junior to spend the summer months at her home in Briarton. Enzo and Carla paid for his train ride from Middleton. Junior said goodbye to Suzanna at the train station and headed to Illinois for three months.

Spending the summer in Illinois was very productive. Enzo asked Junior to work for him again, and Junior readily said yes. Enzo bought Junior a Chevy car that summer to take back with him to New Mexico. Junior paid Enzo back every penny that Enzo invested in it. He also decided to go to summer school while in Illinois to catch up on missed credits from past negligence. He worked hard and focused. At the end of the summer, Junior realized that he had enough credits to skip his junior year and return to New Mexico as a senior at Middleton Christian School.

As promised, the students returned to a brand-new dorm in the fall. The students were excited to walk through the new structure to find their brand-new dorm rooms and bathrooms. They were ecstatic to finally all be under the same roof once more with their peers instead of being scattered here and there throughout the community.

Junior and Suzanna continued to date throughout their senior year. Junior turned seventeen at the beginning of May and graduated later in the month. All of Junior's sisters and brothers came to see him graduate. Gio and Erma did not travel to New Mexico to see him graduate. Junior made a point to call his dad after graduation.

"I graduated from Middleton Christian School this morning, Dad," Junior began the conversation. "I know we talked some about me applying at Oberlin College in Illinois after high school, but I met this wonderful girl at school from Albuquerque, New Mexico. I don't want to be in Illinois when she goes back to her hometown. I am hoping to talk to her mother tomorrow. Instead of Oberlin College, I want to apply at the University of Albuquerque's school of architecture. I will be able to continue my relationship with her in Albuquerque. I wish you were able to make it to my graduation. You would have been able to meet her," Junior told his dad.

He finally stopped talking and waited for some kind of positive response from his dad.

"You're not going to school in Illinois, and you have a girl?" Gio said in a questioning, rough voice. "She lives in New Mexico? That will never work out! Did I hear you say that you are going to architecture school? Didn't anyone tell you at that Christian school that you need to be smart to become an architect? You're never going to make the gra—"

He hung up on his father.

The difference between Suzanna's parents and Gio's dad was day and night. Gio was discouraging and demeaning and always saw the bad in everything. Suzanna's parents were upbeat, positive, and encouraging and exuded love like the love chapter found in 1 Corinthians 13 in the Bible. Junior had been dating Suzanna for over a year now, and he still was in awe over the love he felt from them.

After the high school graduation ceremony, Suzanna's mom approached Junior with a suggestion.

"Junior, I know that you are wanting to attend college and eventually become an architect. Suzanna's dad and I would like to invite you to travel back to Albuquerque with Suzanna and us. You are welcome to sleep on our couch until you found a place to stay and got a summer job. If you come back to Albuquerque with us now, you will have enough time to apply for college at the University of New Mexico at Albuquerque and perhaps begin school in the fall. What do you think?" Suzanna's mom said with an inviting smile.

Junior was stunned. He didn't know what to say. Their love, support, and generosity overwhelmed him. He never knew this kind of love and support from his father.

"Thank you so much," Junior answered in a choked-up voice. "You and your family have been so kind to me. That sounds like a perfect plan. I accept."

Garage Living

Albuquerque, New Mexico
1955–1958

THE FIRST THING JUNIOR DID when he arrived in Albuquerque was go to the administration office at the University of New Mexico at Albuquerque. He applied for college and took his entrance exams. Then he waited. In the meantime, he found a space to live in a converted garage of an elderly widow's home. She was looking for a boy to live on the property. One side of the garage was still used for a car; but on the other side of a sheet that ran down the middle of the garage was space for a cot, sink, shower, and toilet. That was all he needed. It was walking distance to the university, and the price was right. The widow only wanted $1 per day to rent the space.

Later that same week, Junior accepted a job working for a swimming pool company, loading pipes onto trucks. He kept reminding himself that it was only temporary until he found something better and closer to his garage home. He had to take the bus a long distance to get to his job. To make some extra money for the bus rides, Junior started picking up scrap wood from an abandoned lot that was near the garage where he lived. He started making bookshelves out of the scraps and selling them for $10 each.

As time passed, Junior became nervous about his acceptance into the university. The summer was almost over, and he still had not heard if he got accepted. He'd ride the bus back and forth to his job at the swimming pool company praying and feeling the anointing of the Lord come upon him, speaking in his heavenly language as he rode along on the bumpy bus, praying that God would order his steps forward.

Then one day in late summer, he finally heard the news.

"I am sorry to inform you that we are not able to accept your application to the University of New Mexico at Albuquerque at this time. Your entrance scores were too low. Considering a change of career, perhaps in construction, or a career offered at a technical college might be a better fit for you."

Junior could not believe what he heard. He felt numb and discouraged and felt his world was falling down in front of him. Maybe he was just plain stupid, just a stupid big dreamer, like his father told him all his life. Maybe he would never amount to anything. That was what he heard all the years growing up in his dad's home. Maybe it was time to believe what he didn't want to believe.

He decided to take a walk. He couldn't handle sitting in the depressing garage space tonight. He ended up on the UNM campus. He decided to walk out across campus to the school of architecture. He entered the building. It was late summer, so the place was empty. He took his time walking around, looking at all the displays, never realizing that he was being watched. Soon he heard someone call out to him.

"Come in. How can I help you?" the person called out.

"Thank you, but I think it's too late for any help. I just found out today that my scores were not high enough to make it into the architect program," Junior said with tearful eyes.

"Well, don't start crying now, son. What's your name? I'm the dean here. Why don't you let me see your papers? Maybe I can help," he said in a sympathetic voice.

The dean took his time looking over all of Junior's paperwork, and then he gave Junior a shock.

"What if I let you in the program? You would have to begin on probationary status. That means that you would have to maintain a 3.0 GPA or you're out. Understand?"

"Yes, sir, I understand," Junior said, feeling numb all over. He felt his whole body shaking.

"Don't come back to talk to me second semester if your GPA is below 3.0. You will be out! Understand?" the dean continued in a stern voice.

"Yes, I understand. I'll do it. I'll give it my best!" Junior responded to the dean in a confident voice.

He walked back to his small living space in the garage and fell on his face before the Lord.

"Thank you, Lord, for once again covering me with Your grace!"

The dean's required GPA was met both semesters of Junior's freshman year at UNM. He switched jobs to an accounting firm that was within walking distance. His title was "office boy." He picked up trash, swept floors, ran odd jobs, washed the coffee pot, and brewed more to keep the accountants in the office happy.

Junior felt a sense of success after making it through his freshman year at UNM. He switched jobs over the summer and was one week away from starting his sophomore year toward his BS with a major in architecture when Suzanna started acting strange. One night, when Junior was visiting her at her house, he drummed up the courage to ask her if there was something wrong.

"Suzanna, I have noticed the last few times we have gone out that something is on your mind. Are you okay?" Junior asked in a soft voice.

"You're right. I'm not fine, Junior," she started. "I have been struggling with how confined I feel in this relationship. I feel like you have a choke hold on me. Recently I've been feeling like I need some space," she said as honestly as she could.

Junior sat frozen to the couch. He never expected that answer.

"So are you saying that you want to break up with me?" he choked out.

"Yes" was all Suzanna answered.

Junior got up from the couch and quietly walked out the door. There were no words to say. He was broken and confused. He didn't want to suffocate her. If she needed her space, he would give it to her. He only hoped and prayed that this time apart would be a short period of time. However, a few weeks later, he heard that Suzanna had rekindled a relationship she had with an old boyfriend and they were serious.

Summer was over, and ready or not, Junior's sophomore year arrived. He attended college in the day, worked every afternoon, got off work, and studied, only to get up the next day and do it all over again. The next tuition bill was coming due, and he didn't have enough money to pay it. He decided to call his dad for some help.

"I'll send you money this time, but you have no idea the sacrifice I will be making to pay for your tuition," Gio answered in his typical way.

By the end of the conversation, Junior regretted calling at all.

Carla invited Junior to travel to Illinois for Christmas that year. He decided to decline the invitation because he had too much schoolwork to complete before the new semester began in January. He decided to stay in Albuquerque over the holiday to get a head start.

When Virginia and her husband, James, heard that Junior was going to stay in Albuquerque for the Christmas holiday, they asked him if it would be okay for them to travel to him. Junior was thrilled to have them come visit. Once they arrived in town, Virginia asked Junior several questions about Suzanna and their breakup.

"I don't understand why she broke up with you, Junior," Virginia said.

"She said I had a choke hold on our relationship and she needed some space," Junior said, still destroyed in his heart over the breakup.

"I say we go visit her parents. What do you say?" Virginia said in a happy voice.

"If you want to set something up, you go ahead. I'm not arranging the visit," Junior answered.

The get-together at Suzanna's house was set up for the next evening. They arrived on time, and Junior was pleasantly surprised to see that Suzanna was not home. He didn't know what he would do if he saw her. He missed and loved her so much he knew he would start crying in front of her parents and his sister and brother-in-law if she walked into the room. Suzanna's parents were wonderful. They treated Junior as if nothing happened between him and their daughter. They were their usual kind, loving selves, greeting him warmly and making him feel at home.

Everyone was relaxed and catching up on Junior's accomplishments and his new job when they heard someone coming in the front door. Junior looked up, and there stood Suzanna. Junior thought she was even more beautiful than he remembered. The way she dressed and carried herself took his breath away. He was so in love with her he couldn't breathe. She greeted Virginia and James first, wishing them a merry Christmas. She locked eyes with Junior and gave him a warm smile.

Later, when they were ready to leave, Suzanna tugged at Junior's sleeve and whispered in his ear.

"Come by the house again so we can talk," she whispered in her New Mexico accent.

Junior could not get that phrase out of his head. He had no idea what she meant or what a talk would lead to. All he knew was that it was going to drive him crazy until he talked to her. The next day, he thanked his sister and brother-in-law for traveling down to New Mexico to spend the holiday with him and wished them safe travels home. As soon as he gathered himself, he drove over to Suzanna's house.

"I'm back to hear what you need to tell me," Junior said in a nervous voice.

"Let's sit down," Suzanna suggested. "This might take a while. I am sure you know that, after I told you I needed space in our relationship, I went back to dating an old boyfriend. We've been dating ever since the week you and I broke up. I started dating him again because I felt like I needed to be sure that he was not the one I wanted to spend the rest of my life with," Suzanna said with tears running down her face. "I broke up with him last night, not knowing that I would see you here in my house today,"

Suzanna said, stopping to take a deep breath and letting out a heavy sigh. "By dating him over the past few months, I answered my own question. He is not the one I want to spend the rest of my life with. You are the only one I want for that spot in my life, Junior. I love you," Suzanna proclaimed.

Junior sat still and quiet. After a few minutes, he reached out for Suzanna's hand. He held it tenderly between his own. He did not say a word. He held her hand and stared deep into her eyes. He saw honesty and love there like he never saw before. He felt truthfulness and regret. He gently leaned closer and gave her a tender kiss. She reciprocated. They sat holding each other for a long while without speaking. Finally Junior broke the silence.

"Long before I met you, I prayed for God to reveal to me my wife. The first day I saw you from across the room in the student union, I knew you were the one. I loved you from the first moment I saw you. Suzanna, I love you today, and I will always love you," Gio said with tears in his eyes and a heart filled to overflowing. "Will you marry me?"

"Yes," Suzanna whispered.

There was no sweeter moment in time for the both of them.

Junior wanted to start this chapter of their lives correctly. He called Suzanna's father the next day and scheduled a time to meet. Once they were settled and all the initial small talk ended, Junior asked Suzanna's father for her hand in marriage. Her father was overjoyed to give him his blessing on their union.

That evening, Junior called his older brother Mario to tell him the news.

"Well, when are you going to make it official and give her a ring?" Mario asked.

"That might me a while. All the money I have saved has to go toward my tuition. I have no extra cash," Junior explained.

"Julia and I would like to take care of that for you. How about if you go pick out a ring for that special girl and we pay for it?" Mario offered.

"Really? You'd do that for me?" Junior asked in a surprised voice.

"Absolutely. It's a done deal," Mario said with a laugh.

A month later, after taking Suzanna out for a special Valentine's Day dinner, Gio got down on one knee and asked Suzanna to marry him in front of God and everyone in the restaurant. This time, when she answered yes, he placed a beautiful, shiny diamond on her finger. The whole restaurant stood to their feet and applauded. They kissed and held each other for a long moment, knowing that, no matter what was ahead, they would hold tight to one another remembering this day of commitment. Before the end of the week, they set a wedding date for late summer between Junior's sophomore and junior year at the university.

The time went by faster than either of them imagined. Junior worked harder than he ever had before, attending classes in the day, maintaining the required GPA as mandated by the dean, working in the afternoon hours, studying in the late evening hours, and trying to help Suzanna plan the wedding. She was busy too, working full-time as a stenographer. Time together was tight; but somehow they pulled it all together and scheduled the church, flowers, and cake and finally sent out the invitations.

Junior mailed out the wedding invitation with one prayer. "Lord, please make it possible for my family to be able to attend this special day."

His father's wedding response was the first to be returned. He and Erma declined the invitation. With all of his sisters and brothers living in the East and all of them having children now, he was not sure if any would be able to attend. He knew it was a long way to travel all the way across the country to New Mexico. To his surprise, Vincenzo's, Mario's, Antonia's, and Virginia's responses came back marked that they would be attending. Later that week, he got a call from Carla.

"Junior, I haven't returned the wedding response yet because I might not be able to attend the wedding. Robert crashed on his bike in the road on his way to work last week, broke his leg, and is all banged up. His leg is in a big cast, and he's in a lot of pain. We can't travel that long of a distance with him in this condition," Carla said with a sad heart.

"I understand, Carla. It's okay. You can't control that situation. I sure hope he is feeling better soon," Junior responded.

"Enzo and I are desperately trying to find one of his family members to watch him here at our house so we can attend the wedding. So far, no luck. Everyone either has set vacation plans or has other obligations and can't help us out. We will keep trying. I'm not going to give up yet. I'll hate it if I have to miss your big day, Junior," Carla explained. "Oh, and by the way, before I forget, Junior, Enzo and I made arrangements to pay for your wedding tux. This way, if we can't find someone to stay with Robert and can't physically be there, at least we can take part in your wedding by paying for your tux," Carla said with a smile.

Junior was surprised and taken back by their generosity. He thanked Carla from the bottom of his heart. He couldn't find enough words to show her how much he appreciated and loved her, not just for this, but for so much more. After all, she was the one who called the ladies of the church together to pray that her mother would not have an abortion. By that initial action, she gave him a chance at life. She was the first to sacrifice her education and big dreams of a career in math to care for him when his invalid mother was not able to. He wanted her to be a part of this special day. It was as if her attending this day would be a small part in paying her back for her sacrifice. But he had to understand the situation may not permit that.

On the morning of the wedding, Junior still did not have a confirmation if Carla and Enzo would be attending. He gathered up his tux and other items he needed for the wedding and headed to the church with his groomsmen. The pastor showed them to a room at the back of the church where they could dress. Before long, everyone was dressed and ready for the pictures. The photographer came to the small room in the back of the church to take pictures of Junior and his groomsmen. He told Junior that he just finished taking pictures of his beautiful bride and her maids and told him that it was going to be a lovely wedding.

When all the pictures were completed, the photographer and the groomsmen walked to the sanctuary to begin their prewedding duties. Junior was the only one in the room. He sat down on a soft upholstered chair and began to pray. He thanked the Lord for his goodness and grace that covered him over all the years leading to this special day.

In the stillness of the room, he heard the Lord answer, *I did not forget your obedience to My word.*

Junior's thoughts were interrupted by a knock at the door. He heard a familiar voice calling out his name.

"Junior… Junior, are you still in there? It's Carla. Open up," she called.

Junior had never heard a sweeter sound. He rushed over to the door to greet his sister.

"You made it!" he shouted. He hugged and kissed his sister with delight.

"It took us a while to figure things out with Robert, but we made it. I did not want to miss your special day, Junior."

"I am so glad you were able to work things out for you to be here on this special day. I wanted to thank you in person for all that you have sacrificed from a young girl forward in order for me to be where I am standing today. I am aware of how much of your life, education, and dreams you unselfishly surrendered so I would be cared for and loved. You took on the responsibilities of a mom for me so I could grow into the man I am today," Junior proclaimed with appreciation and tenderness toward his oldest sister.

He reached out and grabbed her in his arms. He hugged her with all the love he could muster.

"Junior, you are a miracle baby that, at the very last minute, was given the chance to live. I am fulfilled in your accomplishments. Your accomplishments are my reward!" Carla whispered in his ear.

Junior took a moment to absorb Carla's words. Then after a long, silent pause, Junior whispered back, "*Soli Deo gloria!* Glory to God alone!"

Epilogue

VINCENZO RIVIA HAD A SON and two daughters with his second wife, Ada. He became a deputy tax assessor and president of the real state commission for a state in the South. Ada passed away after sixty years of marriage to Vincenzo. Vincenzo remarried and was married to his new wife until he passed away in 2008 at the age of eighty-six. He was a US Navy veteran.

Carla Rivia had two sons with her husband, Enzo Greco. Her second son sadly passed away as an infant in 1965. She worked as the CEO of Enzo's construction business and later had the opportunity to use her math skills by becoming a licensed realtor. Her love for baking and cooking led her to host many parties for her church and business. Carla had the gift of prayer. She was eager and ready to pray for anyone at any time. She was not shy about sharing her love for the Lord. Besides openly loving the Lord, she loved her family. She passed away in 2014 at the age of ninety-one.

Mario Rivia had a son and a daughter with his wife, Julia. He was the founder and owner of a construction company, where he served as a contractor, builder, and developer. He was the international director and local chapter president of a businessmen's group. Mario had a bold witness for the Lord and used his musical talent to lead worship in churches for decades. He was a US Army veteran of the 882nd Airborne Engineers Aviation Battalion.

Antonia Rivia had four daughters with her husband, Lewis Ricci. She was an exceptional seamstress, sewing custom draperies for an interior designer. She also worked for a short period of time at a fabric warehouse making toss pillows. At the age of forty-three, she finally fulfilled her dream of becoming a licensed cosmetologist and went on to earn her manager's license in cosmetology the following year. Antonia had the gift of hospitality and proved her gift on many occasions hosting parties for friends and family. Lewis passed away after thirty-six years of marriage to Antonia. Antonia remarried and was married for twenty-four years to her new husband until she passed away in 2013 at the age of eighty-four.

Virginia Rivia had a son and daughter with her husband, James Douglas. She graduated from a Christian Bible College in Pennsylvania. She worked as a licensed dietician in the public-school setting for thirty-four years. She was a member of the American School Food Service Association (ASFSA). In addition to being a detailed seamstress, cook, and real estate investor, she was a pastor's wife. She had the gift of encouragement. She used this gift to uplift many children and adults throughout her life who otherwise would have lived in discouragement and despair. Virginia passed away in 2007 at the age of seventy-four.

Junior Rivia had two daughters and a son with his wife, Suzanna. He graduated with a bachelor of science majoring in architecture. He continued on to achieve his bachelor of architecture with honor thesis. Upon graduation, he received a scholarship to Columbia University in New York. There he received his master of science degree in architecture. He was awarded the William Kinne Fellows Memorial Fellowship for travel and study during the academic year. He chose to study in Europe. Today he is a licensed architect in twenty-eight states. Throughout his career, he designed institutional and public buildings. He is a fellow in the American Institute of Architecture (AIA). In 1997, he became a chancellor of the College of Fellows.

About the Author

BRENDA HELTON IS A RETIRED school-teacher that dedicated thirty-five years of service in the public-school setting. Recently she and her husband—along with their papillon rescue dog, Jovie—retired to an active, sunny spot in South Carolina. She enjoys looking out at the beautiful Carolina blue sky and watching the wildlife move about out her back window. She has found the perfect place to write.

Printed in the USA
CPSIA information can be obtained
at www.ICGtesting.com
JSHW020509250124
55705JS00001B/55